Changing Battlefields

Changing Battlefields

The Challenge to the Labour Party

John Silkin

Hamish Hamilton London

HAMISH HAMILTON LTD

Penguin Books Ltd, 27 Wrights Lane, London W8 5TZ (Publishing & Editorial)
and Harmondsworth, Middlesex, England (Distribution & Warehouse)
Viking Penguin Inc., 40 West 23rd Street, New York, New York 10010, U.S.A.
Penguin Books Australia Ltd, Ringwood, Victoria, Australia
Penguin Books Canada Limited, 2801 John Street, Markham,
Ontario, Canada L3R 1B4
Penguin Books (N.Z.) Ltd, 182-190 Wairau Road, Auckland 10, New Zealand

First published in Great Britain 1987 by
Hamish Hamilton Ltd

British Library Cataloguing-in-Publication Data:

Silkin, John
Changing battlefields : the challenge to
the Labour Party.
1. Labour Party (*Great Britain*)
I. Title
324.24107   JN1129.L32

ISBN 0-241-12171-X

Typeset by Pioneer, Perthshire
Printed and bound in Great Britain by
Butler and Tanner Ltd, Frome and London

For Frank Church who would have liked this book
and for Rosamund who does.

Contents

———— ∘∘○∘∘ ————

'Liberty has to be fought for unceasingly, but on changing battlefields.'

The Will and the Way to Socialism, C. R. Attlee.

Prologue

—————————— ooOoo ——————————

Anybody writing a book does not want for free advice. Recently a wellwisher advised me to avoid at all costs producing a book of political ideas. I should, instead, write a straightforward memoir, 'full of spice and flavour'.

Spicy and flavoured memoirs are, of course, commonplace among politicians. They apparently sell well, particularly if disguised as 'diaries'. Dick Crossman, for example, often used to describe his diaries as his life insurance policy. But such books do not help the democratic process; they personalise political philosophy.

It is not that I am short on gossip. I spent five years of my life in the Whips Office — three of them as Chief Whip in a Labour Government, one of them as Deputy Leader of the House of Commons — a place where one learns a lot about one's fellow politicians; more than I could have learned in twenty years' apprenticeship elsewhere. I learned facts about their private lives and their motives that their families and their biographers will never know.

It would be easy to write these things down. But that is the stuff of which gossip-writers, not politicians, are made, and I am not a gossip-writer.

This does not mean that this book contains no comments on personalities, or that I have withheld my views upon them. It

does, and I have not. But this is only because the account of
events would be meaningless without these comments, and the
lessons to be drawn from them have relevance to my theme.
Discussion of personalities is, of course, an important part of
political debate. The late Iain Macleod once said that politics
was a synthesis of the three Ps — principles, party, and
personality. These ingredients give politicians the challenge
and the savour of their work — that and the feeling (strongest
in those who become Ministers) of being brushed by the wings
of history.

If this book is not a gossip column, it is equally not a history
book. It would have been pleasant to write one, for I find it sad
that so few of those who enter politics today actually know
very much about the history of the parties that they are
joining. I am afraid this is true of those who join the Labour
Party, and has been a major cause of the upheavals that
afflicted the Party in the early Eighties.

It is sometimes difficult to get a perspective of time. When I
was a young man in the years immediately following the
Second World War, and attended my first Labour Party
conference as a delegate, it was fairly common for a speaker to
mention the name Keir Hardie. Immediately the conference
rose as one member to applaud. Keir Hardie had then been
dead for over thirty years. He was at once a remote figure from
Labour's early beginnings, and a present inspiration.

A generation later the mention of Aneurin Bevan's great
name would have the same effect on a Party Conference. By
then the memory of Keir Hardie had faded a bit, but was still
part of the Scottish Labour pantheon. No visit to Ayrshire by
a Labour speaker was complete without the ritual genuflection
to the founder of the Labour Party.

Today, the bulk of constituency members have probably
never heard of Keir Hardie. Many of them would be hard put
to tell you much about Aneurin Bevan. The National Health
Service remains his monument, and since it is under threat his
name is recalled.

Everything else he achieved, as much as everything Keir
Hardie achieved, has passed out of folk law. Few recall Bevan's
brilliantly constructive opposition to Government strategy
during the Second World War; few remember that Hardie
risked his leadership of the Labour Party through his support
for Mrs Pankhurst and the suffragettes. Such things can be

learned from history books, but many students prefer to read of more obviously dramatic events, such as the Russian Revolution, or the martyrdoms of Leon Trotsky or Che Guevara. Such readers, vicariously bloodied in violent struggle, often despise those who have sustained the Parliamentary struggle for a mere eight or nine decades. When such people enter the Labour Party — as unfortunately they do — they tend to treat the rest of us with a certain condescension, as they set about rooting out those they think of as 'cowards', 'conchies', and 'cretins'.

When such politics enters the Labour Party, a necessary continuity of purpose is lost. In 1951 I was the Labour Parliamentary candidate in West Woolwich. Supporting my campaign, Clem Attlee could still keep an audience enthralled — an audience of thousands, as we had at public meetings in those days — by his stories of Will Crooks, the first Labour Member for Woolwich, who won the seat in 1903.

Prime Minister Attlee, as he was then, told of how Will Crooks defined the Tory attitude to society. To the Tories, Will said, those who were starving, unemployed, or suffering from avoidable ills were just unlucky. Clem recalled Will's favourite story of a hansom cab driver with a thin and emaciated horse.

'That horse is being ill-treated,' Will said. 'No he isn't,' said the driver. 'He's just unlucky: when I give him his hay I toss a sixpenny piece to decide if he can have more — and he always loses.'

'Just like the working classes,' said Will Crooks.

A nice story, a funny story if told the right way to the right audience. It could not be told on television: the speaker and the audience must be in direct communication, like an actor and his audience. It is not likely to be told at a public meeting: today big public meetings are national rallies, not local events.

If you are advocating a change in society it may not be essential — either rationally or emotionally — to know and understand your history. But roots are as vital to a socialist as they are to anybody else. Settled communities tend to live more stable and productive lives. The crimes and horrors of Victorian London — chronicled by Dickens, Gissing, Morrison, and others — took place in a city peopled by men and women in their millions, frustrated and rootless, who had come from all over the British Isles in search of work. It was a generation or more before a settled, ordered life began to take root in

London. Political movements can similarly attract the frustrated, and suffer similar upheavals.

The roots of the Labour Party lie in trade unionism and in democracy. Both had to be struggled for: our history is not dull or dry; it has its romantic qualities. There was the shy, intelligent, and poetic boy, the son of a Welsh miner, who observed how his father's generation put their pennies together to pay a doctor's fees. It was the start of a dream that became the National Health Service.

Fifty miles away in Llanelli my mother's brother, the foremost dentist in the area, created his own local dental service for a subscription of a shilling a month. Both of them, the miner's son in Tredegar and the dentist in Llanelli, saw beyond immediate remedies. They, and their contemporaries in the movement, believed not only in the right of all to health care, but in equality as a birthright of every British citizen.

In 1950 I was having dinner at my father, Lewis Silkin's house with Aneurin Bevan and Jennie Lee. My wife, as a professional actress, was doing a provincial tour. Aneurin, regretting her absence, launched into a brilliant critique of the British theatre. With his tongue only partially in his cheek, he said: 'People should not have to pay for theatre tickets — they should be paid to attend performances as used to be the case in ancient Athens.'

He went on to tell a story of the miners' welfare hall in Tredegar. One day, he said, the miners came to him and said that somebody wanted to hire the hall once a week for a film show. They were worried: was not charging for the hall a bit 'commercial'? Aneurin assured them the money would be well spent.

Three months later they returned with an even graver problem. The man who gave the film shows had run off with the wife of one of their members, leaving his film projector behind. What should they do? Again Aneurin was constructive: 'If he could make a good income from films, so could you. Run the films yourself.'

Three months later things had got even worse. 'We are worried,' they said, 'because we are making a large profit and somebody says we are liable to income tax.' Nye was up to the challenge. 'What you must do every Sunday is invite some great artist — the pianist Moiseiwitch or the actress Sybil Thorndike. You'll lose money then because they are so highbrow, and you won't have a taxable profit.'

'Three months later,' said Nye, 'they were back again. "You and your bloody ideas," they said. "We're making a bigger profit than ever!"'

If democratic socialism is about the quality of life — in Tredegar as in Covent Garden — it is also about mutual respect and tolerance. The brotherhood of man is not the brotherhood of Cain and Abel — it is a mutual respect and esteem without frontiers. It was Eric Linklater who pointed out in *The Cornerstones* that the only people troubled by the phrase 'love thy neighbour as thyself' were those who had never considered how much they loved themselves.

Not narcissistic love, but nurturing love — we want to be comfortable and well treated. This is the sort of love that socialism expects people to have for their brothers and sisters wherever they may be. It is one of the tragedies of the modern Labour Party that it contains some who do not understand that the brotherhood of man is incompatible with the hatred of other human beings.

To hate injustice, to hate cruelty or poverty or any other avoidable ill is to emphasise one's humanity. But if this hatred is transferred to individual human beings it diminishes one's own humanity. To hate capitalism is understandable; to hate capitalists is a weakness. Today's Labour Party, sadly, contains people who not only hate their opponents, but their own colleagues as well. Perhaps — we socialists must always live in hope — this is a passing phase, which may vanish like any other sickness. If this is true, the future for democratic socialism in Britain looks good. If it is not, we have no future.

This personalised hatred — Aneurin Bevan called it 'demonology' — has even led to a contempt for the very organisation that the pioneers of the Labour movement held in such respect: the institution of Parliamentary democracy. It is a grievous sin in the eyes of some members of the Party for a Labour MP to speak with — let alone to drink, eat, or be friendly with — an MP from another party. To the intolerant, such fraternising smacks of treason. A young friend of mine, working in the House of Commons, told a fiery Labour Party 'activist' that the Left's Dennis Skinner and the Right's Enoch Powell had been known to share a joke. 'The working class,' the activist said, 'would be horrified if they knew such things went on.'

The working class would, of course, understand perfectly. Diversity of political views does not preclude friendship and fellowship in any workplace, any more than it precludes communication across the divide — real or imaginary — between management and employees. It is worrying that such obvious truths are a mystery to some of those who choose to be active in politics.

To explain to such people that Parliament must operate according to rules that guide the conduct of both the major parties is a difficult task — and a sad one as well. Many of the poorest countries of the world are desperate for a Parliamentary democracy that would allow differing interests — which may, in their cases, be as much tribal as political — to debate and dissent while holding to a common cause.

A certain African High Commissioner in London, after listening to a lecture by that great friend of Africa, the late Guy Barnett MP, put his finger neatly on the crux of the British achievement — it was the concept, and the reality, of the 'Loyal Opposition'. For the people of his country, who had looked into the abyss of barbarism, that was their grail.

The central unwritten rule of Parliamentary democracy is that the government must not so oppress the opposition that, when a change of government comes, it will seek revenge. Opposition, in turn, must not so plague the government that it will retaliate in kind when in opposition itself.

Implementing this simple concept is very complicated, and demands all the skills of the party managers — the whips — working through what is known as 'usual channels'. It is among the whips, working together for the common good of Parliament, that affections particularly develop. In a curious way whips, regardless of party, belong to an unofficial trade union. It is twenty years since I ceased being Chief Whip, but I retain a special affection for my old adversaries of those days, Willie Whitelaw and Eric Avebury. None of us was prepared to compromise our political beliefs, but I like to think that the friendship we formed in battles long ago is still alive — as is my socialism.

This book is an attempt to see politics and political life from the perspective of somebody brought up as a democratic socialist by parents who were themselves brought up in that creed. The battlefields have changed, but the principles have not.

Part One

————————— ∘∘◯∘∘ —————————

The Labour Party

Chapter One

ooOoo

Disorganised Labour

In 1974, nearly three-quarters of a century after the birth of the Labour Party, part of its history died, and has now been largely forgotten. What disappeared were the few remaining officially constituted 'Labour and Trades Councils', city-based organisations in which the Labour Party and the trade unions were as one. These councils, lingering on in such Labour strongholds as Sheffield, the Rhondda Valley, Swansea and Norwich, were relics of the days before 1918, when the Labour Party as we now know it was constituted.

'Labour and Trades Councils' have gone but they were for many years a reminder of the origins of the Labour Party and of the roots from which it gained its strength. The Labour Party, contrary to popular legend, was not created by a tiny group of intellectual socialists with nothing but untested theory and ideology to fight with. The mythical image of the pioneering Labour Party — of William Morris proclaiming poetic prophecies in Conway Hall, cheered on by Bernard Shaw, H. G. Wells and Karl Marx's daughter — is if not false at least gravely incomplete. My father as a young man learned his socialism not from the books of the Fabians, still less from Karl Marx, but from listening at the East India Docks to Tom Mann and Will Crooks — Labour stalwarts of the 1900s — who spoke to the dockworkers of the time in the language of the docks.

Of course the Labour Party owes a debt to the intellectuals who met at the Fabian Society in London. Of course there was idealism and thère were gatherings of the faithful. Of course the Independent Labour Party, with its high content of ideology and dedication, was important to the development of the Labour Party. But the powerful reality was that the Labour Party was formed by the trade unions. It was primarily the party of organised labour, growing out of the struggle for workers' rights, out of the Chartist movement, out of the repeal of the Combination Acts and the passing of the Reform Acts. It was the party of freedom and hope for those who did not possess the power and privilege of property and capital.

The founders of the Labour Party knew that the only power they had would come from numbers and that only organisation could create this united strength. It followed, therefore, that the early Labour Party was much more efficient than either the Conservative Party or the Liberals in organisation. At the beginning of this century the best political organisers in the United Kingdom were the Independent Labour Party and the Irish Nationalists. While the Conservatives and the Liberals had to struggle to create a grass-roots organisation to underpin their existing aristocratic and plutocratic parties, their opponents had decades of experience gained in organising to gain the most basic human rights.

At the very beginning of this century the Labour Party came into being as a federation of trade unions, dedicated to extending their industrial organisation into Parliament in order to protect and extend their members' interest — hence the creation of 'Labour and Trades Councils'. Local Labour Parties began to emerge in the Parliamentary constituencies recruiting individual members. These Parties looked to their Trade Union heritage and followed their example. New standards of organisation were achieved by this young political party. It was the pioneer local Labour Parties — in Woolwich first and then in other parts of the country — that pointed the way to the modern Labour Party: a coalition of powerful trade unions and Constituency Parties with large, active and well-organised memberships.

This was once known and remembered. Feats of organisation were revered in the Labour Party because through organisation votes and, therefore, Parliamentary representation were won. For more than fifty years after Woolwich was first captured by

Labour in 1903 (Will Crooks was their first Member of Parliament, Ernest Bevin followed many years later), the Woolwich Party was a shining example to the rest of the Party. As late as 1956 the Woolwich West Labour Party had 6,500 individual members; Lewisham South, a few miles away, had 7,500 members. Today, as the Labour Party reflects on the problems of the Eighties, only a handful of Constituency Labour Parties (or CLPs as they are known) have over 2,000 members. In contrast, just thirty years ago such CLPs were numbered in dozens.

Organisation was vital to Labour's survival in its dark days and to its victories in its good days. It was success built on hard work and dedication and, at the end of the day, on the simple mathematics of Labour unity. A CLP with 5,000 individual members could recruit from its membership an adequate number of active collectors, canvassers, fund-raisers, and others needed to maintain and expand the Party between elections. At election time at least a tenth of the membership — 500 members — could be relied upon to turn out regularly to work for victory. The bigger the Party in a constituency the stronger it would be, but once a Party began to decline so, too, did its active manpower, its competence and its dedication.

A large CLP is an impossibility without full-time staff. The full-time Agent is the key to Party organisation. The best description of the role of an Agent appeared in a Labour Party publication — *Labour Organiser* — in June 1935:

He needs not only to have an intimate knowledge of the Labour Party, its working, rules, personnel and policy, but to possess the personal characteristics embodying drive, tact, staying powers, and to be the optimist of optimists.

He must know how to organise membership and collections, develop money-raising activities, increase affiliations, and to conduct local and Parliamentary elections and do registration work.

On the office side, he needs to be systematic, to be able to keep books, minutes and probably also to handle a typewriter and duplicator. He may also be called upon to run a local newspaper, and to deal with this, not only as an editorial but as a business proposition. He must have an acquaintance with printing and be something of an advertising expert.

All the little knacks of bazaar management and sundry

sideshows that are becoming a feature of Party work must fall to his hand. He must know how to attract and train workers, conduct propaganda and make his Party a hive of industry where goodwill prevails.

That ideal is as true today as it was then, though today the skills of computer programming — and indeed other skills — would be added to the list.

In the intervening years, however, the needs of organisation have not always been taken as seriously in the Labour Party as they should have been. As early as 1945, the great year of Labour victory, changes were taking place. In that year a huge mass of voters — the servicemen — could not be organised in any conventional sense. At the end of the First World War, in the Coupon Election of 1918, the servicemen had been deliberately disenfranchised but in 1945 they were allowed their say and came out overwhelmingly for Labour.

Nineteen-forty-five was the year, too, when the age of the national opinion poll began — not that everyone took notice of it. When *The Times* received the result of the nationwide poll carried out by the Gallup organisation, predicting a Labour victory, it was relegated to a tiny item on an inside page. This was the first general election that Gallup, Britain's first polling organisation, monitored. Founded in 1936, Gallup had correctly predicted the result of the 1938 By-Election in Fulham, which had brought Dr. Edith Summerskill into Parliament, but that prediction and its importance had passed virtually unnoticed.

It was only the newspaper of the Labour movement, the *Daily Herald* — probably more out of enthusiasm than faith — that splashed the 1945 Gallup predictions on its front page. But the pollster mentality was already beginning to show: the editor of the evening *Star*, on hearing the first ten results of the Election, ordered his newspaper headline to read 'Labour Landslide'. A journalist interviewing a Labour agent in a marginal constituency on polling day found the committee room quiet and the agent and candidate chatting peacefully over a pot of tea. No trace of canvassing could be seen. The journalist asked why and the agent replied: 'We've done a straw poll. We have a 10,000 majority.' The prediction, happily, proved to be correct.

The number of full-time Labour agents did expand after the

Second World War to peak at close on three hundred in the early Fifties but the danger signs were already there. Soon began a decline in Labour Party organisation that has not ceased to this day. At the core of this problem, then as now, is a lack of resources — or, rather, a lack of the will to find the resources.

In the Forties a CLP could fund a full-time agent virtually out of its normal membership subscriptions and affiliation fees from trade unions and other affiliated societies. A good agent, keeping the membership up, would cover his or her own wages from these and with money to spare. But the Labour National Executive (the NEC) failed to plan for the future. Subscriptions remained the same as costs rose. The National Union of Labour Organisers pressed, quite rightly, for higher wages to meet rising living costs and then found themselves in trouble as the NEC made no provision to meet these higher wages. The problem was not immediately apparent. For some time after their wages rose a good agent might still be able to raise a quarter of his annual wages with one good Christmas bazaar but the underlying problem was still building up.

Changes in society in the Fifties and Sixties also helped to undermine traditional political organisation. Increased prosperity after the austerity of the war and the Depression gave many people a new attitude towards their leisure hours. Labour Party activities are perfect for people with idealism and nothing except time to spend. Put money in their pockets, give them a range of leisure activities never before enjoyed by the common man and, inevitably, political activism becomes a less attractive way of spending one's spare time. The same process affected the trade union movement. It is significant that whereas in the Fifties three quarters of trade unionists were affiliated members of the Labour Party, by the mid-Eighties this had shrunk to little more than half.

In parallel with these developments came the fashionable belief that organisation was not important. The psephologists — who thought themselves very important indeed and proved it by becoming television stars — were in the forefront of setting this fashion.

'The study of elections by pollsters and academics has steadily eaten into the idea that campaigns change votes,' wrote David Butler and Anthony King in their study of the

1966 General Election. 'But general recognition of the fact that most elections are decided long before a Parliament is dissolved is relatively recent. It becomes reasonable to ask why, if campaigns do not decide elections, so much energy is put into them by politicians . . . In part the answer lies in the fact that there is no proof that campaigns are invariably ineffective.'

No proof — but it was widely believed during the Fifties and Sixties. 'Why bother with organisation when we already know the result from a sample poll?' professional politicians would muse as they obsessively studied the monthly polls. At election time the BBC would feature the late Professor Robert McKenzie and his 'Swingometer' (a clock face upon which an arrow would swing from left to right to indicate Labour or Conservative advantage) to start predicting the result as soon as the first return was in. This was not just show business. Professor MacKenzie, the academic, would proclaim at the London School of Economics that all constituencies and their voters were essentially the same.

This fashion does much to explain why, despite quite a lot of talk, so little was done to halt the decline in Labour's organisation. After the 1955 General Election a committee was set up, chaired by Harold Wilson, to find out what was wrong. Out came the famous phrase that the Party's organisation was 'a penny-farthing bicycle in the jet age'. Yet although the problem had been identified little was done to solve it. Ten years were to go by before the Party set up a National Agency Service, centrally funded, to help stop the decline in the number of agents. By then it was too late. Between 1955 and 1966 the number of full-time agents had dropped from 227 to 204. In just four short years from 1966 to 1970 the number fell to 144. It continued to decline throughout the Seventies with only 81 full-timers available for the 1979 General Election.

This decline in Labour Party organisation and membership had an unexpected result. It enabled the various factions, which were to disrupt the Labour Party in the Seventies and Eighties and almost destroy it in the elections of 1979 and 1983, to gain power in many of the CLPs and to bring in a new system of election for the Leader and Deputy Leader of the Party and of 'reselection' of sitting Members of Parliament. For years the Labour Party had fought against infiltration by organised groups such as the Communist Party of Great

Britain. Armed with proscription lists, which outlawed front organisations of the Communist Party, National Agents and their officers in the regional offices of the Party were able to deal rapidly with any attempt to take over the Party.

By 1970 the mood of the Party generally had moved towards a greater tolerance of dissidents within the Party. It was taken for granted that dissidents accepted the ideas and principles of democratic socialism. While the Communist Party still remained outlawed people who admired many of the Communist achievements in the Soviet Union but remained firmly committed to democratic socialism were left unhindered. The abolition of proscription lists itself followed and it became much easier for people who did not in fact believe in democratic socialism to enter the Party. The weakness of many Constituency Parties, particularly at ward level, meant that disciplined Trotskyites were easily able to take control in CLPs whose membership had shrunk. The newcomers had no interest in the history, traditions or ideals of the Labour Party. They saw it as a reformist movement which had to be destroyed before the revolution to which they were pledged could be brought about. The effect inside the Labour Party was to create an unhappiness not seen since its desertion by Ramsay MacDonald in 1931.

It is little consolation to know that the Conservatives also suffered a decline in their organisation and that local Tory parties, despite having once had a full-time agent in virtually every seat in the country, now have only around 200 full-timers. In the mid-Sixties, when Labour was introducing its ineffectual reforms, the Conservatives were implementing a centrally-funded subsidy to marginal constituencies to allow them to offer higher wages to their agents and thus lure the best agents away from safer seats. They also sought to improve the status of their agents (the then Tory Chairman, Edward du Cann, wrote of them 'as the equivalent of a managing director') and to give them a more political role. So non-political had the Tory agent traditionally been that there were cases of good Labour agents being offered jobs with local Conservative Associations — at twice the salary. It happened, for example, to Walter Brown who later, happily, became Labour's Assistant National Agent.

Such a gloomy picture of Labour's decline raises the question of how Labour managed to win four general elections between

1964 and 1974. It was, of course, partly due to the failures of Conservatism, but Labour did have its organisational and campaigning strengths, which were apparent even during the election loss of 1959.

Labour's superiority at that time lay at the centre: as David Butler and Richard Rose put it in their study of that year's Election: 'The Conservative Party showed itself superior to Labour in the use of public relations and in constituency organisation, while the Labour Party was better than the Conservatives in co-ordinating its national campaign and in its television broadcasts'.

That was the first election in which television played a major role: the majority of homes now had television, commercial television had arrived, and the more staid reporting of politics associated with BBC radio during elections gave way to the exciting immediacy of the television screen.

Labour's Party political television broadcasts in 1959 were, if anything, too slick. The message that it was an eminently respectable party was put across by public school and Oxford-educated Gaitskellites — the only spokesmen who were allowed in front of the camera. A distinguished line-up consisted of Hugh Gaitskell himself, Anthony Wedgwood Benn (as he then called himself), Christopher Mayhew (not yet a Liberal Peer), and Woodrow Wyatt (not yet a *News of the World* columnist of fierce right-wing views). Aneurin Bevan, Harold Wilson, George Brown, James Callaghan — all were kept safely out of the way. None of them spoke with a BBC accent.

After the 1959 defeat there was a real drive within the Party to improve organisation at every level and, despite the underlying trend towards decline, some things were achieved. A new youth section, the Young Socialists, was created in 1960 and brought many young people into the Party. The problem of Trotskyite infiltration dogged it from the start but in its early years it was certainly of net benefit to the Party. Links with the trade unions were strengthened through regional and local liaison committees. In 1961 the NEC formed a Campaign Committee and a plan of action for the run-up to the next election was formulated. When in 1962 the Labour Party hired a new Director of Publicity they chose a public relations professional and paid him more than any other head of department at Transport House. The Publicity Director, John Harris, assembled his own team of expert and experienced volunteers who, together with Labour's private pollster, Dr. Mark Abrams, began to put together firm proposals for winning the coming election. These were approved by the Campaign Committee and the NEC before the death of Hugh Gaitskell.

After the disappointment of the 1979 Election defeat and the chaos of the 1983 defeat, certain myths arose about Labour's past successes. Most of them centred on the remarkable figure of Harold Wilson, winner of four general elections in five attempts. One of the most popular myths was that Wilson won by keeping a firm grasp on the Party machine. This was untrue. Wilson, as even the most gifted politician needs to be, was lucky. He became Party Leader at the right moment in its history and was able to exercise his gifts to the full. He inherited a Party machine that was at least self-confident and motivated. On television — his deliberate persona was that of a family doctor — he faced the unphotogenic Sir Alec Douglas-Home and the stiff Edward Heath.

The 1964 General Election campaign, which brought Labour back to power after thirteen years, was undoubtedly a triumph for Harold Wilson but it was a dangerous triumph. To the astonishment of the Conservatives, Wilson abandoned the carefully formulated campaign plan which had been the theme of all campaign propaganda and went on his own barnstorming pre-campaign. Instead of keeping to the themes that the carefully assembled Head Office experts told him would be most likely to maximise the Labour vote, his speeches covered a vast range of topics, which he seemed to pick up and drop with little forethought. Finally, having totally dominated Labour's campaign, he moved his base from London to Merseyside and his own constituency for the final days of the campaign, almost certainly allowing the Conservatives to pull back some ground nationally by polling day since the main media circus remained firmly in London.

As a virtuoso performance it was greatly to be admired and it had the advantage of giving Labour's campaign an unprecedented look of decisiveness but as an approach to politics it did not square with his ambition to make Labour the natural party of government in Britain. Achieving that requires strategy and organisation. Harold Wilson was not an expert on these. Just as the Labour Government's National Plan, an ambitious programme for economic expansion, was to falter in the July 1966 deflationary measures and die in the devaluation crisis of November 1967, so, too, did the Labour Party's organisation decline catastrophically during the years of Wilson's leadership. Industrial unrest brought the hasty response of a White Paper on trade union law — 'In Place of Strife' — which soured relations with the unions at the very time when their support could not have been more vital.

Harold Wilson can be seen as the most prominent victim of the golden age of the opinion polls. As a statistician he took them very seriously indeed. He left Labour Party head office staff and leaders with a legacy that still is a danger today: a tendency to be mesmerised by the findings of opinion polls and to put excessive faith in the pollsters' interpretation of those findings.

Harold Wilson saw politics as a matter of creating and responding to public moods. He accepted the psephologists' dismissal of party organisation and grass-roots campaigning. By 1970 he had apparently begun to think that opinion polls were more important than actual votes cast. The local council elections in May of that year indicated, when analysed in Transport House, that a general election in the immediate future would not be a good idea. These elections pointed to a Labour defeat nationally. Strenuous efforts were made to talk Wilson out of a June Election. But, unlike the local election results, the opinion polls seemed favourable enough. Wilson was determined to go ahead, and Edward Heath became the next Prime Minister.

The sad irony was that virtually all the polls continued to show Labour ahead right until polling day. (Curiously, the Labour Party's own private poll, conducted by MORI in the last forty-eight hours before the polls opened, actually got it right and recorded a Tory win. The National Agent of the Party, Ron Hayward, was so disturbed that he went to 10 Downing Street to discuss these findings with the Prime Minister, though what he thought could be done at that stage remains a mystery.) Wilson, reassured by what the bulk of the polls were saying, was not troubled and went happily to defeat.

How did the pollsters explain away their inaccurate predictions? Their answers were complex and varied but the most popular one was that the swing to the Conservatives had come too late for the polls to detect it. As an excuse it was a non-sequitur: if the mood of the voters was so volatile surely that was exactly the sort of thing that polls were supposed to detect? The psephologists, forced to admit that polls could not detect national trends as precisely as they had once thought, proceeded on to the next logical conclusions: that 'national trends' themselves might not be as all-powerful as their previous wisdom had insisted.

It must be remembered that in those days psephologists hated regional and local variations in voting. They made life difficult. Professor McKenzie would become very annoyed when his 'Swingometer' was betrayed by the electorate. Voters who did such things to the psephologists were subjected to the sternest possible strictures. They were deemed to be un-scientific. 'In any case, the vast majority of individual results conformed to the national pattern,' insisted David Butler, writing his Nuffield Survey of the 1970 Election in collaboration with Michael Pinto-Duschinsky. 'In 1970, the swing from Labour to Conservative was within 1.5 per cent of the national average in 335 out of the total of 630 constituencies and only in 28 did it deviate by more than 4 per cent.'

The non-academic can be forgiven for believing that 295 constituencies not conforming to the pollsters' prediction might tend to cast doubt upon that prediction and that even 28 seats 'deviating' can give one Party or the other a sizeable majority. Butler went on to mention research carried out in 1964 and 1966 which indicated that well-established and familiar MPs could achieve personal swings of up to 3.5 per cent, and that such results could be decisive. 'In 1950, 1951, 1964 and 1970 a switch of less than 1 per cent of the voters would have robbed the winning Party of its majority,' he observed. 'Unfortunately, there is no equally simple test of the long-term impact of a good local organisation but the . . . study does suggest that — like that of a good candidate — it may be greater in the long term than in the short'.

Since 1970 there is ample evidence to be found that the local factors — the quality of the candidates, the quality of organ-isation in the broadest sense — can make the difference between winning and losing. The major new development has been the growth of local radio and regional television which has changed the whole way in which the public perceives elections. For the first time since the great Reform Act of 1832, candidates for Parliament and for borough and county elections have the chance to become as well-known local figures as if they were

13

running for a parish council in a small village. We are increasingly living in electronic villages. This has the most profound implications for political organisation.

Like many others I tended to ignore the importance of this development until the Grimsby by-election in April 1977, following the death of Tony Crosland. I was Minister of Fisheries at the time and in Grimsby the EEC's Common Fisheries Policy was a burning local issue, so I was asked to speak during the campaign. The meeting I addressed was packed to the rafters in a way I had not seen at a political rally for over a decade. Part of the audience sat among dust and cobwebs in galleries long unused. It was not the issue or the visiting speakers that had brought the crowd: it was the candidate, Austin Mitchell, a well-known presenter with Yorkshire Television.

The audience had turned out to see a television personality who, via the television, shared their sitting rooms more often even than some members of their own families. It was not surprising, therefore, that Austin Mitchell succeeded not only in holding the seat at a time when the Labour Government's fortunes were in decline but actually went on to gain more votes than Tony Crosland had achieved in the general election two and a half years before. On the same day there was another Parliamentary by-election in Ashfield, Nottinghamshire. Labour put up a candidate who had not had previous publicity on regional television. He lost by 15,751 votes. A previously safe seat (22,951 majority in 1974) fell to a youthful Conservative from South London.

Of course there were other factors in the by-elections apart from the fact that Austin Mitchell was a professional television personality and the Ashfield candidate was not. But together the two by-elections proved that local variations in voting could be of overwhelming importance and not of only the marginal interest that the psephologists had traditionally ascribed to them. Nor were they perhaps the most dramatic illustration of local variation in voting.

That came in Bermondsey in South London in February 1983, following the resignation of my successor as Labour Chief Whip, Bob Mellish — an election that was dominated by the press, radio and television to an extent not before seen. A controversial Labour candidate, Peter Tatchell, became the prime target for the media, who both created him as a public figure and then destroyed him. For Labour it was a by-election with all the elements it came to dread in the Eighties: a divided Labour Party, a candidate and agent who played into the hands of hostile journalists, and the emergence of an Alliance candidate who brushed aside generations of Labour Party organisation in the area to win the election with his highly effective style of populist and "community" politics.

Again, it was a by-election where local factors dominated and national trends went out the window. Soon afterwards Labour was to win the next Parliamentary by-election, in Darlington, with a result that if repeated nationally would have won Labour the June 1983 General Election. It was not to be and the Labour Party even lost Darlington a few weeks later in a general election that exposed weaknesses in its organisation at every level.

At national level the highly professional Tory organisation was met by a Labour Party organisation which would have been disowned by the organisers of a village fête. There was the Party Leader, Michael Foot, exhausting himself barn-storming the country as though the electronic media had not yet been invented. There were vast shapeless and interminable committee meetings at Walworth Road. When they failed to work, alternative committees would be invented, adding to the confusion and division of effort. At one stage Mirror Newspapers offered the Party journalists to bolster the Press Department — and had the offer turned down, while thousands of pounds were spent on hiring freelances. Good professionals were hired — and then not used properly. One trade union leader offered the Party a gift of two computers: not the most up-to-date but a whole lot better than not having them — there was no work for them, he was told.

A Labour Party song was written, produced and recorded at a cost of £4,000 — it was considered too bad to be used. A rushed advertising campaign started badly and became worse under pressure. When other advertising agencies with sympathetic staff offered to help in mid-campaign, professional jealousy tore the Party's public relations advisory committee to pieces. The centre did not hold.

But in not doing so it used up an awful lot of paper. Candidates and agents were inundated with mass mailings of minutely detailed research material throughout the campaign which many did not bother even to open until after polling day. On the eve of the election the Party's Scottish researcher based at Keir Hardie House in Glasgow went to the teleprinter to receive the last edition of the daily campaign briefing from Walworth Road in London. As the paper chattered out of the machine the Scotsman took it in his hands and slowly walked backwards through five offices as everyone on the premises collapsed in hysterical laughter. Facing a humiliating defeat, the Party's London headquarters remained convinced that the Tories could be beaten to death with facts and statistics and that the irrefutable logic of Labour's statistical case would still prevail.

That incident is a fitting epitaph to the era — post-Wilson, pre-Kinnock — when the headquarters staff who succeeded Terry Pitt, a research worker with good political instincts, too often thought and acted like a collection of academics playing at being a government in exile, remote from Labour Governments, Labour Oppositions and the Party in the country alike. It was an exile born partly out of frustration with the performance of Labour Governments, partly out of ambition (when the 'Left' controlled the NEC and the 'Right' the Parliamentary leadership, one became the rival of the other), and partly out of physical isolation. When the Labour Party moved from its tenancy of the Transport and General Workers Union's in Transport House in Smith Square, near to Parliament, to a row of eighteenth-century houses converted into offices in Walworth Road, near the Elephant and Castle in South London, the change was not merely geographical. The new premises are attractive to look at from the outside — they are listed as being of historical architectural value — but they have no other advantages whatsoever. They are too big, too costly, and too inconvenient for Westminster and the media. If they were intended to encourage bureaucracy as an act of policy they could not be better designed nor better placed.

The Walworth Road offices are a rabbit warren of passages and rooms, cut off from one another, encouraging fragmentation of purpose and isolation. Many Party members feel out of place when they visit their own headquarters. The staff who work inside the building in their small offices do not get the feeling of communion with the outside world. The social and political contact that used to take place between members of Britain's largest trade union and the headquarters' staff of the

Labour Party — a constant feature for those who wished to take advantage of it — no longer exists.

It was no accident that much of the voting shambles at the 1985 Labour Party conference, where the TGWU voted against the Leadership on the issue of one member/one vote, was simply due to the TGWU not having a clear idea or ample warning of what the Party was up to. In the pre-Walworth Road days that would have been much less likely to have happened.

When the Party's headquarters were in Westminster it was in close and continual contact with Members of Parliament, the trade unions, the press, and even its opponents (Conservative Central Office is also in Smith Square). The whole point of a political party having its headquarters in London is precisely to give it proximity to the people with whom it must deal day in and day out. The pub opposite where Party workers, trade unionists, and journalists met was a valuable grapevine of information. MPs, in particular, took Transport House happily for granted: if a press release needed distributing a ten-minute walk from the House of Commons to Transport House, a word with the Press Office, and things were working. Today, unassisted by modern technology, the journey to Walworth Road is covered rather more slowly than it would have been in Victorian times. A press release is taken down to Walworth Road by messenger and a copy returned hours or even days later. It is small wonder that the service is used hardly at all. This has a serious side-effect — as Shadow Cabinet members use it less, Party press officers inevitably become less well briefed on what the Shadow Cabinet is saying and thinking. The gap between Party head office workers and Parliamentary Party grows even wider.

The working of the NEC was also better in pre-Walworth Road days with quite frequent useful contact between staff members, the Executive, Members of Parliament and trade unionists. Today, the full NEC still meets at Party headquarters but practically every other meeting of its organisational and policy sub-committees takes place at the House of Commons: a significant distance from the headquarters near the Elephant and Castle. Senior staff are forced to spend a great deal of time and money away from the headquarters they are supposed to be running and the once relaxed personal contact between them and the Executive members has tended to disappear. At Walworth Road, junior staff seldom see members of the Executive that acts as their employer. The Party is the poorer for the lack of such contact.

During the 1983 election débâcle this Government in exile poured forth its mountains of detailed policy papers, wasting large sums of money on briefings that were of little practical use to candidates and agents in the throes of battle. These paper mountains came inevitably from a highly qualified and able staff who understandably did not wish to spend their time in idleness. But a party that is short of money must ask itself whether such a large and academically-minded staff is either necessary or advantageous.

In truth, the staffing structure of the Labour Party headquarters has never been thought through. There is little effort to direct resources intelligently. Failing any clear direction from the Executive, staff often wander off in whatever direction suits them, developing some aspects of policy at the expense of others, or pursue a line that may help their own political ambitions rather than the party as a whole.

The staffing structure has just grown over the years in response to various pressures. Departmental heads fight tooth and nail to maintain their empires, or extend them by swallowing other, smaller empires. To keep up with these manoeuvres one really needs to attend the Walworth Road Christmas party, where mainly junior staff perform a series of sketches, laying bare the internal politics of the Labour Party. Everybody laughs heartily, and goes off to another year of doing the same thing.

With the retirement of Jim Mortimer in 1985, Larry Whitty, former director of research for the municipal workers' union, GMBATU, became the new Labour Party General Secretary. As secretary of Trade Unions for Labour Victory, a fund-raising body, he had been closely involved with the Party nationally for a number of years. His priority has been reform at national level. The plan was to bring new people into the headquarters and to this end three new senior posts were created: a new supremo for organisation, another for research and policy, and a third for publicity. It was a hard task and inevitably bitter wrangles ensued: the International Department resented being absorbed into the Research Department; and the staff trade unions at Walworth Road objected to the three new heads being paid more money than the old departmental heads — a rare instance of trade unionists demanding that wage levels be kept down, not put up. They even stood at the steps of Walworth Road and picketed the NEC in pursuit of lower wages.

In the event, the new structure did not bring in the planned new blood. Only the Publicity Chief, the television producer Peter Mandelson, was a new face. Two veteran Labour Party stalwarts, Joyce Gould and Geoff Bish, were moved up to take over organisation, and policy development. The International Department was merged with the Research Department, but the International Secretary, Jenny Little, stayed on minus her department, answering directly to the General Secretary. It was difficult to find anyone who believed that these changes would make a substantial difference to how the Labour Party operates.

Yet the message of the last fifteen years is clear. With the growth of local radio and regional television, with the development of the three-party system, with the knowledge that local and regional variations in voting can be critical and decisive, the Labour Party must learn to devolve if it is to win votes and win power.

The Party must devolve at several levels. At the level of research, publicity, and tactical planning it must devolve into the regions. At the level of grass-roots organisation and expanding membership it must devolve into the constituencies, with resources put into re-establishing full-time agents in the 250 or more seats that have lost them in the last thirty years. Finally, it must devolve back to the individual Party members, including the many who cannot spend endless hours in meetings, arguing about procedural niceties but who are firm socialists on whose votes and work Labour depends for the winning of elections and formulation of practical policies. Members must be given a new relationship and a new sense of involvement with the Party.

Chapter Two

———————— ∘∘◯∘∘ ————————

False Gods

Many of the problems of the twentieth century have arisen because people will persist in treating Karl Marx as a god and not as a man. From this basic fallacy all sorts of errors follow; absolutism, intolerance, contempt for democracy, and the recruitment of lesser gods to populate the pantheon of socialism. Those who cannot live without the supreme god, Marx, often need a lesser god, a living god, to guide them in their day-to-day political activities. This living god may be the guru of an obscure sect, passing on Hegelian wisdom on tablets of stone. It may be a Privy Counsellor running for the Deputy Leadership of the Labour Party. It may be the leader of the Greater London Council, fighting a spirited and costly battle to save that body from abolition. It may be the President of the National Union of Mineworkers, presiding over a year-old strike doomed to end in defeat and division.

The Labour Party's strength over the decades is that it has rejected false gods. It has regarded Marx as a man, not as a deity. It has taken his theories as theories, not as holy writ. Ignorance plays no part in this attitude. Confront a veteran trade unionist of the Left, or his equivalent in Parliament, with the most dogmatic Marxist/Leninist/Trotskyist academic and the academic is likely to get an unpleasant shock. A bright young woman lawyer with Parliamentary aspirations once made the mistake of quoting Marx to such a trade unionist. 'Well,' he replied, 'aren't you going to finish the quotation?' She could not; he could.

The British Labour movement has always seen Marx as a great economist striving in his very Victorian way to create an exact science out of economics. It has viewed his clumsy excursions into politics with a critical eye. It has accepted the steel in his analysis of the capitalist system, but it has forged that steel into a solid link with the trade union movement — a link that Marx, the intellectual, could not have imagined. Indeed, it is impossible to understand the British Labour Party unless that link is understood too.

The trade unionists who formed the Labour Party were concerned with practical empirical programmes for the benefit of their members. Philosophical concepts could aid them in understanding and tackling problems but could never become ends in themselves.

They wanted full employment for their members; they wanted the workers to share in the products of their own labour; they wanted a health service and health and safety standards at work to protect their members in sickness and from injury; they wanted a free and equal education system for their children; they wanted a society in which talent, not money, would be the deciding factor in a citizen's progress through life; they wanted, which is rare, a society which showed compassion to those who fell behind in the competitive race of life, for whatever reason.

The struggle of these trade unionists mirrored that of the suffragists who advocated votes for women. It was only when men began to be aware of the potential of the feminine vote that the social legislation needed to protect women and children began to be put into effect. It was only the growth of the Labour Party that provoked a sudden affection in early twentieth-century Liberals for national insurance, retirement pensions, full employment, and the beginnings of the health service.

But there was for Labour's pioneers a dilemma, an enduring dilemma, in knitting highly practical trade union goals with the concepts of socialism. Sidney Webb confronted this in 1918 when he drafted the Labour Party's constitution, which became its accepted philosophy. In trying to settle for all time the needs of the Labour Party, it may not have entirely succeeded; but in a country that does not like written constitutions and has resolutely refused to have one as an arbiter over its own national life it is impossible not to pay tribute to the lasting quality of that constitution as a statement of aims.

The Labour Party, wrote Webb in his introduction to the Party's constitution, 'is unreservedly democratic in its conviction that only by the widest possible participation in power and the generally spread consciousness of consent can any civilised country attain either the fullest life or its utmost efficiency'.

Fifty years later, in her chairman's address to the annual conference of the Labour Party, Jennie Lee looked back to 1917 at what were then the alternatives to democratic socialism: 'Before the Russian people reached their present level of modest well-being they went all the way to hell and back on a journey lasting half a century. Violent revolution is the slowest, the most costly and the cruellest way of bringing on social change. It is something not to be glamorised but to be strenuously avoided if there is any other way forward.'

There is nothing un-Marxist about this. Indeed Engels in his introduction to the English edition of *Capital* tells us authoritatively that Marx had concluded that England was the only country 'where the inevitable social revolution might be effected entirely by peaceful and legal means'. But that, alas, was only Karl Marx himself speaking. His self-proclaimed disciples are seldom inclined to take his word for it. Rather they prefer their Marxism reflected through the violence of twentieth-century history, as seen by his numerous self-serving interpreters.

To understand the upheavals that have afflicted the Labour Party in recent years it is necessary to understand something of the different strands of twentieth-century Marxism, starting with Georges Sorel, father of syndicalism — or Scargillism, as the press called it more recently.

Sorel posed a simple problem: how does one generate the will among people to carry through a social revolution? His answer: through the creation of a 'myth' that, for the working classes, would be more powerful than the existing establishment 'myths' of the state, nationalism and Parliamentary democracy. He suggested that the ideal 'myth' would be 'the general strike'. It would be a symbol of class struggle and of the need for violence to overthrow the existing system.

It is pertinent that Sorel made clear that this 'myth' was not descriptive but 'the expression of the will'. There might, in other words, never be a general strike or a transfer of power resulting from one. It was a slogan, one that was meant to be so powerful that working people would come to believe in the inevitable need for violence if they were ever to achieve decency in their lives. This could only come about if capitalism was strong and ruthless, thus provoking the workers into action because they became so discontented.

Next, in chronological order, came Leninism, the best-known offshoot of Marxism. It is characterised by the one-party state and by that supreme piece of twentieth-century Newspeak, 'democratic centralism': in practice, dictatorship.

Next Trotskyism, which is a very confused and confusing animal indeed. Leon Trotsky, the supreme opportunist whose gamble finally failed, held so many conflicting views at different times — Sorel was similar in this respect — that almost any political belief could be ascribed to him. But he ended his days preaching world revolution and, in the British context, the theories of 'entryism' and 'transitional demands'.

'Entryism' means that his followers should join the Labour Party, gain as much support inside it as possible, provoke a split in the Party, and should they then do so leave with their faction stronger than it had been when they entered. Meanwhile, they should cause chaos in the Party and in society. In other words, it is not only the enemies of Trotskyism who see them as parasites within the Labour Party — that is how the Trotskyites see themselves.

'Transitional demands' — demands on the transition to revolution — are an echo of syndicalism. They are a programme of demands that are impossible to achieve under capitalism but are, nevertheless, included in the Party programme to create dissatisfaction when they are not achieved and thus to raise political consciousness.

Lastly, there came the latest work of Professor Herbert Marcuse, the guru of so much Sixties student radicalism. Marcuse believed that the working class could no longer become a coherent revolutionary force, having been bought off by post-Second World War prosperity. Marcuse propagated his theory of the 'coalition of minorities' — a coalition of blacks, feminists, homosexuals, students, or the lowest-paid workers — who would form a revolutionary alliance of the deprived. When Paris exploded in the spring of 1968 it all looked quite convincing. Even de Gaulle was temporarily put to flight. Senator Eugene McCarthy's bid for the Democratic Presidential nomination in the same year attempted to bring together a similar coalition of minorities — although clearly for non-revolutionary purposes. He failed, but in 1970 the Democratic Party opened its national caucus to representatives of minority groups.

In identifying these four simple strands of twentieth-century Marxism I will have offended any number of theoreticians, purists, and political activists. Few Marxists today, for example, would accept the company of Georges Sorel — not least because he became a guru of Italian Fascism, inspiring Mussolini on his march to Rome. That is their problem, not mine. (Fascism was also a revolutionary movement and at times borrowed the clothes, ideas and methods of revolutionary Marxism. Mussolini was the son of a socialist father who named him Benito after Benito Juarez, the Republican President of Mexico. Stalin, in later years, used to recall his one visit to London, in 1908, when he attended an international socialist meeting chaired by Mussolini.)

In understanding the recent history of the Labour Party Sorel is particularly interesting as the theoretician of the political slogan: the man who believed that a false slogan could be true. Sorel's instructions to the would-be revolutionary, to create 'myths' that are 'not descriptions of things but the expressions of the will', is today followed religiously by politicians in the syndicalist mould. The slogan manufactured for the 1984-85 miners' strike was 'No Pit Closures', stated without any qualifications or time-limit whatsoever, and under this slogan miners devotedly fought and faced privation for upwards of twelve months. As a declaration of policy it was nonsense; as a syndicalist slogan it fits both the logic of Sorel and the logic of Trotsky's 'transitional demands'.

The problem for those who espouse such politics, which treat ordinary workers and voters as either fellow conspirators or half-witted, is that they do not stand up to democratic scrutiny. To overcome this those who would destroy the democracy and socialism of the Labour Party favour 'democratic centralism'. They would reduce the decision-making process to a small group of professional apparatchiks and so make the problem of wider credibility and support vanish.

'Democratic centralism' is seen in an extreme form in the Revolutionary Socialist League, a tiny secret caucus that does not even acknowledge its existence to the larger grouping it controls and directs — the Militant Tendency. Militant, in turn, denies that it is an organised caucus within the Labour Party — it consists, we are told, merely of sellers and supporters of *Militant* newspaper. A few years ago Militant decided that the Labour Party Young Socialists were ripe for takeover, thereby gaining an automatic seat on the Labour Party NEC. The Young Socialist vote on the NEC was cast according to the instructions of the Revolutionary Socialist League which, through its NEC member and the Party's Youth Officer, had full access to all NEC documents — including those which gave the names of people who recommended the expulsion of Militant members from the Party.

It is doubtful if any of this would have bothered Professor Marcuse. He was all in favour of factions and caucuses. His theory was that if there were enough of them and they were all pointing in the same direction then revolution could be achieved. It is a theory readily adaptable to democratic politics, as it was in America, with the coalitions that opposed the Vietnam War and campaigned for racial equality in voting, civil rights, and job opportunity. But once adopted by democrats as anything more than a temporary measure it quickly becomes a theory of the Right, not the Left, resting as it does on the assumption that the basic problems of the production and distribution of wealth are secondary to the particular problems of blacks, homosexuals, lesbians, and other specific minorities.

It is bizarre that this theory should have been espoused, in time of recession, by such prominent Labour politicians as Ken Livingstone and Tony Benn. For Herbert Marcuse writing in the years of post-war prosperity, it made some sense. Today, the shallowness of such thinking has been exposed. Today, any suggestion that sectional interests are more important than those of the broad working class, of all races, genders, and sexual inclinations, can only undermine the unity that is the basis of Labour's strength. Some people, of course, want to do just that.

It is out of these four strands of Marxism — syndicalism, Leninism, Trotskyism, and the 'coalition of minorities' — that the problems of the Labour Party in recent years have been woven. That is not to say that there would be no problems in the Labour Party if these disturbing elements would go away. Far from it. The Labour Party has created many problems for itself in the last twenty years, but the Marxist solutions to these problems have been a major obstacle and a distraction from real solutions. The real problems and the false solutions have become confused and compounded with every passing year.

To understand the Eighties it is necessary to understand the Sixties and early Seventies, for the generation now rising to prominence first knew politics then. Many of those who took part in the Grosvenor Square anti-Vietnam War demonstration of 1968, or in the storming of the gates at the London School of Economics in the same year, are now approaching middle age.

The Sixties were years of prosperity, therefore they were years of rising expectations. The bitterness of the Sixties generation — even the cynicism of its politics — can be traced to this simple fact: these were the years of the Vietnam War, when many young people abandoned the Labour Party in despair at the failure of the Leadership to condemn American intervention in South-East Asia. This failure fostered a belief in the inherent treachery of Labour Party leaders, a belief energetically encouraged by Trotskyites, who see in every leader a Stalin betraying a Trotsky, and by Communists, whose support for the Vietnamese resistance was understandably uncompromising.

Such divisions were further fuelled by conflict over the Labour Government's wish to introduce trade union legislation as proposed by Barbara Castle's ill-conceived White Paper 'In Place of Strife', and, in the Seventies, by conflicts over Common Market membership and wage restraint, culminating in the 'Winter of Discontent' that helped bring down the 1974-79 Labour Government.

The understandable obsession with Vietnam in the Sixties brought with it an element of the cult of violence. For many campaigners, naive as well as politically motivated, the slogan was not 'Peace in Vietnam' but 'Victory for the Viet Cong'. Trotskyite journals carried on their cover an obligatory picture of a revolutionary guerrilla fighter waving a Kalashnikov.

26

Even the pathetic and ignominious death of Che Guevara in the Bolivian jungle was raised to an heroic event, although in truth it was an object lesson in how not to start a revolution.

This was the time when young activists involved themselves in single-issue campaigns — against the Vietnam War itself, against apartheid, for revolutionary movements in the Third World. Later, activists from that generation were at the forefront of campaigns for mandatory reselection of Labour Members of Parliament, for an electoral college to choose Labour's Leader and Deputy Leader, and thus to make Tony Benn the Deputy Leader of the Labour Party. As single-issue campaigners they were professional and single-minded, but many of them had not learned that there is more to politics than banner-waving. In attempting to prove their credentials as political thinkers most retreated back to Professor Marcuse. Their 'left-wing' thought showed little advance over Senator Eugene McCarthy or any other Left-leaning American of the Sixties.

The Sixties was also the decade when decline of the post-war British economy began to be a subject of concern and debate. The decline of Britain's industry was accompanied by profound social changes. Industrial inner city areas that were once the heart of the Labour movement altered. Factories closed or moved. The inner city became 'de-industrialised' and with that came a break in the organic link between the worker, the shop floor activist, the local community, the local council, and the local MP. As the factories went, so did the younger workers. Their place in the Victorian artisans' dwellings began to be taken by young professional people. The council blocks became increasingly populated by the old and by young women single parents, bringing an increased burden of social services on local councils already hard-pressed by the loss in rates revenue from industry. A vicious spiral set in: rates had to rise to meet the cost of services and new industry was discouraged by the cost.

As Britain's cities changed so did the Labour Party's active membership. The traditional activists, the worker/shop steward/Party members, had the advantage of being accountable in all their waking hours to the community they lived in and served. Any flights of fancy were dealt with very firmly on the shop floor or by their neighbours. In those days 'accountability' did not embrace the standing orders that present-day activists talk about, but a living, day-to-day accountability arising out of life in the locality. With the breaking up of inner city communities this living accountability faded — and with it much of the traditional base of the Labour Party. In many places — indeed in parts of my own constituency of Deptford — the Labour Party became separated from its industrial roots. The bedsit brigade took over.

The profile of the modern inner city Labour Party activist all too often looks rather like this: a student, or somebody with a university or polytechnic degree living with friends of like mind in a run-down Victorian house or in a hard-to-let council tower block flat. These people join the local Labour Party and being young and eager with a great deal of spare time soon control their ward organisation. Soon they form a tenants' association. The council leader, who keeps a close eye on these developments as a matter of necessity, issues instructions to his whip that somebody from this tenants' association should be co-opted on to the council's housing committee. Within the space of a few months this group of young people can gain more influence within an inner city borough than tens of thousands of council tenants and ordinary working or retired people.

Out of this background a new breed of political activist has been born: decent people in the main but with problems getting their political bearings; people who can be far too easily led by unscrupulous leaders who claim in speeches and fringe publications to have all the answers to very difficult problems. If the council after all is to give them a free lease on their squat plus, perhaps, a large grant of public money to renovate it or a speedy transfer to a council flat, who are these young inexperienced people to doubt the wisdom of the council politicians and do anything but support them in their aspirations beyond the local scene? Disdainful of the working classes they see around them, the new political activists prefer to create a mythical working class of their own. Usually this working class exists in books and abroad but occasionally they like to think it is seen close to home. In the miners' strike of 1984-85 these new activists travelled by the coach-load to the mining villages of the North and Wales, where they could gawk at real workers like tourists in a safari park.

This may seem a long way from Karl Marx or even Leon Trotsky and, indeed, it is. But it is out of these minor tragedies of everyday life, of young people searching for a role in life, of the exploitation of the vulnerable by the politically and financially unscrupulous, that so many of our problems arise. A young person of poor education, unemployed, stuck in a council flat with his parents, may turn to the National Front or football hooliganism for adventure. The young intellectuals, trying to reconcile their hopes with disappointing realities, search for their own forms of self-assertion equally unrestrained by elders, betters, or anyone else outside their own isolated sub-culture. What finer ego trip than to believe yourself to be in the vanguard of a revolutionary change in society?

There is just one snag, however: a revolutionary change in society demands a left wing of the Labour Party to achieve it. The trouble is that there already is a left wing; it has its place in history, it has achieved a number of notable victories in the cause of progress, its members date back to the days of Robert Blatchford, and in more recent times Aneurin Bevan and Jennie Lee contributed largely to the achievements of the Labour movement in Britain; but they all believed, as do their modern counterparts, in achieving power and change by Parliamentary means. To the newcomers this is not at all to their taste. This is why the incumbent Left is called 'the soft Left' and the newcomers have adopted for themselves the title of 'the hard Left' — to show that they alone are faithful to the true religion. But, even if one is whoring after false gods, the false gods demand a prophet on earth. For some years there was no candidate but by the late Seventies the hard Left had found one in the somewhat unlikely person of The Rt. Hon. Anthony Wedgwood Benn. For a prophet his immediate ambition was a suitably modest one: he intended to become the Deputy Leader of the Labour Party.

Chapter Three

──────── ∘∘◯∘∘ ────────

Into Chaos

What was the battle over who would be Deputy Leader of the Labour Party really all about? Why so much fuss over a position in the Labour Party that so far had carried little real power? The answer is that the forces that backed Tony Benn saw it as the next logical step in their campaign to control of the Labour Party.

Step one was mandatory reselection; step two was the electoral college; step three was the installation of a Deputy Leader who had become one of them and whom they could control. A Deputy Leader elected by the electoral college would, they reasoned, have more power than one elected solely by the Parliamentary Labour Party (PLP). Tony Benn, they would be able to argue, would have more legitimacy as Deputy Leader than Michael Foot had as Leader, since Foot had been elected by the PLP.

Once elected, Benn would be promoted as the 'real' Leader of the Labour Party. Michael Foot would automatically be treated inside the Labour Party as an ageing figurehead of the old order. To those outside the Labour Party, it may seem confusing that Foot might be regarded in this way: was not he, after all, also a man of the Left? Was he not one of its father-figures, a founder of the Campaign for Nuclear Disarmament, a veteran rebel?

Michael Foot was not, in fact, as popular with all elements of the Left as is often supposed. A socialist literary intellectual, of the tradition dating back to George Bernard Shaw and H. G. Wells — a tradition that had created the most influential journal of the Left, the *New Statesman* — he was envied and despised by many whose education and entry into politics arose from different origins.

His old journal, *Tribune*, had once employed George Orwell as its literary editor and columnist, but thirty years later, when Foot was Leader of the Party, there were those who attacked it for devoting its centre spread to books and the arts. These pages, they snarled, should be given over to "campaigning issues". For those who became politically aware mainly through student politics and the anti-Vietnam War campaigns of the Sixties, politics was mainly about waving banners. In spirit, they were still marching across Westminster Bridge in the autumn of 1968, red banners fluttering in the breeze against the backdrop of the House of Commons, heading for Grosvenor Square and the American Embassy.

They did not know that Foot knew more about campaigning than they did. *Tribune* was always a campaigning newspaper, even if it also devoted pages to books and the arts. It became a great newspaper through two campaigns: the one led by Aneurin Bevan for a second front during the Second World War, and the one led by Foot himself for nuclear disarmament during the Fifties. There are conflicting claims over whether *Tribune* or the *New Statesman* was the true precursor of CND: probably both periodicals can take equal credit.

Michael Foot was a founder member of the Tribune Group in the House of Commons, a group that has always been particularly hated by Trotskyites, who remain determined to prove that nothing in the Labour Party, bar Trotskyism, is truly left-wing. Foot, as a true intellectual, was perfectly familiar with Trotskyite thought, and had indeed been quite friendly for a number of years with Gerry Healy, that old warhorse of British Trotskyism.

Their parting of the ways came at about the time when Gerry Healy was spotted standing in the gutter outside the Labour Party conference as the delegates streamed out for lunch. Beside him was a photographer rapidly using up roll after roll of film. When asked what he was doing, Healy would only mutter: 'We know who the traitors are.' He was bringing his files up to date for use after the revolution when, of course, he would be in charge. There is probably a blurred photograph of a youthful John Silkin stored away in a basement somewhere, along with several hundred others. Mine undoubtedly has 'Immediate Execution' stamped across it. After 1981 it was probably moved to a priority file.

The fate of Tony Benn's photograph would have been different. It would have earned him an 'Immediate Execution' stamp in the nineteen-fifties. He might well have been photographed leaving the hall with his close friend, Tony Crosland, both of them perhaps a few paces behind Hugh Gaitskell — for at that time Anthony Wedgwood Benn was firmly a Gaitskellite, a man of the Right. Another fifteen years were to pass before he began his Odyssey to the Left, and five more before he would make his bid for power as the standard-bearer of the hard Left.

'Standard-bearer' is perhaps not the right word. The flag that Tony Benn has waved for the last decade has resembled more of a patchwork quilt, stitched together out of the numerous enthusiasms that have galvanised him over the years. Like Toad of Toad Hall, it is his enthusiasms that have kept him going.

An enquiry to Eric Heffer for a reading list on the English Revolution and other examples of English rebelliousness led within a few weeks to Benn lecturing an irritated Heffer on the subject. For a while Benn became an apostle of romantic nationalism — not usually a cause associated with the Left. He became temporarily a convert to portable technology, carrying both a camera and tape recorder at all times.

He once secretly took a photograph of a Cabinet meeting, against the rules, but forgot to put any film in the camera. Future historians will be able to consult a Cabinet minute in which an amused Harold Wilson laid down as a precedent for Cabinet Ministers that they should be allowed to take photographs at Cabinet meetings provided that there was no film in the camera.

Benn was a leading campaigner against Common Market membership during the referendum of 1975, but later, as Secretary of State for Energy, his enthusiasms got the better of him. After his six months as President of the EEC Energy Council — a position held by all the EEC Energy Ministers in rotation — he drafted a document on his Presidential achievements. The Foreign Office, not notorious for its opposition to the EEC, vetoed its publication on the grounds that it was far too pro-Market.

Then there was the time when I was due to fly to Brussels for a meeting of the Common Market Fisheries Council. I knew I would be using the British veto several times to stop fisheries policies which would have been disastrous for the UK fishing industry. We were on the point of taking off from RAF Manston in Kent when a radio message came through saying that I was wanted urgently on the telephone. The aircraft's engines were stopped. Civil servants climbed out and sat on the grass while I was driven rapidly back to the CO's office to take the call. It was Tony Benn. He was, he explained, going to Brussels himself the next day to negotiate on the siting of the Joint European Torus nuclear fusion reactor, which he wished to have in Britain. Could I please not do anything, like using the veto, to annoy the other countries? I explained that I had the matter of the future of the British fishing industry to consider. I soared off into the blue, used the veto repeatedly, and, despite my stand, the JET nuclear fusion programme which Tony Benn fought so hard for has been based at Culham in Oxfordshire for some years now.

Tony Benn's redeeming quality has always been his sense of fun, and his uncontrolled enthusiasms are no doubt part of that. But politically they have made him a man of convictions — not of conviction. Before the dramatic events of 1981 there was certainly no animosity between us. When I was Chief Whip I would often listen at length to his latest enthusiasm and would reflect ruefully that I was playing the part of Badger in a production of *The Wind in the Willows*.

To many people on the Left, Benn's very capriciousness was attractive. For Trotskyites, forced for years to listen to such boring gurus as Gerry Healy, Ted Grant (Militant) and Tony Cliff (Socialist Workers Party), he was a godsend. He did not talk about Hegel, was never known to use the word 'cognition', nor indulge in dialectics. On the contrary, he was guaranteed to give only the side of the argument that those listening wanted to hear. Articulate, plausible, affluent, public-school- and Oxford-educated, he could say simple things in a simple way — he had to, because he had probably only read the book the day before. He spoke with the voice of certainty and had mastered the art of saying next-to-nothing with great sincerity on television.

As a former television producer he knew the value of self-publicising. He kept his television and press contacts brightly polished, but not so polished as his own well-rehearsed appearances on television and radio and his cleverly timed interventions in the national press, all the while protesting about the injustices done to him by the very organs of publicity he was so assiduously courting.

Moreover, he brought one other expertise in which none of his rivals could match him: as Postmaster General and later Minister of Technology in the Sixties he was the only politician of his generation in Britain who fully appreciated the advantages of computers. He understood more than anybody that if he was to take over the leadership of the Labour Party he would do it not because he was universally popular, but because he could assess the tactical situation and the numbers involved better than anyone else.

Added to these advantages Benn had made a crucial discovery. He discovered before most people the practical impact of the changes in the Labour Party's rules. The new electoral college reduced the Parliamentary Labour Party's role in leadership elections from 100 per cent to 30 per cent. It became vital for Labour MPs with leadership ambitions to spend much more time talking to Constituency Parties and trade unions, even at the cost of neglecting Parliamentary duties. Benn saw this now obvious fact before most because he had worked for the adoption of the electoral college. He drew his own personal inner cabinet from among activists of the Campaign for Labour Party Democracy, the organisation that was co-ordinating the campaign for change.

This inner cabinet, which met at his Holland Park home on Sunday mornings, consisted mainly of people half his age. They were generally short on wisdom, but they provided Benn with an admirable sounding board for the new electorate of young activists in the constituencies that he wished to woo. Through the network of new pressure groups springing up in the Party — the Labour Co-ordinating Committee, the Rank and File Mobilising Committee — they were able to give access to people who would one day swing Constituency Party votes in his direction in the electoral college or at conference.

Now that the prospect is well behind us we can safely speculate on what would have happened if Benn had been elected Deputy Leader. How would he have coped? Would he have coped at all? Would his undermining of Michael Foot have brought a reaction against him? Or would he have disillusioned his followers? 'Are you really on the Left?' his youthful supporters would ask people at parties. 'Do you support Benn?' His subsequent relations with his supporters would have brought an immediate clash between promises and reality. But in 1981 the atmosphere was still heady. It was a strange period: a time when it was a disadvantage to have been in the Labour Party for more than two years. Any longer than that and you were tainted with the sins of the past — sins that Benn himself catalogued in speech after speech. The fact that he had been in every Labour Cabinet over two decades and, therefore, a party to every sin, real or imagined, of the Wilson and Callaghan years, was forgotten.

He had never, at any time, threatened to resign, even when he was bitterly opposed to actions of the Government. Eric Heffer, his Minister of State, had been sacked over the Common Market issue. Joan Lestor had left over cuts in education. I had offered my resignation at the time of the White Paper on trade union law, 'In Place of Strife' to which I was opposed and had only withdrawn it when it became clear that this would have been used to provoke civil war within the Party. There were other examples — but Tony Benn sailed serenely on, moving from one Cabinet position to another without a murmur.

Such loyalty was thought admirable at the time. It was his total disloyalty after the event, his purging of his own "guilt" by denouncing his former comrades, that put Tony Benn beyond the pale as far as many Labour MPs were concerned.

Through his hard work and tortuous tactics, Benn gained the support of the young, the innocent, and the politically cynical. The young had not been born when he was a Gaitskellite, were babies when he was a pro-Marketeer, were at school when he was a Cabinet Minister. Older persons on the Left supported him because they liked what he was saying and turned a blind eye to the past. They were eager for a messiah to command the Party. The Trotskyites, too, could fit him into their cynical scheme of things. They felt they could control him and as for the divisive effect of his bid for the Deputy

Leadership — that was a desirable part of the scheme of things, too. For the Labour Party to split was, according to entryist theory, a necessity — for it to split with the Deputy Leader as the figurehead of their faction was a superb bonus, a giant step towards the Promised Land of Revolution.

The rise of Tony Benn and the forces behind him inevitably brought reactions. One was the founding of the Social Democratic Party; another was the re-grouping of the Labour Right in the Labour Solidarity Campaign; the third was a left-wing opposition to his candidature for the Deputy Leadership.

The Right and the Left of the Labour Party have another thing in common, apart from being in the same Party. It is that they persist in misunderstanding each other. The Right invents a monolithic 'Left', lumping together people of widely differing views. The Left views the Right in the same over-simplified way. The truth about the Right is that it has never been monolithic. The most obvious proof of this is the fact that Harold Wilson led the Labour Party for twelve years. He was elected in 1963 precisely because the Right was divided then and it remained divided.

At a slight risk of over-simplification, the Right of the Sixties could be divided into the James Callaghan Right and the George Brown/Roy Jenkins Right. The Callaghan Right was the Right of the trade union barons, whose power was just then beginning to wane. It was characterised by a great loyalty to both the trade union movement and to the Labour Party, and a trust in their strength and durability. It was this trust that eventually destroyed the Callaghan Government: he believed that the trade union barons could still deliver, even when they told him very clearly that they could not. The 'Winter of Discontent' followed and then the spring 1979 election defeat.

In contrast, the George Brown/Roy Jenkins Right was the faction not of defenders of the working-class movement but of intellectuals. They saw themselves as the heirs to the Gaitskellite legacy. They tended to be uncomfortable both with the working class and with the word 'socialism'. Tony Benn — or Anthony Wedgwood Benn as he still was in those days — was one of them. So, too, was Shirley Williams when she entered the House of Commons. Roy Hattersley could be seen in their company but though he was with them he was not of them — as he was to prove in 1981 by his refusal to accompany them into exile.

The Brown/Jenkins Right first began to feel extreme discomfort in the early Seventies over the issue of Common Market membership. The Labour Party's decision to review U.K. membership through a national referendum brought Roy Jenkins's resignation from the Deputy Leadership and, therefore, from the Shadow Cabinet. George Thomson, Dick Taverne, David Owen, Harold Lever and Dickson Mabon also resigned from the Front Bench. Of these, all save Harold Lever and George Thomson were eventually to join the SDP. These resignations came in April 1972. In July of that year Dick Taverne was de-selected by his Party in Lincoln. He resigned his seat, forcing a by-election which he won comfortably in March 1973, despite failing to persuade Roy Jenkins and other friends to break with the Labour Party and support him. Dick Taverne retained his seat in the February 1974 General Election, but his efforts to get several other 'social democrats' into Parliament failed and he himself was defeated at Lincoln in the October 1974 Election.

Taverne was the John the Baptist of the SDP. He had experienced de-selection — the fear that helped to push several right-wing Labour MPs towards the SDP — but had bounced back to show that a then-safe Labour seat could be won for the Social Democratic cause. It has been said that Roy Jenkins now deeply regrets not having joined with Taverne in 1972. All the same, it was the Right, not the Left, that won the Common Market referendum battle in 1975. Jenkins himself soon departed for Brussels to become President of the EEC Commission.

After Labour's election defeat in 1979 the inquest began. The most enthusiastic in apportioning blame to others were Tony Benn and his supporters. At the 1979 Labour Party conference Benn made a blistering attack on the Government in which he had so recently served. At the same conference mandatory reselection was approved. The following year conference approved, in principle, the idea of an electoral college for the election of Leader and Deputy Leader. The exact composition of the electoral college was left to a special conference at Wembley Conference Centre on January 25, 1981. Before that could occur, James Callaghan resigned as

Leader and Michael Foot, elected by the PLP, succeeded him.

The Wembley Conference was confusion. The opponents of the electoral college had not done their sums; its supporters, who had after all invented the idea, had. The shopworkers' union, USDAW, put down what its leaders imagined was a wrecking motion. In a series of lunchtime meetings the followers of the Campaign for Labour Party Democracy decided to support the USDAW motion, which was to give 40 per cent of college votes to the trade unions and 30 per cent each to the PLP and the constituencies. The AUEW, the engineering union, whose President — no mathematician — allegedly favoured a 40-40-40 split, decided to abstain. The Right marched confidently to defeat, convinced to the end that they had outwitted their opponents. A journalist who went to ask David Owen's opinion within minutes of the result was startled to find that the former Foreign Secretary was certain that 40 per cent of the vote now rested with the PLP.

Dr Owen's thoughts seem to have been elsewhere. They may have been on the Limehouse Declaration that he, Roy Jenkins, Shirley Williams and Bill Rodgers were to release the next day.

The Declaration was a brief, anodyne statement (it was, after all, drafted by Roy Jenkins) calling for a 'realignment' in British politics. It still did not commit them to setting up a new party, although it could have no other long-term implication. The 'Gang of Four' were taking things slowly. It was already more than a year since Bill Rodgers had said that the Labour Party had only a year to put its house in order; and at about the same time Jenkins, giving the annual Dimbleby Lecture for the BBC, had tried to work out an ideology for 'realignment'.

For those on the Right of the Party, possible recruits to social democracy, it was a time of extraordinary stress. The two organisations of the Right within the Party, the PLP Manifesto Group and the Campaign for Labour Victory (the successor to the Campaign for Democratic Socialism of the Sixties), were divided and effectively ceased to exist. Rodgers was working hard to recruit MPs for the Social Democrats, while a group around Roy Hattersley was trying to keep the Labour Parliamentary Right intact.

It was a time of rumours. There was talk of a third political grouping, a 'New Labour Party' or 'Parliamentary Labour Party', that would pre-empt the launch of the SDP and kill it stone dead. There was talk of the Fabian Society being the nucleus of this new party: it had offices in Westminster, a secretariat, mailing lists. There was talk also, as an alternative, of mass expulsions from the Labour Party. In the fevered atmosphere of the times some people arrived at a definition of 'Trotskyites' that embraced about two-thirds of the membership of the Labour Party.

Roy Hattersley moved to set up Labour Solidarity, a new organisation on the Right. It came into existence in February 1981 with Hattersley and Peter Shore as joint chairmen. It drew a wide membership from the PLP, including four members of the Tribune Group, two of whom, Arthur Davidson and Frank Field, were later to support my bid for the Deputy Leadership. Solidarity secured some financial support from wealthy party members. It had a full-time secretary and considerable help from two trade unions in particular, the EEPTU (which had the Campaign for Labour Victory mailing list on its computer) and APEX.

Solidarity's value was as much symbolic and therapeutic as real. It gave many MPs an opportunity to affirm their support for Labour governments. Worried activists could telephone in from around the country and denounce the activities of their local hard Left. Solidarity could not actually do very much but at least it seemed to its supporters that certain problems were being recognised. It could not really help individual MPs who feared de-selection, some of whom dreaded going back to their constituencies where Trotskyites were in control and exultant. But it gave some MPs a feeling that perhaps they were not completely alone as with heavy hearts they headed towards their constituencies and confrontation with their detractors.

Local Solidarity groups were also formed to try to help. Denis Healey, the Deputy Leader who was soon to be challenged by Tony Benn, kept his distance from Solidarity, and Solidarity, officially, kept its distance from him. It was supposed to be an organisation campaigning for the whole Labour Party, not for individuals within it. This was window-dressing: late in the Deputy Leadership contest it came out publicly for Healey.

Solidarity's attempts to look impartial were somewhat disingenuous. Solidarity was largely Hattersley's idea and he wanted to use it to promote himself and those he agreed with.

Solidarity, in its internal organisation, was the mirror image of Militant but overwhelmingly less efficient. It was controlled by a secret caucus behind its public façade and that caucus had an intense loyalty to Roy Hattersley. The most powerful people who backed Solidarity did so on the clear assumption that Hattersley would be the next Leader of the Labour Party following Michael Foot's retirement. The presence of Peter Shore as joint chairman was little more than a subterfuge to hide the real purpose of the organisation. Shore had polled 32 votes against my 38 in the 1980 Leadership contest, coming last, but was still being spoken of as a future Leader in supposedly informed circles. In reality Hattersley already had the Right's support guaranteed.

What of Denis Healey? He, too, was out. It had been decided by the king-makers of the Right that a generation should be skipped.

Looking back, Solidarity leaders can be seen to have made three mistakes, stemming from their tiny ruling caucus. In their advocacy and threats of expulsion of the undesirable elements on the Left they were often excessively strident and indiscriminate, thus maximising opposition to Solidarity and those they supported. The second mistake came from this same lack of perspective: they disliked the Left too much to understand that Tony Benn was far from being its unchallengeable standard-bearer. Thirdly, like the hard Left, they had become mesmerised by means rather than ends. For them, like the hard Left, there could be no neutrals: if you were not a member of Solidarity you were an enemy as far as many of its keenest exponents were concerned. Far from being the answer to Militant and the rest of the hard Left, Solidarity became part of the problem.

Chapter Four

———————————— ∘∘◯∘∘ ————————————

Belling Benn

Tony Benn's bid for the deputy leadership of the Labour Party in 1981 was not only an indictment of Benn the politician, as a man who put his own ambition above the strength and stability of the Party during a crucial period in its history, but was also an indictment of the electoral system that the party had created for itself at the Wembley conference only a few months before.

To be a serious contender for a party post under the electoral college system you need vastly more money, human resources, and organisations than was ever contemplated under the old system. To gain support from the trade unions you have to cultivate union executives, branch activists, and, in some unions more than others, the membership itself. Gaining support among the CLPs is, if anything, an even more time-consuming business. Cultivating the members of over six hundred parties requires years of work.

In the Parliamentary Party the right of the MP to make his own choice, as before, remains theoretically unchanged, but mandatory re-selection has, in reality, made all MPs more subject to pressure from their CLPs. In the eyes of constituency activists of the hard Left, it is a betrayal for the MP to do anything but vote the same way as the CLP. This means that some CLPs can often effectively have two votes. The double vote was an essential element of Tony Benn's 1981 campaign to encourage his own interpretation of democracy.

To launch such a campaign was akin to a military operation. As in a military operation, it demanded a great deal of preparation, yet at the same time the element of surprise was of supreme importance. Benn's approach to the contest was to keep everybody guessing what he would do next. This approach combined the maximum of publicity with the minimum of risk. He was finally forced to declare himself when his opponents on the Left launched a pre-emptive strike.

It was at 3.30 in the morning of April 3, 1981, during an all-night sitting of the House of Commons, that Tony Benn announced that he was contesting the Deputy Leadership. For Benn this rushed announcement was as near as he came to an admission of weakness: he was not, in the end, able to choose his own moment to launch an attack. Only by sending his panzers rolling in the dead of night could he regain the initiative; but regain the initiative he did.

He made the announcement, after a hurried conclave with his leading advisers, when he realised the strength of feeling against him within the Parliamentary Labour Party. He had joined the Tribune Group shortly before — Michael Meacher had made the initial approach on his behalf — with the clear intention of gaining its support, willing or otherwise, for his Deputy Leadership bid, but he had not received the welcome he had hoped for.

Most members of the Tribune Group were not particularly keen on the incumbent Deputy Leader, Denis Healey, but thought he should be allowed to remain in his post undisturbed. The battle to remove him, in their assessment, could only damage the Party unnecessarily. It was quietly decided that something had to be done to head off the ambitious Benn.

During that all-night sitting of April 2 and 3, the Tribunites were busy circulating a letter and collecting signatories: the letter urged Benn not to stand in the interests of the Party as a whole. The young Scottish MP Robin Cook — later, alas, to capitulate and support Benn — was doing the legwork and it had already been signed by a number of MPs who would have been expected by the Bennites to support him, either out of conviction or because they would be frightened of how their Constituency Parties might react if they did not.

This letter, publicly committing a growing group of MPs to opposing him, was a serious threat to his plans. He moved fast to regain the initiative: as the first contender to throw his hat into the ring, he had months of planning behind him while his rivals — actual or potential — had been left uncertain about his real intentions. Without Benn there would have been no Deputy Leadership contest at all. He had set the agenda for one of the bitterest years of infighting that the Labour Party has ever experienced.

Why did Tony Benn think it was important to run? It was clearly not the post of Deputy Leader itself that attracted him: it is traditionally of little importance within the Labour Party, and this very lack of importance is one reason why the Tribune Group thought the post was not worth disputing. But Benn was after bigger things.

If elected, he was in a perfect position to undermine Michael Foot's authority as Leader. Some of his supporters were already hinting that Benn elected by the electoral college would be the 'real' leader of the Party, since Foot had been elected in December 1980 by the PLP only. It was a silly argument, but for those who saw Benn as a socialist messiah it was a potent one.

It was also irresistible to the media: Benn the challenger to Foot would become a constant theme, damaging the Labour Party's credibility day by day. For those of us who had been brought up in the Labour movement the prospect of Benn as Deputy Leader was chilling.

Benn's supporters and allies had been hard at work in the constituencies and among the trade unions. He had been addressing trade union conferences as early as January. His busy schedule of meetings for the summer was already drawn up. In the constituencies eager acolytes were waiting to commit their CLPs to nominate him and then vote for him. For them it was a crusade, a step towards what they perceived as socialism. Through a network of bodies — the Campaign for Labour Party Democracy, the Labour Co-ordinating Committee, the so-called Institute for Workers Control, the various Trotskyite factions — they could co-ordinate their actions.

The Rank and File Mobilising Committee united many of these bodies: based, like so many other organisations of the destructive Left, at the Rowntree Trust premises at 9 Poland Street in Soho, it brought together a wide range of organisations. The Militant Tendency gained a degree of respectability on the Left by being included on the Committee. 'The Dank and Vile Mobilising Committee' — as it was known — had a hard-working advocate within the Tribune Group in Parliament in Reg Race, but the Tribune Group, its suspicions aroused, decided against seeking affiliation to the Committee.

Those on the Left who wanted to oppose Benn had a very simple choice: they could support the incumbent Deputy Leader, Denis Healey, or they could run a candidate of their own. The problem with the second course was that no machine existed for doing so. Under the old electoral system there was no real need for a machine: the PLP is a very compact and accessible electorate. Bring in the constituencies and the trade unions and it becomes immensely more complex and costly. It also favoured the candidate who was first in the field. At the beginning we were not fully aware of this: the true implications of the electoral college only unfolded as the summer went on.

In the beginning there was another problem as well: no candidate. All that existed after Benn's announcement was an unco-ordinated group of Labour MPs wandering around the House of Commons, all feeling that something should be done. Many thought that somebody of the Left should run against Benn. Nobody was in a hurry to volunteer. Some thought that Healey should stand down in favour of a candidate who could unify the Party: the unpopularity that Healey incurred within the Left of the Labour movement during his period as Chancellor of the Exchequer still clung to him. As a man who did not suffer fools gladly, he had also been rude to too many people.

Healey is, in fact, rude to almost everybody, but it is a jocular rudeness: there is not an ounce of malice in it. Scoring points is one way in which he exercises his sharp mind. This was a major obstacle to gaining broader support from within the party for him, whether from MPs, trade unions, or constituencies. All the same, Healey never had any intention of standing down.

Meetings began to be held to discuss what to do. Nobody will ever be able to unravel how many meetings were held, who called them, who attended them, what conclusions were reached. One Tribune MP can recall attending three in one evening, and, at the third, looking desperately around to try to remember who had been present at the previous two.

Slightly differing groupings began to emerge. The most prominent was the Eric Heffer faction, which, remarkably, had only one member, Eric himself, and one objective, that Eric should stand. Another faction, meeting in some secrecy, did not want Eric at any price and hoped the Labour Party would skip a generation and go for a young candidate. This group — Jeff Rooker, John Garrett, Robin Cook, Andrew Bennett — wanted the newest member of the Shadow Cabinet, Neil Kinnock, to run.

Heffer had offered to stand at a meeting called by me at the request of the Tribune Group itself: this, and subsequent meetings, were the nearest the Left came to an official Tribune Group selection process. Of all the anti-Benn meetings, they were the only ones with written notices and a healthy attendance.

Among those present at that first Tribune meeting — the first of three — were Guy Barnett, Andrew Bennett, Albert Booth, Norman Buchan, Alec Jones, Neil Kinnock, Hugh McCartney, Oonagh McDonald, Kevin McNamara, Stan Orme, Jeff Rooker, and Jack Straw. A number of non-Tribunites were also there — Ted Garrett, Joan Lestor, and Stan Crowther among them.

What emerged at that meeting was a contempt and hatred for Tony Benn. There were long diatribes against him — but the fear was obvious as well. Those present knew how far advanced the Benn campaign was, and how much support was already sewn up. When in due course I came to stand, I was only able to get the nominations of eight Constituency Parties — many of the rest were already pledged and most of them to Benn.

Of those present, Eric Heffer knew Benn better than most of us, and could talk about him with more conviction, having worked under him at the Department of Industry. He told us that the experience had been hell. He wanted the job of belling Benn. The rest of us were willing to let him have his way. His membership of the NEC, having been voted in by the constituency section, indicated that he was popular at the grass roots.

Neither Kinnock nor Heffer was ever publicly in the race. For Neil Kinnock it was the beginning of an anguished year. He had secretly planned to announce his candidature at a May Day rally, but before the end of April he had changed his mind. He had got no open support when his name was floated to the group of MPs who had decided to support Heffer. His loyalty to Michael Foot was also a factor: Foot's public position was always that he wanted Denis Healey to remain as his deputy. Yet, under pressure from his pro-Benn constituency, Kinnock was later, on his own admission, near to taking the line of least resistance and voting for Benn.

Eric Heffer had gone back to Liverpool to consult his constituency — and, as he relayed to us at our next meeting, had got a very rough ride indeed. He told us that his CLP was against his running — they were for Benn — and that his agent was a formidable woman indeed, and had expressed herself very forcefully on the subject. He had decided to bow to this pressure and not run. He had, however, finished the press statement he would have released had he run, and insisted on reading it out to us from beginning to end. In case any of us had missed its nuances, we were also able to read it in next week's *Tribune*. Come October, Heffer would vote for Tony Benn on both ballots.

Who should challenge Benn? Joan Lestor put her name forward, but she too fell by the wayside after consulting her constituency. At a meeting chaired by Judith Hart on May 18, Stan Orme courageously said he was willing to stand, but there was the problem of his trade union, the AUEW, already being committed to Denis Healey. I, on the other hand, was sponsored by a union, the TGWU, that might support me. Stan therefore argued that I should be the one to challenge Benn. With the agreement of those present, I threw my hat into the ring. A long cold summer was about to begin.

Much valuable time had been lost in marshalling the anti-Benn Left to the point where a candidate could be chosen. My own official announcement did not come until May 24 — seven weeks behind Benn. Even then we did not fully realise what a handicap this late entry would be. Only the Benn inner circle fully understood, and were revelling in, the presidential-style campaigning of their hero, as he moved from union conference to union conference and from public meeting to public meeting. The union conferences, with their block votes, were the equivalent of primary elections in the US party political system.

Benn had a machine, the same machine that had campaigned successfully for changes in the Labour Party constitution, which not only enabled him to mount such a campaign, but inhibited others from trying. Others had already decided the challenge was too much for them. There were grumbles within the Deptford Constituency Party from Benn supporters. In the week my campaign was launched I met my General Committee, which passed a resolution 'regretting' my lack of consultation with them.

They used what was to become the common Bennite argument during the campaign: that I was 'splitting the Left'. In the end they voted for me. I have never been able to establish whether Tony Benn's General Committee had got out of bed en masse to meet in the early hours of April 3 to endorse their MP's hurried decision to contest the Deputy Leadership, but somehow I doubt it. I doubt also if they condemned his lack of consultation with his Parliamentary colleagues.

My first task was to spell out why I was standing and to show that I had a body of support within the Labour Party. 'Working together' was the title of my mini-manifesto: it consisted of 'My 10 points for a Labour victory', a brief résumé of my record in Parliament (I was the only trade-union-sponsored candidate, and the only candidate to have opposed the 'In Place of Strife' legislation), and a statement supporting me signed by fourteen Labour MPs, all of whom were Front Bench spokesmen, members of the NEC, or Privy Counsellors.

The ten-point plan was as follows: (i) Rebuild Britain's industries and create new industries; (ii) Repeal Tory anti-union legislation; (iii) Get out of the EEC; (iv) Give priority in investment to regions and inner city areas; (v) Restore power to local government; (vi) Provide the funds for a mammoth advance in public housing and the NHS; (vii) Maintain a strong non-nuclear defence policy; (viii) Bring in import controls on manufactured goods; (ix) Increase aid to the Third World; (x) Guarantee full tolerance for every Labour Party member to express his own views.

The statement of support took up the theme of tolerance. John Silkin, it said, 'is the candidate who at the same time wholeheartedly supports the party's policies, demonstrates the courage and the stamina to carry them out in government, and has an unrivalled record of tolerance within the party.

'Labour must win the next election, for the country's sake. But we shall do so only if we reject internal party strife and concentrate on policy . . .

'John Silkin is the only candidate whose election will end the bickering and squabbling that has gone on in the party since the last election. He is the only candidate who will help to lead us into the next election as a party committed to the policies passed by conference but committed also to tolerance, understanding, and comradeship within the party.'

The signatories were Guy Barnett, Albert Booth, Norman Buchan, Don Concannon, Arthur Davidson, Frank Field, Judith Hart, Alec Jones, Hugh McCartney, Charles Morris, Stan Orme, Tom Pendry, and Harold Walker — all Front Benchers, and people of considerable influence in the PLP.

Benn's support extended to the leadership of a number of large trade unions, who exerted all the pressure they could. The unions had, by 1981, largely abandoned the stabilising role they had once had on the Labour Party: they had begun to feel almost guilty at the power they could wield. They began to believe that the constituency activists, not their own members, were the real grass roots of the movement.

At the annual conference of the National Union of Public Employees, during the session when delegates could question the union's sponsored MPs, the bulk of the questions from the floor were not about Parliamentary activities that might affect NUPE members: they were from Benn supporters, whose assigned task in his campaign was to try to force the NUPE MPs to vote for their man.

The Yorkshire MP Peter Hardy stood up and said it was a grossly improper question: his Constituency Party might have a right to know, but not a sponsoring union. Later he was taken aside by the triumvirate of Alan Fisher (the general secretary), Bernard Dix (deputy general secretary), and Ron Keating (an assistant general secretary) who ran — or thought they ran — NUPE. Peter Hardy was told that, if he did not support Benn, he would lose his NUPE sponsorship. In the event he supported Healey, and the threat was carried out — after the NUPE membership itself had voted for the union to support Healey.

Such pressures were directed most violently at my supporters, real or potential. Some, such as Heffer, capitulated completely; others found it easier to keep their heads down. The effect of this on my campaign was dramatic. Whereas Benn had a group of MPs willing to speak on his behalf when he could not be present himself, I had almost none. Benn's strength was particularly vital when he became ill, and had to rest throughout August. His campaign scarcely faltered at all. Most of the MPs who voted for me on the first ballot in October, and scuppered Benn by abstaining on the second

ballot, played no part in my campaign at all. They understandably did not want to be placed under constant pressure
throughout the summer. Many a meeting took place with a
Benn representative and a Healey representative, but nobody
from my side.

I myself could not attend all meetings simply because of the
impossibility of being at several venues at the same time.
Union conferences, constituency meetings, regional meetings,
all began to pile up inexorably. So too did the expenses. It
became increasingly obvious that under the electoral college
system a candidate needed a big team of supporters and a lot
of money.

There was the problem of producing all the articles requested
by newspapers, magazines, and trade union journals. Some
union journals wanted a standard article setting out my
objectives; others wanted one tailored to the interests of their
readers. I could not in the event supply a standard size article.
Journals had their own individual requirements and differing
lengths needed differing articles.

There was the problem of getting the names of Constituency
Party secretaries: Labour Party headquarters refused to hand
over a list until I was nominated as a candidate, therefore our
ad hoc anti-Benn committee could do no preparatory work
pending our choice of candidate. Benn and Healey, as members
of the NEC, would have had no trouble getting a list at any
time. Better still, Benn could use the files of the Campaign for
Labour Party Democracy, which were probably more accurate
and more extensive than those at Walworth Road. His own
files were on a computer.

I had trouble getting details from Labour Party regional
offices. One regional executive instructed its staff not to give
out a list of constituency secretaries — one of them gave it to
me secretly, by telephoning the details to my adviser, Ann
Carlton, at home one evening: the staff were too afraid to
supply a written list. Trying to produce my election address
for all who should have seen it was an enormous and expensive
task.

The CLPs that were introducing one member, one vote
naturally wanted a copy for every one of their members. This
meant over a thousand being printed and posted for each of
these constituencies.

The question of expenses led the Labour Party Chairman,

Judith Hart, to ask questions about the source of Tony Benn's funding, and to urge me to do the same publicly: he was clearly spending many times more than I was, and his extra resources could have a very real bearing on the outcome of the election.

His supporters even took a full-page advertisement in the Party newspaper, *Labour Weekly*, costing £700, with a tear-off slip at the bottom for others who wanted to support him: 'cheques payable to "RFMC Deputy-Leadership Campaign"'; 'I am/am not willing to be contacted in the future in connection with this and allied campaigns.'

This seemed to me a totally unacceptable way for the Labour Party to run an internal election. It was at odds both with the British tradition of electoral law, which imposes statutory limits on spending by candidates in both national and local elections, and with the Labour Party's proud belief that it is not a party that sells its favours.

Denis Healey's campaign was also spending a lot of money. A glossy booklet of his speeches appeared, bearing the imprint of Giles Radice MP. I demanded that all three candidates should publish their accounts.

I was to send mine, in a most detailed form to Judith Hart on October 29, with a covering letter. My expenses, I wrote, 'amount to £1,282.28p, which taken together with pre-nomination expenses of £694.36p, totals £1,977.14p.

'I have urged on the other candidates that they publish their expenses but they have chosen not to do so. This is a pity because the rumours, for example, that one candidate's supporters spent over £20,000 in trying to get him elected could have been subjected to open examination.'

The few figures that did finally appear from the other camps would not have satisfied any auditor. Some time later a Benn acolyte accused me of attacking Benn for spending his own money. That was untrue. I was not too worried about what he did with his own money, since I do not believe he spent much of it.

What really concerned me was that he was spending large sums of money from undisclosed sources. Perhaps all the money he spent came from members of the Labour Party; but then, perhaps it did not. The mystery has never been solved, although it did emerge during the campaign that the newspaper *Socialist Challenge* — not a Labour publication — had had 15,000 'Benn for Deputy' badges produced at a cost of £779.80 plus VAT. The paper denied that any profit would go to the

Benn campaign, but the mere printing of these badges was a contribution to that campaign.

It is clear that ground-rules are urgently needed. The experiences of the 1983 Leadership and Deputy Leadership elections, although less contentious, have underlined this message. A limit must be imposed on spending by candidates, and a tight control placed upon meetings and literature to ensure that all candidates are present and afforded equal exposure. The Labour Party itself should organise the major televised debates between candidates, and ensure that they are fairly conducted and televised. Tee-shirts and lapel badges, which were long-running props of the Benn campaign (and to a lesser extent the Healey campaign), should be prohibited.

Such ground rules would not only ensure a degree of fairness, but also raises the standard of political debate. Benn, with so many platforms to himself, was too often able to put his case across unchallenged. I and all those who supported me were accused of 'splitting the Left', with no chance to explain that our concept of 'the Left' differed from the cause Tony Benn was now espousing, and with no opportunity to spell out what socialism meant to us. The Euro-MP Janey Buchan reacted most strongly to accusations of 'splitting the Left': in an article in *Labour Weekly* she pointed out that Tony Benn's claims to being on the Left himself were decidedly thin, and of very recent origin.

I was accused of being very rich and employing a vast staff to help me with my political ambitions (for the campaign I had exactly three paid helpers, only two of them paid full-time, my loyal secretary Margaret Jack and my political adviser Ann Carlton, and they had to deal at the same time with my work as an MP and Front Bench Spokesman). Phil Wyatt, a college lecturer, was my unpaid researcher. Benn, a journalist himself, had journalists among his inner circle, and they were not shy about using the gossip columns of the capitalist press. Denis Healey bore the brunt of these smear tactics initially, but soon the fire was turned on me, when it was realised that I could deprive Benn of victory.

For all Benn's complaints about the media, his relationship with them was excellent. He was, after all, their big story. A BBC 'Panorama' programme in June was called 'Vote, vote, vote for Tony Benn', which could have done him no harm at all, even if it was supposed to be a study of his campaign. Balance was not a strong point of the media coverage. One

BBC interviewer told me I was an 'unsuitable' candidate. Another, when interviewing all three candidates, talked at length with Healey and Benn before turning to me and saying: 'As a matter of courtesy, we should bring John Silkin into the discussion.' 'Not as a matter of courtesy,' I retorted, 'as a matter of democracy.'

The hard Left made it perfectly clear how it defined democracy. At the Scottish Miners' Gala on June 13, Arthur Scargill, in an all too characteristic speech, said that anyone who criticised Benn was 'sabotaging not only the candidature of Tony Benn but the principles of socialism which are basic to our movement'.

Statements such as Scargill's only confirmed the idea, relentlessly put out by the media, that the Labour Party was irrevocably split. That, as far as the media was concerned, was the story. Since my candidature did not fit this theory, it was viewed with puzzlement and even derision. Even the pro-Labour *Daily Mirror*, in an editorial entitled 'The Silkin Trap' (May 27), saw the battle in black-and-white, Benn-versus-Healey terms, although it did at least address what it thought would be the result of my winning. My candidature was 'not so much a compromise as a putting-off of the real decision. Not an alternative but a postponement.

'His success would be a catastrophe for Mr Healey but it would hardly take Mr Benn out of his stride.'

In this the *Mirror* proved to be absolutely wrong. The Benn campaign itself recognised the threat I posed, even if I could not win. Benn could survive any number of confrontations with the Right: such challenges were to be expected. What he could not survive was a challenge to his self-proclaimed supremacy on the Left.

What Arthur Scargill said shrilly from a rally platform, Michael Meacher said much more smoothly in the pages of *The Times*. Citing *The Times* itself as his authority, he wrote on June 18 that Mr Healey could not be trusted with Labour Party policy, and that the election was necessary 'to help determine rather more clearly what the next Labour government will actually do'. The Benn campaign was about 'consolidating the main policy positions of the last Labour Party conference', which Denis Healey 'utterly rejected'. His comments on my position? There were none. I did not publicly enter the equation.

My campaign, such as it was, struggled on, surviving on the dedication of a few individuals. And I do mean a few: the MPs were Guy Barnett, Andrew Bennett, Don Concannon, Ted Garrett, Hugh McCartney, Stan Crowther, Kevin McNamara, Oonagh McDonald and Jeff Rooker. Andrew Bennett was canvassing support among left-wing MPs for the tactic of abstaining on the second ballot. Andrew's work had to be carried out in considerable secrecy, because it would do me no good at all to concede in public that I had no hope of coming anywhere but last.

By mid-September about twenty MPs had privately agreed to abstain. Neil Kinnock, who was in the process of joining us, wanted to reveal publicly how many potential abstainers there were, but the best tactic was clearly to leave that unsaid. To concede that the fight was already lost would have ended all hope of support from the TGWU. Without that crucial support, all credibility would have been lost.

The televised debates, particularly the one at the Trades Union Congress in Blackpool, chaired by the Labour Party General Secretary Designate Jim Mortimer, enabled me to put my case across more effectively than many people expected. Tony Benn's supporters were placed strategically around the hall, clapping his every utterance. They could not, however, blot out among the audience the critical faculties that are inevitably aroused when three politicians are asked to respond as intelligently as they can to a series of questions carefully selected for their pertinence.

It was my adviser, Ann Carlton, who suggested that the debate should be based on written questions. This had been decided at a meeting with Jim Mortimer at Walworth Road, where Ann had represented me, Tony Banks had represented Tony Benn, and Richard Heller had represented Denis Healey. Ann argued that it would counter the effect of any faction packing the meeting (everyone knew the Bennites, and to a lesser extent the Healeyites, would do just that), and give a proper balance. It would also avoid the use of roving microphones, which never work well. A second meeting with Mortimer was held in Blackpool on the eve of the debate: he was extremely worried that something would go wrong. In fact, it went very smoothly.

Faced with the challenge, I found myself enjoying the experience. 'John Silkin was the only one to emerge from that

with any credit,' the eminent Labour movement historian
Walter Kendall told a friend of mine after that debate, which
cheered me up no end. But then, of the three I was the only one
fighting in a cause and not out of ambition, since I had not
sought the nomination in the first place.

By the time of the Labour Party conference, I was able, by a
whisker, to gain the vote of my union, the TGWU, despite a
number of Communist Party members opposing me from
beginning to end. Alex Kitson, the Deputy General Secretary,
was a loyal supporter, and did all he could to swing the
delegates' votes in my direction. The TGWU President, Walter
Greendale, was a strong Bennite, and Alex Kitson had to put
up with much abuse. I had similar valuable support from Sam
McCluskie, then Assistant General Secretary of the National
Union of Seamen, and Jack Boddy of the National Union of
Agricultural and Allied Workers: both these small unions
backed me, and both Alex and Sam spoke on my behalf.
Support came as well from the two MPs on the TGWU
delegation, Kevin McNamara and Stan Crowther.

But the unions as a whole had abdicated their traditional
responsibilities to the Labour Party: they felt it was their duty
to respond to the changes within the Constituency Parties, and
not to use their block votes in the interests of common sense
and stability.

Until a few hours before the poll it seemed that Benn would
still win: it all depended upon the final union to make up its
mind, NUPE. Its leadership and executive was pro-Benn, and
most observers thought that settled the matter. The lobby of
the Imperial Hotel, next door to the Brighton Conference
Centre, was crowded with delegates and journalists, all
awaiting the result of the NUPE membership ballot. On the
stairs above, two white-faced figures appeared: the *Tribune*
journalist Chris Mullin and Benn's former adviser Frances
Morrell. Their faces answered the question: NUPE had gone
for Healey.

On the first ballot the voting was Healey, 45.369 per cent;
Benn, 36.627 per cent; Silkin, 18.004 per cent. I was eliminated.
But to have gained half as many votes as Tony Benn was more
than any of us had dared hope for. With no real organisation
and no machine, we had shown that the non-Bennite Left was
a significant force. This gave heart to others: Benn could be
beaten, even with the odds stacked against us.

On the second ballot, despite the shouting and the threats, more than three-quarters of the sixty-five MPs who had supported me on the first ballot (Benn had the support of fifty-five; Healey of 125) refused to support Benn. Thirty-five abstained, fourteen voted for Healey, sixteen for Benn. It was just enough, even though the TGWU, after much confusion, decided to vote for Benn. Benn lost by 49.574 per cent to Healey's 50.426 per cent. Benn had got over 80 per cent of the constituency votes, but had lost decisively in the other two sections.

From this narrowest of defeats can be traced the decline of Tony Benn and his supporters. When the remnants of the Benn machine were cranked into action two years later in an effort to gain Michael Meacher the Deputy Leadership, Meacher was decisively beaten on the first ballot, by 67.3 per cent of the vote to 27.9 per cent. Most significantly, Roy Hattersley won a majority of the CLP votes. The Benn power base was no more.

The shallowness of support for Benn among the PLP can be seen if one looks closely at those who supported him. Of the sixty-five MPs who voted for me on the first ballot, sixteen switched to Benn on the second. They were no more pro-Benn at heart than those who abstained. They included Robin Cook, who had taken that anti-Benn letter around the House of Commons back in April. The others were Judith Hart and Albert Booth (both of whom had signed the initial statement in support of me), Neil Carmichael, Lewis Carter-Jones, Frank Dobson, Alf Dubs, Ken Eastham, John Fraser, John Garrett, Roy Hughes, David Lambie, Maurice Miller, Gwilym Roberts, Jock Stallard, and Jack Straw. All backed Benn out of expediency, rather than from conviction.

Among the MPs who supported Benn on both ballots, the same lack of conviction was prevalent. Eric Heffer could not have been a happy man as he cast his vote for Benn twice. A dedicated core of Benn supporters can be identified, some from what can be called the old Left (Frank Allaun, Sid Bidwell, Norman Atkinson, Bob Edwards, Martin Flannery, James Lamond, Joan Maynard, Ian Mikardo, Jo Richardson, Ernie Roberts, Stan Thorne), some who were ambitious young turks (Michael Meacher, Stuart Holland, Reg Race), others less easy to categorise (Christopher Price, Dennis Skinner, Dennis Canavan, Allan Roberts).

But this hard core was balanced, or even outnumbered, by a group who, to a greater or lesser extent, were uncomfortable bedfellows with Benn: Hugh Brown, Tam Dalyell, Don Dixon, Alex Eadie, Ted Fletcher, Bob Hughes, Ron Leighton, Frank McElhone, Andrew McMahon, John Prescott, John Ryman, Renee Short, Clive Soley, John Tilley . . .

On the evening of that dramatic Sunday Chris Jones, a *Tribune* journalist, ran into a very gloomy Norman Buchan outside his hotel in Brighton. The threats were still being thrown about. 'I'm sure I will be de-selected,' he said, trudging off into the night. Many others felt the same way. Most were wrong: Norman Buchan was finally re-selected unopposed and unanimously.

One thing, unfortunately, has not been confronted: the deficiencies of the electoral college system that had made Benn's adventurism possible. In 1983, when Kinnock became leader, its deficiencies were masked by the fact that it was not a closely fought contest: the momentum for Kinnock was so great that his election was not in doubt, and the resources thrown into the battle by the various campaigns had ceased to matter. This momentum was partly the result of what Kinnock had learned from observing the events of 1981: his decision to contest the leadership in succession to Michael Foot in 1983 followed two years of touring the constituencies.

But the deficiencies of the system had, if anything, got worse. The Hattersley campaign struggled on without being able to get an up-to-date list of constituencies until far too late in the day. More CLPs had gone over to one-person, one-vote, thus increasing the demand for election addresses. More magazine articles were needed, more meetings needed a larger crew of MPs to address them.

With so many other problems for the Labour Party to face, it may not seem to be an urgent priority to reform the Electoral College system. But reform cannot be delayed forever. The deficiencies of the system are far too obvious not to be exploited again.

Chapter Five

——————————— ooOoo ———————————

Organising the Future

The diversity of views within the Labour Party need not always be a weakness, it can be a strength; but only if the Party wants it to be so, and has the will to make it one. Some people in the present Labour Party do not, of course, want that. They want their own faction to be strong and they despise everyone else's views. In some people this derives from over-enthusiasm and misplaced idealism, in others from stupidity, in still others — the conscious entryists — from a deliberate policy.

Most members of the Labour Party are to some extent involved in factions — most call themselves 'Left' or 'Right', a few would describe themselves as in the Centre — but usually members realise that the broad interests of the party are more important than factional interests.

The Party holds together not because there is a Parliamentary Labour Party or a NEC with a supporting bureaucracy, but because there is some degree of communication and mutual respect between the different factions and between the different tiers and official groupings within the Party. Without these links this unity of purpose would collapse. In 1981 the Party was nearly destroyed. One faction, which became the SDP, left the Party, another, the Bennites, did almost mortal damage to it.

A political party, at the end of the day, is a network through which people with mutual interests communicate. Conversely, those who choose to manipulate and damage the Labour Party do so by restricting and controlling the flow of information. This can be done at any level.

At the grass-roots level one of the most common ploys is for CLP officers to let meetings get longer and longer. This, in theory, could mean that more and more time is available to impart information to Party members, but the practical effect and the intention is the opposite. Long meetings create problems for people: they may have family responsibilities, other obligations, an early shift in the morning, or perhaps the normal human weakness of getting tired after a long day.

The net result of over-long meetings, made as boring and unpleasant as possible, is that fewer people attend, and so decisions get made by a tiny caucus. When Pat Wall, then a member of the Militant Tendency, stood up at the 1981 Wembley conference and spoke in favour of the 'democracy of the committed', that was what he was talking about. People who are not prepared to attend political meetings to the very end and to the exclusion of all else in life are deemed to have sacrificed their right to a voice. As a political principle, it is Leninist 'democratic centralism' applied to pluralistic democracy. To consolidate this principle, some Trotskyist-led CLPs have even invented a new mythical rule of the constitution, which deems that anyone who has missed three General Committee meetings is no longer a member of the GC. This constitutional myth is used to bully opponents off the GC. It can be used very effectively by well-educated people against less well-educated Party members. An apparently effective grasp of procedural matters can hide lies and bullying under a smooth veneer.

There are other tactics too. If the officers of a constituency want to have their MP de-selected, and wish to persuade their GC that this is the correct thing to do, the over-long meeting will only be the start. In this situation, meetings have been known to go on literally all night. Long agendas mean that the MP's report has a habit of falling off the end. If this happens too often, the MP may decide to submit a written report. 'Ah ha,' say the Party officers to new members — 'why is our MP refusing to talk to us and answer our questions?'

If a written apology for absence has been sent in by the MP, it will not necessarily be read out. If there is a meeting in the

constituency, the MP may not be invited, or be invited so late
that there are problems in attending. His invitation may have
been posted to arrive after the meeting had been held. The
problem of attending mid-week evening meetings when there is
a three-line whip in the Commons are sneered at as putting
Westminster's needs before those of the constituency.

By destroying communications between an MP and his CLP
the MP can be made to seem remote and uncaring. Should the
MP respond by neglecting Parliamentary business, control of
information can still be used against him. Suddenly a list of
'key' divisions in the House of Commons will be waved at him.
Why did the MP miss these votes?

What, in this context, is a 'key' division? It is one that an
MP missed and that the self-appointed guardians of conscience
have decided should be made a symbol. It may have been
important, it may have been of no importance at all: that is not
the point. The MP may have been at a vital meeting about a
factory closure in his constituency, or seriously ill: that, too, is
not the point. The point is to have anything at hand as
ammunition against an MP whom Party officers wish to de-
select.

A booklet, *How to Select or Re-select your MP*, published by
the Campaign for Labour Party Democracy, was based on this
principle. It included a score-card of votes in a number of
House of Commons divisions. The information could be used
in a variety of ways, any one of which was calculated to
embarrass the sitting MP. Later the GLC even published such
lists at the ratepayers' expense.

It follows that if Labour Party politics at the grass-roots
level are played in these terms, only those who enjoy this sort
of politics will be attracted to the Party. Factionalism begets
factionalism. If Militant could control constituencies, why
should not the International Marxist Group pitch in as well?
They did. If the hard Left can play the game successfully,
why should not the Right try as well? It did, with the creation
of local right-wing Solidarity Groups. They, too, sent out
model resolutions from their national organisation, and
members in the constituencies were expected to support them
automatically.

Through control of agendas, control of meetings, control of
newsletters, control of recruitment, control of membership, a
local party can be both directed and stifled, becoming irrelevant

to the local community and destructive to the Labour Party as a whole.

The key to reversing this trend lies in the way the Party approaches its individual members. Labour Party members are at present shamefully neglected. In some cases they are denied contact with their MPs by the GC of their local party. In 1983 I attempted to get a list of Deptford party members — four years later the list had still not been supplied.

Having gone to the trouble of tracking down the local Labour Party (no easy task in many cases, with the telephone directory no help at all), and joining it (which can take months), a Labour supporter may never hear from the Party again. In theory regular notices of meetings should arrive, with in some cases some sort of newsletter. But there is no guarantee that the member who applies to join will see either. Communications between members are based on attendance at meetings and calls from 'collectors', who distribute whatever a branch wants distributed and collect subscriptions, although many people nowadays naturally pay by cheque or standing order.

The truth is that credit card companies treat their members with more respect than does the Labour Party. Hardly a week goes by without cardholders getting some communication through the post. They are continually reminded of why they are a cardholder and of the benefits of membership. A friend of mine grumbles that often when the post arrives in the morning he feels more involved with American Express than he does with the Labour Party.

The postal service is hardly a new invention, but it is astonishing how little the Labour Party uses it. With modern technology a national membership register and regular mailings to every member of the Labour Party are not only practicable but could be profitable. With a circulation of over a quarter of a million, such a mailing could certainly be financed from advertising.

The next question is: what should the individual Labour Party members be sent through the post? The answer is: up-to-date and accurate information about the activities of the PLP, the Party in the country, and the trade unions as they affect the Labour Party, that would help them to maintain their commitment and enthusiasm, and serve the Party to the best of their ability. It must avoid the type of reporting that sees the Labour Party as a battlefield of Left and Right factions on the NEC.

In 1971 the Labour Party decided to put much of its communication resources into the publication of *Labour Weekly*. Other Party publications were absorbed into it. It was hoped that it would prove an effective and profitable way of communicating with Party members, and with interested people outside the Party.

It was an experiment that has persisted for a decade and a half, despite the fact that it has never worked. Fewer than one Labour Party member in ten buys it. It has never come near to breaking even. In no area of news — whether internal Party affairs, Parliament, the trade unions — can it be said to supply a first-class service. Its news values are frequently as bizarre as they are dull. It has not been a stabilising or loyal influence during times of turmoil within the Party. It is a sad little publication, unread and unloved. The fact that other political parties produce equally dull publications is no excuse.

In all its publications the Labour Party must aim for the highest possible quality, matching in quality and bettering in content anything published by its rivals. Again the comparison with some credit card companies is apt. Their journals are of high quality, and geared to their customers in every country. They care because it pays them to care. It would pay the Labour Party too. Whether Party members should receive one journal weekly or monthly, or a variety of perhaps more specialised journals on request, is a matter for detailed planning.

This does not mean that traditional Labour Party organisation, through branches, GCs, and executive meetings, through up-dating electoral registers and canvassing, should be neglected. On the contrary, they should be strengthened. The key to doing this is the re-establishment of full-time agents.

Full-time agents, like MPs, have been a target for those who entered the Labour Party in order to destroy it. The impact of a good agent on a CLP is immeasurable. Meetings are better organised, become more interesting, and therefore attract more active members. Canvass returns are more accurate: the Party is better able to find its support when an election comes along. Elections themselves find the Party in good heart, with the agent calmly in charge, knowing who his best helpers are and where their efforts should be directed.

Ideally there should be a full-time agent in every constituency. If that is impossible, the priority must be to have agents in marginal seats and in safe Labour seats that are undergoing demographic change. Yet in the Labour Party today the distribution of full-time agents is largely haphazard. Organisational resources are not allocated in any rational way.

The Labour Party is aware of the problems created by the shortage of full-time agents. A ritualistic deploring of the deficiency is as much a part of the annual Labour Party conference as the eulogies to Aneurin Bevan. But nothing is done. Instead the Party meekly assumes that Labour's organisation is not as good as the Conservatives' in general elections, and not up to Liberal standards in by-elections.

Full-time agents are not created by talking about them at annual conferences. Results will only come when the right people are recruited and the money is found to pay them adequately. The Conservatives do this, and this factor — and this factor only — accounts for the superiority of Conservative organisation. Once upon a time it was the secret of Labour Party efficiency, and the reason Labour once beat the Conservatives and the Liberals.

The key question is: who should be responsible for creating Labour's network of full-time agents? There is a school of thought that believes in a national agency service, funded centrally. Such a service was, in fact, founded in the Sixties, but was never given the resources to tackle the problem of the disastrous decline in full-time agents.

There is another school of thought that believes it is entirely a matter for the CLP. This view is strongly held among entryists into the Labour Party. Given local power their response, however, is not to create local agents, but to do away with them.

This is totally cynical. The Militant Tendency, by far the most successful of the entryist sects, is based, like the Labour Party itself, on a combination of full-time agents and part-time volunteer helpers. Some chroniclers of Militant have claimed that it actually has more full-time agents than the Labour Party itself. A priority for these Militant agents is clearly to dispose of their rivals on the Labour payroll.

When a full-time agent is removed, the finances and

membership of a CLP change dramatically for the worse. This is in part due to losing the positive benefits of having a full-time agent, and partly due to the desire of the infiltrators to destroy the backbone of the old membership, who are an obstacle to their plans.

The decline in the number of full-time agents has also seriously weakened the skilled human resources available to the Party as a whole. When a job at regional or national level needs to be filled, there are fewer experienced and skilled applications to draw upon.

The truth is that the problem can only be solved with the combined efforts of the Party at all levels. Certainly no individual agent should be imposed upon a reluctant party by a national agency service — but no CLP should have the right to veto the appointment of an agent in principle, nor dispose of an agent unless an overwhelming case can be presented to regional and national officials. The potential loss or gain of a seat in Parliament, or control of a council, is not a matter for local party officers to play with at the expense of the Party as a whole.

To revive the agency service, and improve the organisational skills of the Labour Party as a whole, I believe there must be a major revival at city and regional level.

Reviving city parties would demand a change in Labour Party rules, since they were abolished in 1974. The reasoning then was that city parties were obsessed with local government at the expense of winning seats in general elections. They were getting all the money and the CLPs, in some cases, were virtually non-existent. The abolition of city parties was a very crude way of forcing money and organisation into the CLPs.

In the short term it was a successful tactic — some seats were certainly won as a result — but the overall strategy can only be called negative.

Cities are real. Cities are where most people in Britain live. Cities should have Labour Parties. Of course the mistakes of the past must not be repeated. The city parties must devote much of their energies to nurturing and guiding the CLPs in their area. In partnership with regional and national officials, they must work out the priorities for organisation and campaigning. They must work out what resources are needed, and where they should be directed.

One priority must be the appointment in the large

conurbations of a paid city press officer, who would not only work for the city party, but would liaise with and help the CLPs. It would not be an easy job.

Some CLPs would no doubt send the press officer lengthy resolutions, based on model resolutions sent by pressure groups in London, and demand that the press officer issue them verbatim to the local press. Militant supporters might want advice on becoming television stars like some of their former colleagues.

But, with patience and professionalism, a good city press officer could do an immense amount of good. Local weekly newspapers are a very effective way of communicating with the voters, since they lie around the home and are read and re-read. Local radio is equally important. The press officer must have radio experience, and be able to coach local politicians in microphone technique.

Agents themselves must become better versed in dealing with the press, radio and television. Old prejudices about the 'capitalist media' must be abandoned. Agents must be skilled at speaking as the professional and impartial voice of the Labour Party. If journalists learn they can go to an agent for facts and a good quote, they will be less inclined to quote some dubious statements from an unrepresentative sectarian source.

The agency service has a long tradition of impartiality. Good professional agents are not members of groups, whether Solidarity, Tribune, or Campaign, and it is vital that this tradition be maintained.

One tradition that should not be maintained is the attitude of the agents' trade union, the National Union of Labour Organisers, to recruitment from outside its members. In the days when NULO's membership numbered several hundred, it was practical to fill every organisational post from among its members. The Party in those days had a career structure: from recruitment as an agent or an assistant agent, a NULO member could move upwards through city parties and regional offices to the national headquarters.

With fewer than eighty constituency agents in place, this becomes nonsense. There are too few points of recruitment, too few experienced agents, and, as a result, too few agents of sufficient ability to staff all senior organisational posts within the party. NULO must allow candidates from outside its ranks, whether part-time agents or trade union organisers, to be considered for posts at all levels. NULO will oppose this at first, but in the long run it is in the union's own interests to see a large and effective agency service.

It is particularly vital that NULO changes its attitude towards recruitment to regional posts. The regions must become greatly strengthened links between national and local organisation. A region is a very attractive organisational unit, not as cumbersome as national organisation, broader than city organisation, not as parochial as a constituency. The major trade unions have considerable funds available at regional level, and would have few problems switching resources from their central funding of the Labour Party to regional funding, if they were convinced that the organisational skills were there to enable the funds to be used effectively.

Political parties have their headquarters in London for only one reason: it is the seat of Parliament and Government. Labour's headquarters should move back to Westminster. Much of its organisational and research functions should be devolved to the regions, where they would be able to respond much more effectively to local needs.

The main role of headquarters should be liaison and communication — most vitally of all with the individual party member through direct mailing, reminding them all that Labour is a national political party, and of what its aims and objectives are. On the research side the present gulf between headquarters staff (usually academically inclined) and those working for the Cabinet or Shadow Cabinet (usually personal political aides, but also having academic qualifications) must be bridged.

Today some headquarters researchers are deeply involved with Parliament, some are not — it is as much a matter of personal inclination as anything. In future they must be involved as a matter of course, and new recruits must be chosen for their interest in and understanding of Westminster, Whitehall and practical politics.

The creation of regional research staffs — today the Scottish and Welsh offices are the only regional offices with researchers, and they only have one each — would be a step towards creating a career structure of sorts for political researchers, and a better appreciation of the peculiar skills that go into the job. Regional researchers must not be confined to their region. They should be in Westminster whenever their regional group of MPs meets. So too should the regional press officer. Front Bench spokesmen visiting a region should automatically receive a brief beforehand, filling in the details of local industries and local problems. Trade union researchers at regional level are often of a very high quality: they too should be formally part of the regional Labour Party organisation.

This approach to organisation, research, and press and publicity is the best antidote to factionalism within the Party — a factionalism that can only flourish by stifling debate and destroying communications, and which has sadly been the motor of all the recent constitutional changes within the Party. None of the changes has increased the collective strength of the Party. They have simply given added strength to one section at the expense of other sections. The most obvious sufferers have been Labour MPs.

Chapter Six

────────── ∘∘◯∘∘ ──────────

The Labour MP

The position of a Member of Parliament in any democratic party is a difficult one. The keener he is to do his job in Parliament, the more difficult it is for him to do it with thoroughness in his constituency. If the MP is a Minister as well, he is burdened with a three-tier job: his constituency, Parliament and Government.

Many democratic countries have constitutions that avoid many of these pressures. National assemblies may contain members elected from national party lists, not by constituents. This is an excellent system for politicians, but less fair to constituents. In other countries — France and the United States are the most obvious examples — Ministers are not elected by anybody at all. Again, this is a splendid system for politicians, but not for constituents.

When I was Minister of Agriculture, I had to deal with important negotiations in Brussels while crucial divisions were being held in Westminster. Unfortunately, in those days of a minority Labour Government, every vote counted. As a consequence, on a single day I overflew the North Sea four times. I had ample time to reflect on the advantages of not being accountable to any assembly, or perhaps, as in the Netherlands, of being allowed a substitute to vote for me in Parliament.

If one is Prime Minister or Chief Whip, the problem is greater still. The pressure of work is greater, and so too is the need to make decisions that may be unpopular in the country and in the MP's own party.

Under the British system of government there is no escape from this dilemma, nor am I proposing that there should be. Any alternative system breaks the link between the ordinary citizen and the national parliament. A list system presupposes some form of proportional representation — again, a system much favoured by many politicians and parties, but offering few advantages to the voter. The arguments over 'fairer' voting systems are usually based on self-interest. All voting systems are 'unfair' to those out of power, and changing the system to institutionalise coalition governments will not change that. It may keep a few more politicians employed in government, but that should not be the object of any political system.

The problem of the overworked British MPs, with conflicting demands on their time, should be met not by changing the system but by providing more resources and by defining with greater clarity the role of MPs. The first is a matter for Parliament; the second for political parties.

When I became the MP for Deptford in 1963, no MP for that constituency had ever held an advice surgery: I introduced a weekly surgery, which, of course, is considered quite normal today. Over the years I have been fortunate in receiving very good support from the local council — first Deptford, then Lewisham — who provide a room for surgeries and whose Town Hall officials do everything they can to help.

When you are sending out some six hundred letters a month on constituency matters, as I did, such help is vital. I firmly believe that this should be the right of all MPs: that councils should have a statutory obligation to provide every MP with accommodation and support, independent of the MP's party organisation. The accommodation needs to be in a place to which the public has ready access.

Such a reform would not only allow the MP to work more effectively within his constituency, but also, by placing him in the town hall, would help to define his role in relation to the council and local politics. An MP is not a jack-of-all-trades welfare worker, but one vital link in the democratic process — that between the citizen and Parliament.

The difficulties created for Labour MPs by mandatory reselection must also be tackled. The problem is not that it allows MPs to be de-selected — that was always possible — but the way that it has changed the relationship between the MP and his CLP. Under the old system an MP could only be de-selected if there was something like a consensus within the CLP that he should go. Under the new system it automatically becomes a matter of counting votes and influencing them, and finally controlling them when re-selection time arrives.

Any faction that commands any votes at all on the GC — it might be only a handful — is elevated in importance. Expediency in dealing with them may take precedence over principle, or the wider interests of the Labour Party or of the electorate.

If an MP finds himself in disagreement with his GC about any matter, he has a simple choice: to acquiesce, to ignore the difference and hope for the best, or to organise against those who oppose him. The choice is all too often between becoming the prisoner of a faction, or whatever coalition of factions holds sway at the moment, or becoming a factionalist oneself. Much time is spent in organising a loyalist faction. There is a price to be paid for that, and not just in time and effort, but in becoming a prisoner of a different sort.

The result, however the MP responds, is destructive. It wastes time, it leads to bitterness and in-fighting. Some people, of course, thrive on that. Most normal people do not, and the electorate quite rightly treats such antics with contempt. It has certainly been a factor in Labour's disastrous general election showing. A party that does not appear to love itself is not going to be loved by the electorate.

The effects of this destructiveness came out when Labour's Chief Whip, Michael Cocks, and I organised a reception for new Labour MPs after the 1983 General Election. As we moved from group to group, we soon discovered that the common topic of conversation among those who had been in Parliament for less than two weeks was their prospects of re-selection.

There was only one other major topic of conversation at that reception: the dearth of facilities in the House of Commons. Most of the new MPs had had some authority and experience before their election. They knew what an office looked like, and had experience of working with staff. They were consequently surprised to arrive to do the biggest job of their lives and find that there was no office waiting for them. At best, they might already have been allocated a desk in a room with three or four other MPs. A desk for their secretary was even more problematic.

Disillusionment was already setting in, conflicting with a robust desire to change the workings of Parliament for the better — and, whisper it softly, sometimes a desire to change the workings of the Labour Party as well. New Members are impatient with the antique rituals of Parliament — the apparently interminable signing on of Members, the repetition of arcane phrases — and are usually very disgruntled indeed at the long hours that Parliament sits. Their first all-night sitting is not a happy occasion. New women Members are inclined to blame all deficiencies of the House on its 'male' traditions. Demands for a 'normal working day' also come up.

It is almost impossible to counter such complaints without being labelled a reactionary. I am, of course, totally in favour of expanding the facilities of the House. When I entered the House in 1963 I had no secretarial allowance and negligible accommodation. We were all crammed into the Palace of Westminster, which could never provide enough rooms.

In 1969, as Minister of Public Building and Works, I one day ran into Iain Macleod. 'You look happy,' said the eminent Conservative. 'I have the plans for a new Parliamentary building,' I said. 'Every ten years someone comes up with plans for a new Parliamentary building,' said Macleod. 'Every ten years they are turned down.'

But by the mid-Seventies the former Metropolitan Police Headquarters at Scotland Yard had been converted into Parliamentary offices. The library became more accessible so that Members' researchers and secretaries could use parts of it freely. In the Eighties Iain Macleod's cynicism has been comprehensively disproven: new facilities are being built behind the old façades of Bridge Street and Parliament Street. I chaired the New Building sub-Committee of the Commons that brought this into being, with all deadlines being met. It will provide, for the first time, proper accommodation for all MPs, either in the Palace or the new complex, in offices equipped for modern technology, and greatly expanded library and staff facilities. As part of the overall scheme, the Shadow Cabinet will be adequately housed in the Palace itself.

It is traditionally the Conservatives who have done most to

improve pay and conditions for MPs. Labour has always been sensitive to charges that MPs are 'feathering their own nests' — Conservatives take a more relaxed view of public opinion. It was the Conservative Government in 1970 that introduced free postage, along with the first secretarial allowances and improved pay.

Back in the late Sixties, when I was Chief Whip and Dick Crossman was Leader of the House, we tried to introduce morning sittings of the Commons. The Conservatives would have none of it, although there was the obvious precedent of morning sittings on Fridays — but that was largely for Private Members Business and was considered special. You do not have to turn up if you do not want to.

There are, in fact, two strong indications that the present system will not be changed. One is that Parliaments abroad that sit in the morning tend to go on into the late evening, just like ours, and this results in even longer hours. The Australian Federal Parliament in Canberra, which sits in the morning and has less business to conduct than ours, regularly sits a twelve-hour day. The other factor is the growth of the committee system. Standing Committees sit in the mornings, adding two and a half hours to many MPs' days.

With the best will in the world the bizarre working hours of an MP seem destined to continue. Yet the grumbles and the lack of understanding of the system have the effect of diminishing the status of MPs. Some people expect them to be in the Chamber at all times, others expect them to devote every minute to constituency or to party affairs. These misunderstandings make Labour MPs more vulnerable to those who think they should be subservient to outside manipulators.

It was the understanding of this vulnerability that led to the Bennite attack not just upon individual MPs and those groupings that the Bennites saw as right-wing, but on the organisation of the PLP itself.

The Shadow Cabinet, the Bennites said, and the Campaign Group continue to say, should be more 'accountable' to the PLP. A Labour Shadow Cabinet, or Parliamentary Committee as it is more properly called, is in fact elected by the PLP. What the Bennites wanted to do was apply more Party discipline to all Labour MPs.

I am a strong libertarian, and so was Harold Wilson, despite his occasional pretence that he was a dictator as Party Leader.

When I was Chief Whip in the Sixties a number of reforms were introduced to give backbenchers more freedom to express their views, with the proviso that dissent must never threaten the survival of a Labour Government. In 1966 and 1967 these reforms were opposed by the Chairman of the PLP, Manny Shinwell, who had spent the first sixty years of his life being a rebel, but was by then a fierce authoritarian. The atmosphere became more harmonious when Manny resigned, and Douglas Houghton, a believer in the right of dissent, took his place as Chairman of the PLP.

The Bennite line was to sweep away the reforms of the Sixties, and introduce a discipline such as the PLP has never seen. Members of the PLP would be forced to accept majority decisions on everything, and would speak and vote accordingly. Individual MPs would, of course, be mandated on how to vote by their CLPs — including on whom to vote for in Shadow Cabinet elections. It was all beautifully simple. With both the PLP and the Shadow Cabinet so mandated, they would accurately reflect the views of CLP activists — those same activists who ensured that Tony Benn received 80 per cent of the CLP vote in the 1981 Deputy Leadership election. If it worked, it would clearly ensure that Tony Benn was elected to the Shadow Cabinet.

The scheme never got off the ground. Although another idea pushed by Benn — to increase the number of Shadow Cabinet places from twelve to fifteen — was implemented, it still did not get him on the Shadow Cabinet. Not voting for Tony Benn became something of a ritual in the PLP.

Before this situation came to pass, two more resolutions came before the PLP. The first, passed by a large majority on 1 April, 1981, decreed that the elected Shadow Cabinet in the last year in opposition should automatically become the actual Cabinet in the first year of Labour Government. The freedom of former Labour Leaders to choose exactly who they want within their Cabinet has gone, although the power to allocate portfolios, and change the Cabinet in subsequent years, remains.

The second resolution, soundly defeated, called for the Shadow Cabinet to be elected by the Party as a whole — which would mean, of course, a first-year Cabinet elected by the Party outside Parliament. If the Leader and Deputy Leader are elected by the Party as a whole, why not the whole Cabinet? The Labour Party would become like an American town, with elected sheriff, judge, dog-catcher, school janitor, and the rest.

The problem is that the Labour Party is not a small, compact community. Its electorate is in a weak position to monitor and judge the performance of a Cabinet Minister, with the exception, perhaps, of the very senior posts: Chancellor of the Exchequer, Foreign Secretary, Home Secretary. The average Labour Party member, like the average citizen, could not name the entire Cabinet, nor are they in a good position to judge Parliamentary performance. Their perception is inevitably gained from the media, which gives prominence to crisis and showmanship rather than to statesmanship.

To have Shadow Ministers elected by the Party as a whole would put power into the hands of the factional lobbyists, with their slates, disciplined supporters, and printing equipment. They have discovered, as Claud Cockburn did in the Thirties, that the mimeograph machine is one of the most powerful political weapons of the twentieth century. Cockburn, with his newsletter *The Week*, used the mimeograph to undermine the British political establishment; it is an even better means of undermining a political party from within.

Another ploy that keeps bobbing up is the idea of recorded votes for Shadow Cabinet elections. This reveals the political philosophy of the hard Left in all its shallowness. The proposal is a subterfuge, a deliberate tactic, to change the political complexion of the Shadow Cabinet. It implies that one of the basic tenets of democracy — that secret ballots are essential to allow votes to be cast without fear or favour — should be put aside in the interests of the authoritarian Left.

Some people who support recorded votes are, of course, out-right enemies of democracy: they support Leninist 'democratic centralism'. Others, alas, are just short-sighted and ignorant. It is sad that in a country where universal suffrage is only sixty years old, in a world where the vast majority of people do not have an effective vote, that there are people in our own Party who have such a cavalier attitude towards democracy. The Campaign Group in Parliament records its members' votes in Shadow Cabinet elections. Its members no doubt feel they have nothing to fear from showing their marked ballot form to one another. The other side of the coin is that they endorse, tacitly or deliberately, the use of fear to influence elections.

The PLP has had its periods of intolerance before. When the Right exercised authoritarian control over the PLP, dissent could only be excused by religion, pacifism, or teetotalism. A Labour MP could abstain on the Defence Estimates on pacifist grounds, religious or otherwise, but not simply because he disagreed with them. Failure to obey this rule could, and frequently did, result in the removal of the whip and expulsion from the PLP.

Over a period of thirty years many distinguished Labour Party members were cast into outer darkness. One actually went on to become Party Leader, and two of them became Deputy Leader. Others reached Cabinet rank. Michael Foot, Nye Bevan, Stafford Cripps, and George Strauss were all disciplined before they reached Cabinet rank.

The procedure, which existed up until I became Chief Whip in 1966, was that the Cabinet or Shadow Cabinet, at the request of the Chief Whip, recommended to the PLP that the whip be withdrawn. The miscreant was able to defend himself before the PLP — which would then, invariably, follow the Chief Whip's recommendation and vote for expulsion.

Under Hard Left authoritarianism it would clearly be a little different. The call for expulsion would start in the constituencies — probably in the constituency of the MP the authoritarians wanted thrown out. It would be taken up by the PLP, who would hand the Chief Whip the axe to do the job.

The effect of all these ploys inside the PLP has been to weaken morale and to damage the delicate structure of the Party in Parliament. Normally the machine is kept running by a series of intricate checks and balances. Empirical decisions and plain trust are the lubricants that have kept the machine running. Destroy them and you help to destroy the party itself.

The fear of de-selection and the quest for high Party office has led many Labour MPs to spend far too much time outside the House. This, in turn, undermines the ability of the Chief Whip to muster an effective force in Parliament, which further diminishes the standing of MPs. The loss is a cumulative one. Today even the Chief Whip himself has to work with an elected deputy, rather than with a hand-picked deputy. In my own day as Chief Whip I sacked my deputy because it was impossible to make him understand that the new regime was not like the old. Such a conflict has fortunately not occurred since elections for Deputy Chief Whip were instituted, but some day, unless the system is changed, it is bound to happen.

The role of Chief Whip is not sufficiently understood. By its history and development it is a peculiarly British institution, and does not translate easily. I discussed this with President Nixon in 1976, when he was in London as a guest of Harold Wilson. He came as near as any foreigner I have known to understanding the role, but agreed there was no real equivalent in Congress.

A few years ago I was asked to give my advice to the newly-appointed Chief Whip of a former British protectorate in Africa. Sir Freddie Warren, the Chief Whip's Secretary during my period in that office, had arranged the meeting. I asked my new colleague how I could help.

He told me of the recent democratic revolution in his country, and the decision to appoint a Chief Whip. Unfortunately neither he nor his colleagues knew what a Chief Whip should do, so they had sent him to London to find out. Had there, I asked, ever been a Chief Whip in his country's history before? 'Yes,' he said. 'During the previous democratic government, before the revolution.' So what was the problem? Unfortunately all records had been destroyed in the coup — along with the Chief Whip — so could I please explain the duties of the job? I did, in some detail, but he left looking almost as puzzled as when he arrived.

The difficulty is not so much the duties of the job, but the very special qualities needed to carry them out. Disraeli thought these qualities were 'an amiable flexibility, a masterly self-control and a consummate knowledge of men'. All the Chief Whips I have known certainly possessed these qualities. Two of them became effective Secretaries of State for Northern Ireland — a job that is exacting in the extreme — and two of them became good Leaders of the House.

Only two Chief Whips that I can think of became Prime Ministers. Ian Smith in Rhodesia, whatever his politics may have been, was undoubtedly an effective Prime Minister. To preserve a rebel regime with a tiny minority of adherents for over eight years was a considerable achievement. Edward Heath possessed considerable courage and integrity, but failed through lack of the quality that Disraeli put first. Many things can be said of Edward Heath, but not that he possesses 'amiable flexibility'.

In British politics the Chief Whip's unique position is sustained by force of personality, since many of the powers of patronage he once possessed have gone. At one time he could distribute honours, and he even had £10,000 in gold from a secret fund to spend as he wished. When my time came this admirable means of securing a majority had, alas, disappeared, and in 1966 Harold Wilson decided that no more political honours would be given by Labour Governments. Nor, since my time, has the threat of expulsion from the PLP been available.

Nevertheless, a Chief Whip ought to be able to inspire enough affection and enough fear to see that he is listened to. If he succeeds in this, then many of the problems of the PLP today — such as voting against a three-line whip, which was once unheard of — would disappear.

Traditionally, Government Chief Whips, along with all Ministers of the Crown, are automatically entitled to a peerage. This is because the secrets with which they have been entrusted, and which none of them has ever divulged, put them in a unique position — even, in some cases, giving them knowledge that even Prime Ministers do not share. When Edward Short became Chief Whip in 1964 there was discovered in the Chief Whip's Office at 12 Downing Street a book that Conservative whips had kept during thirteen years of government. Familiarly known as 'the dirt book', it contained information on scandals affecting MPs. Edward Short's first action as Chief Whip was to burn it.

Whether or not the 'dirt book' has been revived, the Chief Whip is well aware of almost everything in the lives of his fellow MPs. A good Chief Whip never forgets, and a good Chief Whip never tells. He is in a position of trust, and in turn can demand trust from his colleagues.

I come back to the first quality that Disraeli spoke of — amiable flexibility. If Disraeli meant, as I believe he did, a tolerance of human frailty then I am sure he was right. When I had to deal with the first great back-bench rebellion of my period as Chief Whip I had only held the job for a few days. A number of Labour MPs refused to support the Government in its attitude towards the Vietnam War.

I had a great deal of sympathy with them, but Harold Wilson's ambitions to bring an end to that war — never, unfortunately, achieved — required that he remained on friendly terms with President Johnson while seeing that no

British troops went to Vietnam. This balancing act was not helped at this stage by extreme anti-Americans or extreme pro-Americans voicing their views too loudly. A large-scale rebellion was the last thing the Labour Government needed.

Accordingly, I summoned a dozen of those who had rebelled to see me in my office. I picked them at random: most of those were surprised to find themselves being interviewed — the press, too, could not understand why these MPs had been singled out. I merely told the MPs not to do it again, and then issued a press release stating that I had dealt with the leaders of the revolt. Subsequently I received a dozen letters from outraged rebels, claiming that they were the real ringleaders and deriding the 'nonentities' I had seen. But it was quite some time before another revolt was organised on this issue.

Harold Wilson, for all his great qualities — and he was undoubtedly one of the best Party Leaders I have known — could not grasp the tactics I had used. To him a Chief Whip was merely the loyal henchman of the Leader. In fact, a Chief Whip is not accountable to anybody within the Party — not to the PLP, nor the Party Leader, certainly not to anyone outside Parliament.

His task is to act as a channel of communication between the back benches and the Front Bench, to tell the back benches what the Front Bench wishes it to do, and to tell the Front Bench what the back benches believe should be done. On every single issue of policy when I was Chief Whip I saw that a sounding of the opinion of every single Labour MP was taken. I was able to give the Cabinet a detailed account of how members of the PLP viewed Cabinet policies.

Sometimes the duty that the Chief Whip owes to the backbenchers transcends any duty he owes to the Cabinet. In December 1967 I was approached by two backbenchers, Kevin McNamara and John Ellis, who had just attended a meeting of the Under-Forties Group of Labour MPs. They were greatly perturbed because the Group had been asked by the Home Secretary, James Callaghan, if it thought the Party would object to strategic arms being supplied to South Africa. In the aftermath of the Six Day War in the Middle East, with the Suez Canal closed, the Simonstown naval base in South Africa was considered to have increased in importance — and the sale of arms to anyone would help to ease Britain's balance of payments problems. But arms sales to South Africa had been banned by Britain since 1964, in line with United Nations policy.

James Callaghan himself was strongly opposed to supplying arms that could be used internally, but many of those present doubted if such a distinction between strategic arms and arms suitable for internal suppression could really be made. Kevin McNamara and John Ellis wished to put down an Early Day Motion condemning any attempt to supply the South African regime with arms. They asked me, as Chief Whip, for permission. I immediately gave my consent, and went to see the Prime Minister.

I told him that I thought I should get my whips to encourage every PLP member they could to sign the Motion. Harold Wilson not only agreed: he was enthusiastic. Within twenty-four hours the Order Paper was swamped with names.

Next Thursday in Cabinet I was personally attacked by a number of Cabinet Ministers, including Ray Gunter (Labour), Denis Healey (Defence), Tony Crosland (Education), and George Brown (Foreign Secretary) — the group that the *Spectator* approvingly called 'the junta' after the Greek Colonels who had recently seized control of their country — all accusing me of disloyalty. Later Harold Wilson was accused of not accepting collective responsibility, after he, with the steadfast help of Michael Stewart (Economic Affairs) and Willie Ross (the indomitable Secretary of State for Scotland), had won the day. I have never had any regrets about this episode: I spoke as the mouthpiece of the backbenchers, and accurately reflected the strength of their views.

But there are times when the Chief Whip has to do the opposite: make the policies of Cabinet clear and acceptable to backbenchers. This can involve the Chief Whip in some unpopularity, especially when he appears to be pushing a policy that he does not particularly like himself. But a Chief Whip cannot resign over every disagreement on policy: he must tell the Prime Minister if he disagrees with the policy, and, if the Prime Minister overrides his objections, continue to carry out his duties.

The greatest duty — and service — that a Chief Whip can do the party is to warn the Prime Minister that a policy cannot be implemented. For me, such an occasion happened over the trade union White Paper 'In Place of Strife' in 1969. I had to tell Harold Wilson that while I could guarantee that legislation based on it could pass through the House, it would split the Party in the country, perhaps irrevocably. I was dismissed immediately and replaced by Bob Mellish.

My resentment lasted about a day. If the Prime Minister felt as strongly as he did, he had no other choice of action. Logically he should perhaps have sacked Bob Mellish as well, since the new Chief Whip told him that the legislation could not even get through the House. But it is an almost immutable law of democratic politics that successive occupants of a post are not sacked for the same offence. Bob Mellish survived as Chief Whip for seven years, outliving Harold Wilson's tenure as Party Leader.

What can be done to improve the position of the Labour MP, following the introduction of the present system of mandatory re-selection?

Since we cannot go back, we must go forward. It should not be for a GC to decide if there will be a re-selection procedure: every Party member must have a say. If a majority of CLP members vote for re-selection, the GC would then draw up a short list, automatically including the sitting MP, as at present. This would both increase the power of the ordinary member, and reduce that of the officers and the GC, and make them more responsive generally to the feelings of Party members. It is quite wrong that an 'ordinary' Party member who may have served the Party loyally for a lifetime, but is not on the GC, should have no say while an ambitious youngster, who may only have been in the Party for a year or so, has a vote by virtue of a GC position. I would not go as far as favouring a postal ballot. It is the system used by the SDP, where it has not been conspicuously successful. It is open to abuse and can reward candidates with the most money and the best access to the media, regardless of other qualities.

One member, one vote would greatly strengthen Labour's work in Parliament. It would improve morale and attendance, and reduce factionalism within the House itself. MPs accountable to a broader electorate within the Party would have less incentive to join a group within Parliament. There is no doubt that the Tribune Group's membership over the years has been boosted by token members, who have joined to give themselves

79

spurious left-wing credentials and keep their constituencies quiet. Their subscriptions are no doubt welcome to the Tribune Group treasurer, but it is hardly a dignified way for an MP to behave.

Even unhealthier are the attempts to establish a cradle-to-the-grave factionalism within the Labour Party, extending from the CLPs, through to meetings of candidates, and on into Parliament. The Tribune Group, named after the newspaper, has had unofficial local groups for years, but they have been largely innocuous. The Campaign Group is the Parliamentary manifestation of the old Bennite Rank and File Mobilising Committee, a rag-bag of authoritarian Left groups.

Campaign's distinguishing feature is its willingness to work with every group of entryists, including the Militant Tendency. Its extra-Parliamentary wing, now called Labour Left Liaison (a year or so ago it was called Campaign Forum — next year, who knows?) is the same old collection of authoritarian Left groups — but formally excluding Militant. Militant's two MPs are, however, members of the Campaign Group. This confusion is a symptom of the weakening of the hard Left, and its increasingly desperate attempts to stitch together a workable coalition.

If factionalism has weakened in the PLP, the slate system has not. It has come more and more to dominate Shadow Cabinet elections, to the point where, during the period 1979-86, there was only one MP not on a slate at each election to the Shadow Cabinet. First it was me, and Denzil Davies took my place when I decided to stand down.

It is the Right who are the arch exponents of a slate, and will continue to be so until their often irrational fear of the Left diminishes. I fear it will be a long time before old habits are broken. It should be the personal task of all Labour MPs to break down factionalism and build trust with fellow Labour MPs who, by conventional analysis, are on a different wing of the Party from themselves.

Part Two

————————— ○○○○○ —————————

Home Affairs

Chapter Seven

—————————— ooOoo ——————————

Dancing round the Maypole

National leaders — and British Prime Ministers are no exception — like to see themselves as actors on the world stage. It is a desire that grows stronger with every passing year in office, especially if things are not going well at home. National leaders fervently believe that voters are proud of them when they appear on the television screen, talking to other national leaders about important matters in some foreign capital. In reality, voters are generally uninterested in foreign affairs — unless it is a part of the world where they have relatives or which they have visited that hits the headlines. This is a fact that politicians ignore at their peril.

In this judgement, the voters show more imagination and realism than their leaders. They understand, with de Tocqueville, that foreign policy is merely an extension of domestic policy. Rulers who think that foreign adventures can be an escape from decline at home always find they are mistaken.

It was this lesson that Aneurin Bevan tried to teach me when, as a young man recently demobilised from the Royal Navy at the end of the Second World War, I was advocating Labour fighting an election on foreign policy.

'When Jennie and I were in New York,' Nye said, 'there happened to be a rent strike on New York's East Side. The landlord was a man named Murphy, and his tenants were parading around the tenement block that he owned with signs reading "Murphy unfair to tenants", "No rent rise".

'Soon others began to move in, who were not tenants. The placards began to multiply but now began to read "Hands off Cuba", "Support China", "Leave Russia alone".

'Finally,' said Nye, 'Murphy himself came down and said to the protesters: "All right — I'll keep my hands off Cuba, I'll support China, I'll leave Russia alone — but you pay the rent."'

No nation can make a powerful contribution to the future of the world if its economy is weak and fragile. The history of Britain is a continuing illustration of this fundamental truth. A relatively small island, on the road to nowhere in particular, possessing little in the way of natural resources, she became a force in the world through the development of trade and manufacturing. Britain became 'the workshop of the world' and created a world empire through trade. In the eighteenth and nineteenth centuries, as her Empire expanded, Britain sent engineers and scientists to every corner of the globe. Throughout the world British products and British methods became the foundation of British influence. Of all the empires, Britain's strength has depended remarkably little on military conquest.

But from the last quarter of the nineteenth century a decline set in. Two new manufacturing nations arose to challenge Britain's supremacy. In Europe, following the Franco-Prussian war of 1870, a newly-united Germany began to threaten the British monopoly of trade in Asia and Africa. After the Civil War in the United States of America that nation began to lose her dependence on British imports and went into business for herself. The United States had what Britain did not have: a vast treasury of natural resources and a deficiency of labour, which put a premium on methods of mass production, and on the nurturing of a working class skilled in these methods. Henry Ford not only gave the world the mass-produced motor car, he also gave his workers — from similar humble backgrounds to his own — welfare schemes and other incentives to make the transition from farm labour to production line. The twentieth century was being invented.

With the coming of this international competition, the British ruling classes began to neglect manufacturing and started to concentrate instead on making Britain the financial centre of the world. The City of London, which for centuries had housed the most adventurous traders in Britain, from the days of Dick Whittington on, became increasingly the home of banking and insurance. The next generation of British traders began to concentrate on exporting these 'invisibles', rather than upon promoting the products of British factories.

At the turn of the century, although Britain exported more manufactured goods than she imported, the decline was in full swing. The quality and number of skilled engineers and workers grew fewer and fewer. At the same time the quality and design of the products of British factories began to deteriorate. New centres of manufacturing excellence began to take Britain's place. They were despised at the time. Englishmen joked about the man who cut his throat, but fortunately used a German razor blade and so survived. The same condescending attitude was later evidenced in attitudes towards goods from Japan and Hong Kong.

As the years went by, Britain's heavy industries — coal, steel, shipbuilding — lost their dominant position in the economy. Large areas of unemployment arose in parts of the country that were once bywords for industry and prosperity. A temporary reprieve came in the Thirties, when the National Government of 1931-35 introduced import controls, boosting output and cutting unemployment. Protectionism became Government policy in 1932, and by 1934 unemployment, at 3.2 million when the Government came to power, had begun to fall. Without this recovery, the Second World War would have been swiftly lost. As it was, the coming of war gave these industries a further temporary reprieve, although it was not until 1941, two years into the war, that unemployment fell below one million, even though rearmament had been going on since 1936.

In 1945, with the coming of peace, Britain appeared to be more powerful than she had ever been. With the industry of Continental Europe in ruins, Britain and the United States had a free ride. The Fifties saw a new optimism, as the hardships of war and its immediate aftermath were forgotten. In 1954, when the Chancellor of the Exchequer, R. A. Butler, boasted that the standard of living would double in twenty-five years, few doubted it. When Harold Macmillan told the British people that they 'had never had it so good', they believed him and rewarded him with a large majority in the Election of 1959.

But under the surface things were going badly. By the Sixties a regenerated West Germany was once again dominating the Continent of Europe. Germany had undergone what was called an 'economic miracle'. Another name for it was Marshall Aid, the pumping of American money into Western Europe.

The United States, whose mighty production had been essential to the winning of the Second World War, was now geared to full peacetime production, and to serving a world market. The Soviet Union and the other Eastern Bloc countries were increasing their industrialisation day by day, often aided by investment and technology from Western nations that professed to despise the Soviet system. Japan had arisen to take the mastery of steel and consumer electronics, and had created new world markets for such products as motorcycles and cameras. The new centres of manufacturing — Hong Kong, Taiwan, Korea — were challenging British industry and winning. While their strength increased, the British economy once again faltered.

By the early Sixties there appeared to be two roads open to Britain. She could succumb to the competition and settle down, as other former imperial powers had done, to a period of decadence and oblivion, or she could plan to win back her share of world markets, using the undoubted skills and expertise that she still had.

Both these options were distasteful to the Governments of the Sixties — Conservative and Labour alike. Labour initially tried planning and created a Department of Economic Affairs in 1964. The new department drew up an expansionist National Plan, of the sort that countries as diverse as Japan and France have thrived upon. Both department and plan soon sank without trace. The plaque that had identified the headquarters of the Department of Economic Affairs was taken down and hung for several years in a nearby public house.

Some looked for a softer option. To them joining the European Economic Community seemed attractive. They managed to enlist the support of the leaders of both the major parties — Harold Wilson and Edward Heath. They argued that the mere act of joining this Western European trading bloc would bolster Britain's faltering economy and enable her to exist in accustomed affluence without having to face any of the unpleasantness involved in the other options. The power of the EEC was growing; merely to be a member of that organisation, the argument went, would give Britain a new dynamism.

By 1973 Britain had joined the EEC; but 1973, to students

of economics, was not primarily the year of 'British entry into Europe'. It was the year when oil prices started to go through the roof. From that moment the decline of the British economy accelerated at a rate not seen since the Twenties. The EEC's response to the oil crisis was confused and divisive. To the particular British crisis there was no response at all. The British public found, suddenly and sickeningly, that membership of the EEC was no easy option.

They found, instead, an organisation that promised to its members future glories, while taking credit for fifteen years of European economic expansion that would have taken place anyway, had the EEC existed or not. Confronted with a crisis, the EEC proved to be a clumsy and ineffectual giant, unable to make decisions or even to make up its mind about what the crisis was really about. The individual nations of the EEC, bound by the organisation's treaties, laws, and directives, have little room for manoeuvre. Within the British Labour Party there was pressure for an 'alternative economic policy', harking back to both the aborted National Plan of the Sixties and to the National Government's policies of the Thirties. But such a strategy demands import controls and widespread Government aid and intervention in industry. All are clearly illegal under the Treaty of Rome, which holds that such matters are not within the competence of national governments.

Any country that relies upon the export of goods for its survival must cope with international competitive pressure — its goods must not be too expensive compared with those of its rivals. Britain, in common with another island, Japan, has an additional difficulty to face. Because she must import much of her food and practically all of the raw materials needed in the manufacturing processes, she must have a favourable balance of trade in manufactures to compensate for this, in order to avoid an overall deficit.

The problem that has faced Britain for the last quarter of a century, and the solution to which is ever more urgent, is: what should be done when this favourable balance of trade is not being achieved, or is being dangerously eroded? There are several courses of action: to direct import controls to keep out foreign goods (illegal under EEC law); to deflate in order to reduce the purchasing power of the nation as a whole (which leads to large-scale unemployment); or to reduce labour costs by using a statutory prices and incomes policy. It is the last of these three options that has deluded British Governments during the last twenty years, and caused much of the industrial unrest during this period. The use of devaluation was tried in 1947 and 1967. It may be a temporary necessity. It is never a cure since its longer-term effect is to increase the cost of these essential imports which the nation requires.

The idea of government action to make labour costs a smaller percentage of production costs is a very old one. Slavery is its most extreme manifestation. For centuries governments of various descriptions in various parts of the world have been able to impose a temporary cut, or standstill, on wages and prices. Sometimes, it is true, this has had a beneficial effect upon the economy of these countries, but it is not practical to maintain such a policy for any length of time.

The belligerent powers in the two World Wars tried to control prices and incomes, and more or less succeeded for the duration of hostilities. But all the administrative systems of control built up during the war were unable to prevent an explosion of wages and prices when the war ended. Even totalitarian governments able to bring the whole machinery of the state to bear on the problem have been unable to maintain an effective control of prices and incomes, as the recent history of Poland amply demonstrates.

In Britain, peacetime controls over prices have never been particularly satisfactory, despite efforts to sell prices and income policies to the country as promoting fairness among income earners. Wage earners soon found that it was not at all fair. They first complained about the policies, and then tried to destroy them. While wage earners who had PAYE deducted had their incomes controlled, they saw that the self-employed and the mobile were able to evade regulation. Nor could any government hide its inability to control dividends from shares. It was easy enough to decree that no dividend should exceed a particular level: but that usually meant that the market value of shares themselves increased, as profits went back into the business. One way or another, the shareholder gained. The burden of rising prices continued to fall on the wage earner.

In 1975 the Labour Government succeeded in getting an agreement with the unions limiting increases to £6 a week. This benefited the lower-paid worker, who in comparison with skilled workers was grossly underpaid. This was popular, and aroused little protest. But by the next year skilled workers began to complain that the differential in wages, which they regarded as their reward for their training and their skills, was being eaten away by flat-rate increases. For the next two years, therefore, the Government's policy turned to percentage increases. By the fourth year the whole wages policy was breaking down, causing industrial disputes on a scale that had not been seen for years. It was this, more than anything else, that lost Labour the election of 1979. I remember attending a meeting of the TUC Economic Committee towards the end of 1978 and hearing Jack Jones, the General Secretary of the TGWU, and Hugh Scanlon, the General Secretary of the AUEW, warn a Treasury Minister that their members were thoroughly discontented with the incomes policy. Jones and Scanlon said very clearly that they could no longer greatly limit demands for pay. This warning was ignored.

Ten years before, the same policy was abandoned after a similar period when the Prime Minister, Harold Wilson, decided to promote legislation intended to limit the powers of the trade unions. The trade unions liked this even less than they liked wage restraint, so Harold Wilson decided that he could not afford to fight on two fronts at once. Roy Jenkins, the then Chancellor of the Exchequer, accepted the abandonment of wage restraint with as much nonchalance as he had approved its appearance. He said that it made a difference in prices of only one penny in the pound. I wondered at the time: why had he made us suffer so much for so little reward?

It is hard to understand the fanaticism of those academics who are obsessed with the theory of wage and price control, or the docility with which some politicians have listened to them. Usually such controls are brought in mainly as window-dressing to try to persuade foreign bankers that something dramatic is being done. Such measures no doubt have some influence on the financial markets, but bankers tend to be much more interested in the industrial well-being of the nation.

When Harold Wilson made me Chief Whip in 1966 he told me that it was essential to have a statutory prices and incomes policy in place before the summer recess if the Government was to stop a decline in the value of the pound. The Bill received the Royal Assent on the day the House rose for the recess. It had no effect whatever on the value of the pound. What did steady the pound was the settlement of a strike by merchant seamen which had been holding up British exports for a number of weeks. The ending of this strike and the ending of the strikes in the winter of 1979 — the so-called 'Winter of Discontent' — had a real effect on stabilising the pound. Industrial harmony is much more effective in restoring confidence than any incomes policy.

When Margaret Thatcher came to power in 1979, she had her own version of an incomes policy. As the biggest employer in the country, the Government could hold down wages in the public sector. Under its deflationary policies it could also rely upon unemployment to force workers to accept lower wages.

Deflation was the key to international competitiveness for Mrs Thatcher. The best that can be said for this policy is that it is virtually the only one legally available to a member state of the EEC. It relies upon depressing the national economy. By cutting public expenditure, including benefits to the poor, it is designed also to cut private expenditure on imported goods. With less money in circulation, labour costs theoretically fall, thus making exports cheaper and more competitive. Such policies are not protectionist in the terms of the Treaty of Rome. Deflation is therefore the economic policy traditionally favoured by the EEC. Despite the fuss Mrs Thatcher has made over the EEC budget from time to time, she has no fundamental quarrel with the basic tenets of the EEC.

Like any form of protectionism, deflation is competitive. Once one country deflates, others are forced to follow, lest they suffer a huge increase in imports and thus experience a rapid worsening of their balance of payments. The laissez-faire free-trader may then argue that things will correct themselves: the value of that country's currency will fall, making imports more expensive and exports more competitive. Prosperity will then return. That is what the textbooks and the pundits say: but nobody seems to believe them, least of all the free-trader theoreticians themselves. They lose their nerve long before their theories are truly put to the test. Workers who successfully follow the economic imperative and gain more money for themselves are castigated (Marxists tend to do the same thing in reverse, their materialism giving way to moral indignation over profits that are, by their own logic, inevitable). On the 'European' level, the idea of floating exchange rates compensating for economic diversity is rejected. Competitive deflation is supposed to coexist with the stable exchange rates that the

European Monetary System is intended to supply to its members.

European double standards do not stop there. Subsidies to manufacturing industry are outlawed by the EEC, while those to agriculture proliferate. Import controls are to be avoided — unless they are controlled from Brussels. Dual pricing for home sales and export, together with exchange rates for different commodities (popular before the Second World War), are anathema for industrial products, yet are the lifeblood of the Common Agricultural Policy.

The EEC failed to meet the challenge of the oil crisis and the subsequent recession of the Seventies because it had no mechanism for doing so. Its founders worked on the assumption of expansion forever more. Only one national government, that of the French Socialists of the early Eighties, has ever tried to break away from competitive deflation. They introduced a wide range of protectionist measures — subsidies to industries, dual pricing — and immediately the writs from Brussels began to rain down on Paris. The Socialists' expansionist policies were modified, emasculated, and then abandoned. Even the French could not, in the end, defeat the power of Brussels.

These developments were naturally followed with great interest by the Labour Opposition in Britain. At one meeting at the House of Commons between a French Government economic adviser and a number of Labour Front Bench spokesmen, one spokesman, on hearing the French tale of woe, said: 'Doesn't that mean you should withdraw from the EEC?' Since the Frenchman's Cartesian logic could take him nowhere else, he had to say 'yes', but then add: 'It's politically impossible.'

The British economy has suffered greatly from our membership of the Common Market. By 1983, for the first time since the sixteenth century, Britain's trade in manufactures moved into deficit. There is a view, which owes much to that pioneer monetarist, Mr Micawber, that this is not a matter for concern. Those who hold this view believe that there is a fixed amount of trade any nation can undertake. To the laissez-faire free-trade purist, this doctrine has a mystical quality. To anybody else it sounds like nonsense, yet there are those who point to North Sea oil as proof that something always turns up.

They ignore the lessons of history. The Spain of Ferdinand and Isabella is most instructive even after five centuries.

'Until Spain found the wealth of the Indies,' wrote Dudley Pope in his biography of Sir Henry Morgan, the seventeenth-century privateer, (*Harry Morgan's Way*) 'a nation had to depend upon its trade and taxation to put gold into the treasury, with the result that a wealthy nation was one with a healthy trade. Spain's discovery of gold had changed all that for her; merely mining the gold and silver brought her undreamed-of wealth, and trade and industry were neglected, so that it withered. The long-term effect was that soon Spain could exist only from the gold shipments because she had no prospering industry to fall back on if the gold ever failed to arrive. She had become dependent, like a drug addict.'

Granted that the use and consumption of oil follows a different pattern from that of gold, and has different economic consequences, a basic similarity remains: both are finite resources. Like seventeenth-century gold oil will one day come to an end. And, like seventeenth-century gold, oil's finite quality is too often overlooked. The net effect of drug-addict economics is to fuel an economic cycle that destroys jobs in Britain. Oil is exported to Britain's continental competitors and plays its part, therefore, in promoting the very imports that help to destroy Britain's manufacturing base. It does more: it makes Britain ever more dependent on the receipts from oil sales rather than looking to her manufactures. Thus as the jobs disappear, so too do skills and abilities.

Britain cannot console herself with the prospect of a prosperous future based on service industries or tourism. Service industries depend upon manufacturing. It is possible to imagine an economy that is based entirely upon manufacturing; it is not possible to imagine one based entirely upon services. We cannot sustain ourselves and our society by cutting each other's hair — nor by dancing around maypoles to the click of tourists' cameras. Tourism is a useful component in any economy, but in the age of mass tourism it is the countries with low standards of living, and consequent low living costs, that have tourism as a dominant part of their economy.

Britain's decline has been a long one: for a hundred years her share of world exports, compared with other major industrial nations, has been dropping. A century ago a third of all exports from the major industrial nations were British: today the figure has dropped to 8 per cent. This decline has not been continuous. On two occasions it has been reversed: by the Labour Government that came to power in 1945; and by the Labour Government of 1974-79. It is not a coincidence that these were periods of Labour Government. The measures taken during both periods were remarkably similar: economic planning on a national scale coupled with national investment and a firm lead to the bankers. Looking back, the measures taken may have been inadequate, but they did work. Mistakes were made, as over incomes policy, but the net results were beneficial. To say that Labour's policies were the right ones is not to make a narrow party point, for they are broadly similar to the policies pursued by the most successful manufacturing economies of the post-war years. The blunders of Thatcherism, with its tragic experiment in laissez-faire economics, has tended to obscure the fact that there is no great mystery about how to run a successful industrial economy. The models are there for us to study. Some of the models lie in our own past, others, the more recent ones, lie abroad. The real problem is one of will, not of method.

To succeed, an industrial nation needs investment, it needs infrastructure, it needs education and training, and it needs planning to bring these first three factors together.

It is a paradox that the advocates of laissez-faire point to the United States of America as the supreme example of free enterprise. They cite America's virtues and the many advances in science and engineering made in that great country. But they ignore the fact that for the last forty years these advances have been critically dependent on state planning and state funding, both in the defence industries and in the armed forces themselves. Education plays a role in this strategy: the armed forces like to take the cream of science graduates in their early post-graduate years. Later they can be assisted, through what President Eisenhower accurately called the military-industrial complex, to obtain privileged positions in American industry.

Many of the dividing lines that exist between civil and military manufacturing in Europe do not exist in America. It is not surprising that the Boeing 707 airliner dominated the new world market for jet airliners after it went into service in 1958 — the US Airforce had ordered four hundred of the military tanker version four years before. In America, army tanks are not built by heavy engineering works or government ordnance factories, but by motor manufacturers such as

General Motors and Chrysler. (West Germany to some extent follows this pattern: Porsche designed that country's current battle tank. Saab of Sweden build military aircraft as well as cars.) California's Silicon Valley, that talisman of free enterprise, would not exist today had not the micro-chip been developed to meet the needs of the US military and the NASA space programme. Development is sustained to this day by military as well as by commercial needs.

It is a myth that free enterprise alone will promote and generate new ideas and technologies. The Victorians have been overestimated. They provided a network of railways that even George Stephenson thought was too large, and in the wrong places — and they neglected road transport, leaving it to the Germans and the French to develop practical automobiles. They applauded Isambard Kingdom Brunel's grandiose schemes, but they ignored Charles Babbage's invention of the computer. When the coming of electricity made Babbage's ideas practical, these ideas had been forgotten in Britain. It was a government contract in the United States, for a machine to tabulate the results of the 1890 census, that led Herman Hollerith to build his successful electro-mechanical tabulator — and create the company that became known as IBM.

When Charles Babbage was struggling to build his vast mechanical analytical machine, one person who came to visit him was the aged Duke of Wellington. As a military man he understood planning, and thought that a machine to collate and analyse information was a splendid idea — every bit as sensible as Wellington boots. In the Second World War it was military needs that made the British Government assemble a crew of eccentric scientists to build the code-breaking computer known as Colossus. It worked, and was one of the great achievements of public-school and Oxbridge amateurism, an alliance between academia and old chums in Whitehall, but the momentum was immediately lost after the war ended. The equivalent American computer, built at Harvard, was the result of an alliance between that university, the US Navy, and IBM. Government funding, the cream of education, planning that embraced public and private sectors, it was this alliance that gave America the lead in computers. The transistor and the micro-chip were to follow, both American in origin, both richly exploited.

American public investment and public planning is marked

by an ideological rejection of public ownership — instead, America puts its faith in its elected representatives to monitor public expenditure. At their best, Senate and Congressional committees can be fierce watchdogs of the public interest, and a model from which other democracies can learn much. However they are better at uncovering abuses after they have occurred than at playing a constructive role in decision-making. Under the American system Congress can say 'no' to vast blocks of public expenditure, and it can complain bitterly after the event — in between it can do very little.

Within the British Labour Party there has been, in marked contrast, an enduring faith in public ownership. This is not the same as a blind belief in state ownership. Clause IV of the Labour Party's constitution, drafted by Sydney Webb in 1918, calls for the 'common ownership of the means of production, distribution and exchange'. The constitution might have used the words 'public ownership' or the single word 'nationalisation', but instead it chose two words that imply a variety of methods of transferring privately-owned industry into the community's hands. The constitution calls for 'the best obtainable system of popular administration and control of each industry or service'. Nationalisation, in other words, was envisaged as existing alongside municipal ownership and co-operative ownership. Centralised state ownership was clearly inappropriate in many cases.

But for Webb and his generation of democratic socialists it was the transfer of ownership out of private hands that was essential. They regarded it as morally unjust that important industries should be run for private profit rather than serving the interests of the country as a whole. Workers in industry, they reasoned, would be better treated under community, not private, ownership. Greater efficiency would come about when common need, not profiteering and nepotism, became the criteria for management. With a commitment to the country as a whole, service industries under common ownership would see that there were no disadvantaged geographical areas. No longer would private profit dictate that remote rural hamlets in, say, the Lake District would be without basic services because the capital expense of bringing these services to such places would destroy any hope of profit. An equal and beneficial service would be available to all those who dwelt in these islands.

Equality of services is vitally important, and well demonstrates the point that the crude profit motive will always come into conflict with the needs of the nation and the community. Britain has, on the whole, had a history of understanding this point. When Sir Rowland Hill introduced the Penny Post in 1840, he made the price of a letter the same whether it was sent to a remote corner of the country or half a mile across London. The result was the best postal service in the world. Sadly, in the last twenty years the erosion of the traditional postal service has led to a two-tier postal system: couriers and telexes for those who can afford it, or who cannot survive without a rapid service; a declining postal service for the rest.

The Second World War, with its direction of capital and labour, and an overwhelming sense of common purpose, made the task of promoting common ownership in Britain very much easier. When Labour swept to power in 1945, state ownership and state control were familiar to everyone after six years of war. The methods the 1945 Labour Government used to extend common ownership were uniform and monolithic, and it was these features that later led to the unpopularity of common ownership.

Large public corporations were set up, run very much on the lines of private corporations, however different their economic goals were supposed to be from those of private capitalism. These corporations satisfied the moral imperative that any profit should be preserved for the community, but hardly satisfied the aspirations of those who worked for them and those who used their services. Improvements were made — the mines became more mechanised, amenities and working conditions improved — but the gulf between workers and managers still remained. To some extent this was the workers' own fault. In most nationalised industries they were offered a place in management, through their own representatives, but preferred to remain separate — with some exceptions, such as the post office and later the steel and shipbuilding industries, where trade union officers became directors.

But in general the trade union leaders insisted upon distancing themselves from management — while in practice taking over many lower managerial tasks through their shop stewards. Thus developed the strange paradox where an Arthur Scargill could be a strong opponent of the whole idea of 'workers' control' (as a distraction from true socialism), while officers and officials of his own union, the National Union of

Mineworkers, had for years drawn up duty rosters and carried out other management tasks at pit level. Similarly the print unions, who worked mainly in the private sector, would not, as a matter of principle, take an equity stake in a Labour movement journal, but saw no contradiction in controlling recruitment, manning, and other equally important management functions in Fleet Street. It is hardly surprising that unions operating in this schizoid manner eventually found themselves in the forefront of major industrial disputes.

The mutual antagonism between management and workers prevents a British counterpart of the Israeli Histradut from operating — a trade union federation that would itself own a large part of the industry of its own country. The trade union movement believed that nationalisation would be enough to bring the interests of management and workers together. It was therefore with a sense of shock and betrayal that the leaders of the old trade unions found that state management treated striking workers with the same autocratic ruthlessness as they had experienced from the old private owners.

Little effort has been made by the Labour Party since the fall of the Attlee Government to explain the logic and morality that lies behind the belief in common ownership, while often the Conservatives have met no coherent opposition when they have indicated the bureaucratic errors and follies of state ownership. In the popular mind, one dirty railway carriage has been enough to condemn the entire nationalised railway network. Any rise in gas, electricity, and telephone charges — whether justified or not — equally condemned these nationalised services. At local level, the same unimaginative bureaucracy in house repairs and building has often made people despair of municipal enterprise. In recent years, the Conservatives have been able to denationalise industry after industry (leaving aside for a moment their attacks on local government) with hardly a murmur from the workers involved and near total apathy on the part of the population as a whole.

The Labour Party has viewed this development with incredulity. For forty years it has assumed that the basic industries in the public sector were a permanent feature of national life. The strongest opposition to Mrs Thatcher came, if anything, from other Conservatives, who were not opposed to the principle of denationalisation, but to the way the country was being robbed by sell-offs at bargain-basement prices. The

97

former Prime Minister Lord Stockton complained of the family silver being sold off. As for Labour, not only was it unprepared for Mrs Thatcher's successes in rolling back the frontiers of the state; it was also hopelessly divided on what a future Labour Government would do about these denationalised industries. Nationalisation on the old lines was losing favour, but what to put in its place was not fully considered. The sheer scale and cost of renationalisation was awesome. The family silver may have been sold off at cut-price, but buying it back will prove very expensive. Nor is repurchase a popular issue on which to fight an election.

In the Fifties Aneurin Bevan identified the limits of common ownership as 'the commanding heights of the economy'. At that time these heights were dominated by the large heavy industries, coal and steel, and the companion manufacturing industries of shipbuilding and aircraft production. These industries, far from remaining the motors of economic growth in Britain, have declined in relative importance. The miners' union found this to its cost when in 1985 its attempt at a national strike collapsed in humiliating defeat. A union that for three generations had regarded itself as constituting 'the shock troops of the trade union movement', and which as recently as 1974 had had a profound impact on the general election result, no longer represents an industry so vital that a widespread strike can put the economy at risk.

In times of expansion and economic stability, the trade unions can be the Labour Party's greatest strength. In times of decline and necessary reconstruction, they can become a weakness. By their very nature, they represent workers in established industries: those with high employment and an important place in the national economy. Conversely, they do not represent the unemployed, thrown on the scrap-heap by the vagaries of laissez-faire capitalism; nor those able and willing to seek employment in the industries of the future, on which the future health of the nation will ultimately depend. This is not to say that these two areas will be ignored. Some voices will speak up for them, but the weight of votes at a Labour Party conference or a Trades Union Congress will always be in favour of workers in established industries. In times of decline and uncertainty, as jobs are threatened, the voice of these workers gets louder as their very industrial strength gets weaker.

This dilemma leads to the Labour Party's weakness in developing an industrial strategy and its failure in economic planning. The Party may believe in a planned economy, but it devotes astonishingly little thought to the practicalities of carrying this out. On the Left of the Party there are calls for more public ownership; the Right limits itself to calling for Keynesian reflation. The Left reverts to Marxist-inspired fundamentals; the Right harks back to the post-war consensus politics of Macmillan, Butler, and Gaitskell. Depth of thought and a willingness to face up to new challenges with new ideas are conspicuously absent. There is more likely to be radical thought on peripheral social issues than on economic ones. This is evident when one reads the agendas for annual Party conferences or looks at the lists of fringe meetings held during Party conferences.

Such indifference to Britain's economic decline is not, of course, confined to the Labour Party and the trade unions. Britain's failures in economic planning have been identified by many commentators, at home and abroad, as something approaching a national malaise. Entering the EEC was an attempt to avoid the burden by joining in a wider economic bloc. Equally futile has been the attempt to place the entire burden upon market forces. Both were attempts to run away from reality. Both, in short, were symptoms of a failure of national will.

This is the central problem, to which economists usually fail to address themselves. How does one create, or recreate, the necessary national will? How does one reverse a century-old decline brought about by the abdication of Britain's ruling class and the lack of cohesion of its working class? The question is easy to formulate; the answer is more difficult. The Labour Party has still not answered it fully. In the campaign for the 1983 General Election, it harked back to the successes of the Attlee Government, and tried to revive that immediate post-war spirit. That can never be brought back: the situation today is entirely different. The Second World War concentrated the national will into a fight for survival, and that spirit lingered into the post-war years, but it has long gone. Nor is there much sign of the British gaining inspiration from trade wars. The Government, aided by the *Sun* newspaper, may talk of bringing the Japanese to heel. There is no answering echo in the country. These days the British rather admire them.

It is an admiration that is very understandable, for the Japanese are also an island people. They also export to feed themselves, but they do so very successfully. We can learn a lot from them, as they once did from us. Two aspects of Japanese success should be especially noted.

First their emphasis on education as an integral part of economic planning. When Japan decided some fifteen years ago that new technology was the way ahead for their economy, they launched a ten-year programme to steer industry in that direction. Between 1975 and 1985, seventy billion US dollars of public money went into technological development, and of that three billion dollars a year went on education. Educational standards in Japan are among the highest in the world: 94 per cent of pupils complete their school education. In the UK the figure is 18 per cent. In Japan 38.6 per cent go on to university; in the UK the figure is 7 per cent; of the Japanese percentage a vastly higher percentage emerge with science degrees than in the UK.

This in turn has created a high level of innovation in Japanese industry, and innovation in products and their application is the way to obtain new markets. The Japanese did not set out to conquer the British motorcycle industry: they created a new, hard market for motorcycles in countries where Britain had previously sold only a handful of machines to a few wealthy, Westernised enthusiasts. Similarly, the Japanese decided that amateur photographers would like cameras to professional specifications at low prices: they created that market, and have continued to dominate it ever since. The European camera industry has all but vanished. The six British camera manufacturers who were in business thirty years ago have disappeared from the scene. In car manufacture, the Japanese have shown similar originality. The staid conservatism of their designs serves a profitable purpose: they have launched their attack on European and North American markets from a base of voluminous Third World sales. They built simple, solid cars for the rapidly expanded Third World market, which European and American manufacturers tended to despise.

Such success is a creative process. It can only be achieved by people with ideas and imagination, and above all an education that enables them to put their ideas into practice, and a commercial environment that encourages them to take a genuine pride and pleasure in making things, not just in making money. Workers and management both have a sense of pride which comes from involvement and participation. People must feel that their brains and their skills are contributing to a common good.

Yet the irony is that the people of Britain have the means to imitate the Japanese miracle. They already own much of their own industry. They are still unaware that they have an equity stake in many industrial concerns through pension funds invested in industry. Pension funds and insurance companies today own over 60 per cent of British industry. The people have absolutely no say in how these investments are managed. That task is performed by professional managers and advisers, whose attitudes to investment is not related to the long-term needs of industrial development.

The managers inevitably put short-term gain before the long-term needs of society. Like the trade unions, the pension funds have no effective mechanism for looking ahead. Yet tomorrow's industries, jobs, and profits will only come about if the investment is made today.

A coherently argued case for public investment in industry, using the British people's own money, put across with flair and imagination, could generate wide support. It is an exciting idea and an exciting venture, one with the potential of cutting through the apathy and rekindling the national self-confidence.

People instinctively feel that the world economy has changed. The image of the tycoon, the wealthy man who both owns and controls his own company, lingers on, but today such persons are rare. Very few workers know exactly who owns the company they work for, and there must be many managers who have no precise idea either. The professional manager is as much a hired hand as the worker on the shop floor. He tends to be much better paid, and all too often isolated from the workforce by a carefully fostered mystique of managerial status, and is all too often inadequately trained.

The decline in British manufacturing has caused a decline in the status of those who work in industry. Status is now focused not on people who make things, but on people in the media, on people who manipulate, and on people who make money. A young merchant banker will earn more before he is thirty than most engineers can expect to earn in the last five years of their working life.

Nations can be judged by the priorities that they award to the occupations of their citizens. The decline of the Roman empire became obvious when it lacked the engineers to maintain and repair the technology that had once made it great. When roads became pot-holed, buildings decayed and the public baths no longer worked — when, in other words, the infrastructure was gone — then the empire was finished.

The danger for Britain is not the absolute disappearance of the skills needed to maintain a prosperous industrial society. We face rather the problem that afflicts many Third World countries: that of the dual economy, of prosperity existing within poverty. It means that there is a complete industrial economy, with managers, bankers, engineers, skilled workers, which has no connection at all with the mass economy surrounding it.

While the term 'dual economy' is comparatively new, the phenomenon it describes has been observed from the beginning of industrialisation. Disraeli, in his novel *Sybil; or, the Two Nations*, wrote of once prosperous artisans pushed aside by mechanisation. When the hand loom became redundant, so too did the weaver. Both were thrown on to the scrap-heap.

'Two nations; between whom there is no intercourse and no sympathy, who are as ignorant of each other's habits, thoughts, and feelings, as if they were dwellers in different zones, or inhabitants of different planets; they are formed by a different breeding, are fed by a different food; are ordered by different manners, and are not governed by the same laws. "The rich and the poor."'

Disraeli argued that a nation that had depended for its wealth on these now-redundant workers has a duty to look after them once their economic usefulness is at an end. Disraeli wanted one nation, not two. So too do the more compassionate Tories today. Whether they want one economy or two is another matter. The attitude of most prosperous Conservatives towards the state playing a creative role in bringing the two nations together is ambivalent at best. They fear that it may put the country on the road to socialism, as indeed it may.

It is not a fear that anyone, least of all a socialist, can brush aside. Behind it lies a genuine fear that socialism could lead to totalitarian communism, with the loss of many democratic freedoms. The frontiers of the state must be a matter of greater concern and study for socialists than for Conservatives.

Conservatives tend, as a matter of principle if not of practice, to regard any extension to the powers of the state as regrettable. Socialists see the state as potentially an active and creative force for good.

The choice between conservatism and socialism is a choice between fatalism and hope. Britain has endured a century of economic decline; she is facing a crisis of two nations.

Education in Britain is very much a case of two nations. There is a deep divide, not just between state and private education, but between science and arts. If Britain's economy is to be restored, there is an overwhelming need for more and better engineers. In 1980 the Finniston Report on engineering training was published. It came out with a clear recipe for education in the profession. The report was ignored by the then Secretary of State for Industry, Sir Keith Joseph, largely because it demanded action by the state. But apathy towards its recommendations was much wider. The report was debated in the House of Commons on a Friday. There was a poor attendance in the chamber and even fewer in the press gallery. The press was just not interested, and the public was given no opportunity to read what was said by either of the Front Bench spokesmen, William Waldegrave and myself, still less by any of the acknowledged experts who had spoken from other parts of the House.

Britain spends 5.2 per cent of its Gross National Product on education. The figure is 5 per cent for both France and West Germany, 6 per cent for Japan, 6.7 per cent for the United States. The central problem of British education does not, comparatively speaking, appear to be lack of resources — classes in Japan are bigger than those in Britain — but the way these resources are spent. Priorities are often confused. The binary system of the Sixties was intended to encourage engineering and science by promoting degrees in these subjects in polytechnics, which were intended to have equal status to universities. This has not worked. Polytechnic degrees have never enjoyed equal status with university degrees, nor have the polytechnics stuck to the industry-linked priorities. For most students a place in a polytechnic is very much second best.

This failure — both a symptom and a cause of our problems — has been compounded, to Britain's long-term detriment, by the absurdly mean treatment of overseas students. Blame for this must be shared by the Labour Government under Harold Wilson, when Tony Crosland was Secretary of State for Education in 1965-67, and by subsequent Conservative Governments. By making it financially impossible for all but the wealthiest overseas students to study at British universities, they have cut a link that for generations has preserved British influence overseas.

Young men and women, as they grow older, will tend to preserve the contacts of their youth. If they no longer go to British universities, but instead study in France or Germany, it is towards France or Germany that they will turn in later life when they have political and economic power or influence. Some students will eventually become the leaders of their countries. Others, with knowledge of languages and contacts abroad, will control trade and commerce. The contacts they made in their student days will inevitably influence their thoughts and actions in later life.

In the totality of planning, the treatment of overseas students is a relatively minor matter. The problem can be put right at relatively small cost. I mention it to illustrate that planning must be long-term, and, for a nation that depends on trade, it must be outward-looking. It must, if Britain is to throw off its century of decline, ask fundamental questions about Britain's place in the world. Too much of what has happened since the Second World War is taken for granted.

Britain's future does not lie in becoming a mere adjunct of some Western European economy, any more than it lies in dependency on the United States. It is a myth to think there is any security in size. The countries that have been most successful in creating new jobs over the past decade are Australia, Austria, Canada, Japan, Norway, and the United States. They are a mixed bunch of nations, varying greatly in size, population, natural resources, and the types of industry they specialise in. But none, it should be noted, are members of an organised trading bloc. They are countries with, in one way or another, a high degree of national independence.

Membership of the EEC put us outside this category. The EEC controls our trade policy, our agricultural policy, and much of our industrial and regional policy. This cannot be ignored. It is not practical to accept EEC membership and not comply with its rules. 'Britain should stay in and cheat, just like the French do,' has often been advanced in argument. It is nonsense. The EEC has legal powers to enforce its policies. The first importer to be aggrieved by an import control imposed by a Labour Government would go straight to the courts. When he arrived he would be trampled underfoot by a horde of EEC Commissioners and representatives of other EEC nations, all there to obtain writs against the British Government. The unfortunate reality is that the French have no need to cheat — they simply play the game successfully, within the rules they themselves had a large part in formulating. If we as a country do not like the rules we must get out.

International constraints do not, of course, end with the EEC. There are the international agreements of GATT. In theory a Britain outside the EEC could impose what import controls it wanted, so long as they did not discriminate against any particular country or countries. In reality things work the other way around. A country can impose discriminatory controls so long as it does so to another country that is too small to fight back, or to a disparate group of countries who are not going to gang up together to fight back.

Non-discriminatory tariffs, on the other hand, tend to offend everybody. Some of them, in particular the industrial power blocs, are in a position to fight back. The United States and the EEC are particularly adept at this. It is by this means that the EEC can virtually dictate industrial policy in some sectors to European countries outside the EEC. If Brussels decides that a company in, say, Norway is being unfairly subsidised against rivals within the EEC, it can get very tough indeed.

It is from this fact that some argue that it is better for Britain to be inside the EEC, where it has a say in EEC policy-making, than to be outside where it has none. The argument is wrong on two counts: in reality Britain has almost no influence over the main thrust of EEC policy; and Britain is still a big enough force in world trade to look after itself in international bargaining. This may sound like a complete contradiction, but it is not. Inside the EEC Britain can bargain only within the restraints of EEC treaties and laws, which dictate the main policies. Outside she would have much more freedom. Her large market is needed by the industries and farmers of the other EEC countries. Now they have guaranteed access; if Britain were outside the EEC, they would have to bargain for it.

Within the restraints of EEC membership Britain could do

much to improve our education and industrial training. She could invest in improved infrastructure: transport, communications, the quality of numerous public services. But, in the vital area of investment and planning for the future industries and future jobs, EEC membership will prove an insuperable handicap.

Withdrawal from the EEC would take great courage. But, as a number of wise men have said, that is the one virtue that makes all others possible. It is the only course that allows a return to wisdom in economic policy for the UK. It is the only course that makes economic planning and economic strategy possible.

Chapter Eight

—————————— ooOoo ——————————

Democracy and the Centre

Back in the days of the Fourth Republic, before de Gaulle came to power in 1958, I was discussing the role of the civil service with a diplomat from the French Embassy in London. 'We in the French civil service,' he said, 'regard the politicians as lodgers in our house. We are the people who run France.'

In mainland Europe the existence of a strong civil service guarantees a continuity in politics regardless of the ideologies of governments. This phenomenon is to be seen in the institutions of the EEC — not just in the Commission, where it might be expected, but in the national delegations to the Council of Ministers. In most EEC countries civil servants have the rank of junior Ministers — or State Secretaries, as they are called — and will take the Ministerial chair in all but the super-restricted sessions.

These civil servants speak for their country at the Council and in the accompanying press conferences. As might be expected, British civil servants have no objection at all to this system. There have been permanent secretaries who have been regarded by the other delegations as the real British Ministers, and courted for their support more often than their political masters.

Similarly, within British Government, there have been civil servants who have run their departments with such skill and forcefulness that some Ministers have been content merely just to follow their instructions and neglect their own party's political objectives in doing so. A junior Minister once complained that his civil servants would not let him give the answers he wanted to give to Parliamentary questions. Another, more senior Minister asked his permanent secretary whether he needed a political adviser. The permanent secretary generously offered to give the Minister all the advice he needed, so the Minister felt he could do without.

On the other hand there are Ministers who see constant overruling of civil servants as proof of their loyalty to their political cause. They like to boast about it afterwards. Carried to extremes this can lead to a mentality that sees civil servants as disloyal if they tender advice contrary to what the Minister wants to hear. The temptation for the civil servant is to tell the Minister that everything is practical even when it is not.

If the Minister's judgement is poor, this can lead to a loss of morale among civil servants in his department. Some Cabinet Ministers have been known, for example, to choose their information officers not from among those qualified for the job, but from among civil servants who showed a sufficiently fawning loyalty, regardless of professional skills and the ability to deal fairly with the press.

In some countries the interchangeability of civil servants and Ministers is not a sign of civil service domination, but of subservience. In Sweden, for example, survival in the career structure means becoming, in effect, a party political officer. Clearly this works in Sweden where it has been possible to go from university to retirement during a period of uninterrupted socialist Government. The United States is the other extreme: political appointments predominate, but there is little security or continuity.

Britain has always tried to achieve a compromise, and there is a lot to be said for this. A political civil service, by excluding the experienced career civil servant from top posts, can limit the intellectual resources of Government. An all-powerful permanent civil service, such as that created by the French, despite the intelligence and ability it can muster (and the French civil service is among the best), will lack creativity and imagination.

The British civil service has been based on the principles of impartiality and fairness, and on the pride it takes in serving

Governments of different ideologies. But this philosophy is open to many different interpretations. One permanent secretary I knew believed that the ideal permanent secretary was a Conservative during a Labour Government and a Labour one during a Conservative Government. He thought this gave 'balance', and it is certainly true that a civil servant's duty includes the necessity to acquaint his Minister with the pitfalls and difficulties of his party's policies.

Not that the advice given is always of the calibre one would like. When I became Minister of Planning and Local Government in 1974 I was asked to produce a policy on the municipal ownership of development land. I asked the civil servants in charge of the relevant section of the department if they had studied Labour's policies. The reply was as succinct as it was inaccurate: 'Yes, Minister: you want to tax profits.'

We were a minority Government at the time, and it was clear that a new election would follow in a few months. With the possibility of another change of Government, the civil service back-pedalled on Labour's policies. When I instructed my officials to produce a White Paper on development land I was told that it would take eighteen months, possibly two years, and was therefore a pointless exercise until the next election had been held.

I went to Harold Wilson and asked if he would object if I wrote the White Paper myself. He was delighted at the idea and gave me all the encouragement I needed. I had written about half of it when the civil servants capitulated and took over the task of completing it.

The identikit permanent secretary would be scrupulously fair, at ease with both Labour and Conservative Ministers, putting forward reasoned objections to policy changes, but happily withdrawing them if the Minister's mind was made up. In real life, of course, permanent secretaries have their individual prejudices and abilities. But every permanent secretary I have come across, whether he was happy to work with me or not, preferred Ministers with minds of their own. Indecisive Ministers tend to make life very rough for their advisers and blame others when the going gets rough.

It was during the 1974-79 Labour Government that political advisers were first introduced into Whitehall on a large scale. There were drawbacks in this, of course, but it did lead to better political decision-making by Ministers. The Conservatives, who initially opposed the idea, had by 1983 adopted it. I was one of the first to advocate that the idea should be extended by creating a cabinet system, as used in Brussels and Paris, giving every Minister a team of political advisers.

It does not have to be a big team: what is needed is a few political advisers, plus two sympathetic, hand-picked civil servants, the team being serviced by the Minister's private office. The contact with the permanent secretary and the civil service would be preserved and augmented by a team capable of uniting the political and bureaucratic positions. Government would be both more efficient and more in tune with party policy.

A British tradition that foreigners find hard to understand is the abrupt loss of status of a Minister who has lost power. A British Prime Minister has only to concede an election and the furniture van is at the back door of Number Ten. The new occupant is inside within hours. In Britain, unlike in most other countries, a Minister loses his title on relinquishing power. With the title goes the deference. This system, harsh as it seems in foreign eyes, is an affirmation of democracy and strong government. Once the electorate withdraws power from its elected leaders, there is no cosy retention of status or power.

But the weakness of this system is that it results in a weak Opposition which, when its turn to succeed the Government comes again, in a crisis is too often ill-equipped to assume power. The first few months are dangerous ones for any new Government taking office after an interval of years. In 1974 Labour assumed power after opposing the reorganisation of local government — a reorganisation that had yet to be implemented. The new Ministers were told by their civil servants that it was too late to make any changes or to scrap the reorganisation. This, they later discovered, was untrue, and they would have known that it was untrue had they not lost touch, in Opposition, with the real situation.

If the civil service requires a degree of continuity, so too do political parties as they move in and out of Government and Opposition. It is important, therefore, that a Shadow Minister of any department has his own *cabinet*, consisting, like the real Minister's, of one or two political advisers and perhaps two seconded civil servants, who would be able to retain their civil service rank and seniority. In this way not only would the transition to power be made more smooth, when in due time

110

the Opposition *cabinet* became the Ministerial *cabinet*. The Shadow Minister himself would be sufficiently well informed to put forward Opposition policies that could be quickly implemented by the new Government.

When a Government taunts an Opposition by challenging it to say what it would do in government, and scores a point by getting a hesitant or evasive reply, it carries a great deal of force. Over the years of Conservative Government I have seen this taunt made again and again by Ministers, smug in their belief that an incoming Labour Government would not be able to do anything radically different from what the Conservative Government was already doing within the current constraints. The problem is compounded not just by lack of resources, but by the need to reconcile the aspirations of party members and the commitments of party policy with the harsh realities of being pitched in to run a major industrial democracy, limited in both resources and Parliamentary time.

Additional pressure has been put on Ministers and Shadow Ministers alike by the development of Select Committees. The Agriculture Committee, set up by Dick Crossman and myself in 1967, was the first of the new committees. Its establishment coincided with the Labour Government's decision to seek membership of the EEC, at a time when most agriculturalists were opposed to British membership. The new Committee set about proving the unsuitability of joining the EEC, a proposition which the Cabinet did not like at all. The Agriculture Committee was allowed to die, but the precedent had been set. Other Select Committees have since emerged, and became increasingly vociferous.

There are those who would like to take things a stage further, and create committees on American lines, powerful bodies that are watched on television and make national figures out of their chairmen. This would not really square with Parliamentary Government, where Ministers are part of the legislative body and face frequent scrutiny on the floor of the House. The American system has emerged as a check on the overwhelming power of the Presidency.

Logic should lead the House of Commons to merge the Select Committees, which scrutinise departments, with Standing Committees, which scrutinise Bills. As it is, the lack of connection between the two is wasting the expertise built up in the Select Committees.

The present Standing Committee system militates against proper scrutiny of legislation. Members on the Government side are instructed to say as little as possible to avoid delaying the passage of the Bill; Opposition members talk as much as possible in order deliberately to delay its passage. On controversial Bills, which should have the most rigorous scrutiny, this problem is at its most acute. The Opposition gives long, facetious speeches, a mixture of procedural wrangling and filibustering, while Government Members yearn for the day when a timetable motion, the so-called guillotine, will rescue them.

Two reforms are needed. Select Committees, singly or, when necessary, two in harness, should scrutinise Bills; and all Bills should be timetabled from the beginning. Procedure Committees have long recommended this course of action. Backbenchers would welcome it. All experienced Chief Whips are in favour. The problem is inexperienced Leaders and Shadow Leaders of the House, who continue to think that mandatory timetabling is somehow an erosion of Parliamentary democracy. It is nothing of the sort.

The truth is that no controversial Bill is ever discussed to the end in the House of Commons. Each Bill goes instead to the House of Lords, where, having been inadequately and only partially scrutinised in the Commons, its passage will inevitably be slow.

It is a myth that the filibuster, the deliberate using up of Parliamentary time, is an effective weapon of Opposition. If the Government really wants to get a Bill through it will do so, regardless of filibustering, simply by voting through a guillotine motion. It will even do this on a constitutional Bill, which would have been considered improper a generation ago.

It would be better, therefore, to accept that the best scrutiny of legislation is obtained if all political parties participate fully in the process and accept that the legislation, as amended, will go through if that is the will of the House. The Opposition should certainly use what gifts of time are made available to it, and, once a termination date has been set, the Opposition should be able to dictate how much time is spent on the Bill up to that date.

But that is not the end of the story. We have a two-chamber Parliament. Some people argue in favour of a single chamber, such as exists in New Zealand and a few other Western-style democracies. Most democracies favour two chambers, since they allow scope for a second, detailed look at legislation.

But arguing for the preservation of a second chamber in Westminster raises problems within the Labour Party. The existence of the House of Lords seems at total variance with socialist ideals of equality. The very word 'Lord' is also emotive. The Labour Party has always officially favoured abolition of the House of Lords. In office, Labour Governments have shown little enthusiasm for the idea. Of eight Labour Governments, only one made any attempt even to reform the House of Lords, and that reform died from lack of interest and the consequent inability to find the minimum number of MPs — at a time when Labour had a large majority — to stay in the House to vote on the issue.

The pragmatic Labour view of the House of Lords, as opposed to the official policy, was succinctly put by Mannie Shinwell: 'Who do you blame when things go wrong?' After decades of attacking the Lords from his seat in the House of Commons, but never, in his later years, in favour of abolishing it, he eventually became a peer himself.

Labour's theoretical opposition to the House of Lords is also blunted by the fact that the Lords does not, contrary to popular belief, have a built-in Conservative majority. Many peers are cross-benchers. The traditional backwoodsman may be deeply conservative in instinct, but he is not a party political animal, and cannot be relied upon to be lobby fodder. On every social issue of the last thirty years — capital punishment, abortion, homosexual rights — the Lords have been in advance of the Commons, in some cases by many years. The small-'c' conservatism of the Lords has also been a restraining influence on Margaret Thatcher's right-wing radicalism, and they have shown much more determination in opposing many of her policies than they ever did in frustrating previous Labour Governments. Having no popular mandate, no manifesto commitments tested before the electorate, the Lords can only be ruled by common sense and consensus.

But is the House of Lords really the right sort of second chamber? All socialists would agree that the automatic entitlement through heredity to act as a legislator must be wrong. To end this entitlement would leave us with a House of Lords composed of peers selected for life, or perhaps for a shorter period.

The argument that socialists often use against the concept of life peerage is that the peers are beholden to nobody, and are likely to go their own way, not following the party line, perhaps even switching to another party in the course of their political life. But this independence applies equally to peers of all political persuasions, as Margaret Thatcher found when Conservative peers blocked and amended some of her most cherished legislation. Such independence could be curbed by restricting a peer to perhaps the period of two Parliaments, but there would be the danger that it would encourage servility on all sides.

Peers would then owe their political existence to the party machines. Such a system exists in the Australian Senate, and it was a minute majority of anti-Labour Senators that destroyed Gough Whitlam's Labour Government in the Seventies, by preventing the elected Government from pursuing its programme. This was possible because the Australian Senate has parity of power with the elected chamber, combined with Senators who had every incentive to put their party first.

Tony Benn, who renounced his father's hereditary title in order to retake his seat in the Commons, informs us in *Who's Who* of his authorship of a 1957 Fabian pamphlet entitled 'The Privy Council as a Second Chamber'. Writing in this pamphlet of his scheme he concludes that 'it accepts the need for a Second Chamber while absolutely rejecting the hereditary principle. It offers an alternative basis of recruitment and yet gives a sufficient overlap of membership to guarantee continuity of legislative experience.'

This would be achieved by ensuring that 'All Privy Counsellors, whether Peers or Commoners, shall be entitled, regardless of sex, at the beginning of each new Parliament, to a Writ of Attendance to the Second Chamber, which Writ shall confer upon them the right to a seat, voice and vote in that House . . .

'The Privy Council, meeting as a House of Parliament, shall enjoy all the powers and privileges at present enjoyed by the House of Lords . . . Members of the Privy Council who have taken their seats in response to a Writ of Attendance shall receive a daily concessionary allowance for each day on which they attend the House.'

All that Tony Benn really achieves with this scheme is to get rid of that emotive word 'Lord'. What appears to be a point of principle boils down to a semantic discussion. At the end of the day a non-hereditary second chamber with a legislative body that can scrutinise legislation, but with only the most minimal powers of delay, is the most sensible policy for Labour. Merely to call Lords Privy Counsellors or Senators is to ignore the real questions of principle.

Of far greater importance is to consider what the work of the second chamber should be. At present too much time is lost in the House of Lords on Second Reading debates, which duplicate the Second Reading debates in the Commons. This is unnecessary and time-wasting. To justify their existence Lords must concentrate on the scrutiny of legislation, not on debates on points of principle. The Lords anyway have numerous opportunities to debate matters of principle. As long as Britain remains a member of the EEC, for example, time could usefully be given to examining in detail the legislation that at present gets little or no scrutiny at all — the vast tide of EEC law and directives.

This would be a valuable and legitimate function for a reformed House of Lords. Their reports on EEC legislation could be debated in the Commons, and their recommendations put into effect where the Commons agree. The Lords should not be able to initiate public legislation, but there is no reason why Private Members' Bills should not start there and then proceed to the House of Commons.

Chapter Nine

$\cdots \circ \circ \bigcirc \circ \circ \cdots$

Local Democracy

At its best, democracy is the means whereby men and women can organise their country's affairs with equity, fairness, and efficiency. But it requires instruction and practice in its proper use. It can be used destructively as well as constructively.

Democracy takes almost as many forms as there are attitudes towards it. Some of those who most strongly profess their reverence for it merely seek to attack any form of democracy that does not appear to provide them with a road to power. Those who wish to destroy democracy completely often attempt to use democratic means to achieve power, usually by what is known as populism — of pandering to the lowest common denominators of prejudice and fear. Others, on the fringes of politics (sometimes called 'ultra-democrats') attempt to stifle democracy through endless procedural and legalistic nit-picking, all in the name of 'accountability' and 'consultation', two words that came into particular vogue in the Seventies.

Democracy began in ancient Athens with direct democracy: the citizens were themselves the legislators. They did not elect representatives but came together to decide issues for themselves. Such a system survives today, in a modified form, in Switzerland. At local level citizens still gather in the town square to vote directly. At national level referenda decide virtually every issue. Elected representatives play a much smaller role than in the more typical Western democracy. Even the Swiss President, their head of state, is a comparatively obscure figure who travels to his office by tram.

Switzerland is also a federal state: the cantons that form the state enjoy a high degree of independence, which they guard jealously against encroachments from central government. The use of referenda helps them greatly in doing this, since it limits the development of central government.

The modern world's first constitutional republic, the United States of America, is a very different federal state. Its history has been strongly marked by conflict between the independence of the states and the power of central government. Early in the nineteenth century President Thomas Jefferson claimed to favour the rights of the states. For the next half-century or more the European view was that Americans were an impossibly unruly lot who would probably never be able to govern themselves effectively. Eventually, through the railway, the telegraph, the will of Abraham Lincoln, and civil war, the USA became a highly centralised state, although the structures and the aspirations of state rights remain.

Many God-fearing Americans would be appalled to hear it, but the doctrine of federalism has always been closely linked with that of anarchism: with the belief that people should be left to govern themselves free of *diktats* from rulers or the state. Anarchists, whether theoreticians such as Pierre-Joseph Proudhon, the French philosopher, or practitioners such as Emiliano Zapata, the Mexican revolutionary, usually came from the peasantry. They wanted land and freedom, and could only see the centralised state as a threat to both. But not every human need could be met by a local commune; therefore a federal state, built from the bottom up as a gathering of communes, was needed to meet these needs while avoiding the dangers of a centralised state.

The anarchist analysis is basically correct. Those federal states that have been most successful — Switzerland, the United States — have been built from the ground up, evolving into unitary states over centuries. Those imposed from above — the Central African Federation, the United Arab Republic — have swiftly collapsed. They have withered because the roots of democracy have not been there. There are those who believe the European Common Market will wither away for much the same reason.

British democracy, too, has been largely built from the

ground up. The English tradition of local government is as old as the coming of the first Saxons, after the fall of Rome. English local government ante-dates central government by over five centuries. When the Normans invaded England and established a centralised government they retained local administrations — indeed, they extended them to Wales and subsequently to parts of Scotland. The Normans realised that local administration was needed to cater for local needs. A central administration that attempted to do so would become so vast that it would break down under the weight of its own bureaucracy.

In government and administration there is an ideal size for most functions. There may be some tolerance at either side of the ideal, but in general an organisation that is too big will collapse under the weight of bureaucracy; one that is too small will collapse through petty in-fighting and divisions as personal and community needs become confused. The first is too far away to cope with the real problems; the second often too close.

Human organisations conform to Professor J. B. S. Haldane's axiom of evolution — the essential need to be the right size. Dinosaurs vanished from the face of the earth, Haldane maintained, because they were too big to cope with changing circumstances; the success of mankind came about because we were the right size, both physically and mentally. What is true of species, and hence of mankind, is equally applicable to institutions created by mankind, which are after all merely the expressions of our physical and mental attributes. Institutions, like species, must be the right size.

The neighbourhood council movement that grew in the late-Sixties and early-Seventies has largely disappeared (although it continues to have a few supporters) because they were too small and their functions too limited. At the other extreme, many people in the Fifties and Sixties were excited by the prospect of the European Common Market. Its sheer size was held to offer solutions to problems that overwhelmed nation states. But where solutions have been tried on a Common Market-wide scale, such as in agriculture, the results have been disappointing. The giant has tottered, unable to support its own weight. There is a growing feeling that the Common Market should be a grouping of independent nations, with certain common economic and political organisations, but without the thrust to be a superstate with a centralised bureaucracy.

The idea of the Common Market had been around since the late nineteenth century, but it was no accident that it should actually come into being after the Second World War. The Fifties were an era marked by the philosophy that big was beautiful. The United States and the Soviet Union had emerged from the war as the dominant world powers. In Europe the vast problems of reconstruction turned people's minds to the best way to organise it. An MP, in the Fifties, standing on the terrace of the House of Commons, looking south across the river, could scarcely pick out an undamaged building as far as the eye could see. Central funds and central direction seemed the only way to cope. In industrial reconstruction the term 'economics of scale' became a by-word. Marshall Aid from the United States encouraged Europeans to think — as it was meant to — in terms of Europe-wide reconstruction.

The post-war Labour Government adopted a centralised structure. The planning laws introduced by my father, Lewis Silkin, under the Attlee administration put development land under centralised public control. Attempts were made to localise the Land Board by setting up local offices, but nobody felt it was really local or accountable. In contrast, when I put through the Community Land Act thirty years later in 1975 I sought to put development land under the control of local government.

In nationalising industries, the Attlee Government placed them under the control of regional boards, not local government. Thus the Gas Act of 1948 took the control of gas away from local authorities and put it under twelve area gas boards. The British Electricity Authority was set up with fourteen area boards. Hospitals were taken away from local authorities.

The worship of largeness expressed itself strongly in town planning and development. Typical of the Fifties and Sixties, in every Western country, was the large-scale redevelopment of city centres. Enormous shopping centres were built in the centre of cities, surrounded by even bigger car parks and office blocks and sports centres. To link these new-style cities, vast new motorway systems were built, on which people travelled in bigger and bigger cars. These in turn created bigger and bigger accidents and the victims were carted off to bigger and bigger hospitals.

It is fashionable to blame all this on the planners, who are held to be remote individuals living in ivory towers. The truth is that the planners were merely implementing the commonly-held view that this brave new world was for the best. The planners got to work not in defiance of human happiness, but in order to further it. What they were doing seemed logical. Bigger meant more facilities for more people, more wealth created, more opportunities to enjoy it.

It was not until this new world had been experienced that doubts began to set in. But other attitudes were also being moulded by this new environment. As all towns began to look increasingly alike, and the goods and facilities that could be bought in them were produced increasingly from the same production-lines in the same factories, people began to ask themselves if local government any longer had any relevance. Were our local habitats not just identical slices of the great national cake?

This attitude was highly popular with civil servants. Whitehall had always believed that local government was unnecessary. As the years went by central government, encouraged by civil servants, began more and more to regulate local government, and increasingly to formalise the relationship between local and central government. This was not a new process: the original Rate Act, establishing a permanent system of local government finance, dates from the time of the first Queen Elizabeth. Rates were at first levied for ad hoc purposes: to build a new bridge or road. With the industrial revolution and the explosive growth of our cities, local government as we recognise it today came into being. The Municipal Corporations Act of 1834 was followed by a succession of local government statutes over the last century and a half.

At the heart of the relationship between central and local government has always been the control over finance. What separates Britain from any federal state is the fact that no local authority has ever had a completely free hand in raising money. It can only do so under laws passed by central government. Subsidy is another form of control: a rate support grant given by central government is a rate support grant that can be taken away. The control over first how much money can be spent, and then over what rate can be set — as imposed by Conservative Governments after 1979 — are a continuation of a process that is centuries old. The 'freedom' of local government in Britain has always been circumscribed.

The Labour Party, for the first thirty-odd years of its existence, was a strong supporter of the idea of independent local authorities. A typical Labour complaint was that local authorities were not fully using the powers given to them by Parliament. A 1927 Labour leaflet on public enterprise had this to say:

Parliament has given certain powers to Councils or arranged for them to obtain certain powers, to conduct some of the necessary services.

35 Urban District Councils have their own **electricity** supply.

50 Urban District Councils have their own **gas** supply.

110 Urban District Councils have their own **water** supply.

50 Urban District Councils have their own **markets**.

50 Urban District Councils have their own **tramways**.

Urban District Councils may build and own **houses**, establish **hospitals**, provide **parks** and **recreation grounds**, have their own **cemeteries**, own **slaughterhouses** . . .

Powers have been given to District Councils to be **used**. But often District Councils include members who do not believe in using these powers.

Labour believes in using the powers given by Parliament to conduct these enterprises.

At this time local authorities in Britain operated nearly £700,000,000 in revenue-earning capital plant. They were responsible for four-fifths of all water supply and tramways, two-thirds of all electricity supply, and two-fifths of all gas supply. The Labour Party revelled in the powers and achievements of local government. An earlier Labour Party leaflet (1923) had this to say about Poplar Council:

'So efficient is their Electricity Department that they have a higher revenue per unit sold than any other London undertaking. The number of consumers in 1923 has increased 49 per cent in the past three years. In Poplar they have municipal baths and wash-houses, and people like them! In four years the number of bathers has increased 94 per cent, the number of washers 280 per cent — that's business and efficiency in Poplar!'

Labour at that time also favoured home rule for Wales, Scotland, Ireland. Labour believed in a decentralised form of socialism: partly this was from force of circumstance — power in local authorities was more easily achieved than power nationally — but it stemmed also from a genuine distrust of national planning. That was favoured by the Communist Party, not by Labour.

But the Communist example was gaining influence, and in the long term this was to have an impact. The young left-wing activists and intelligentsia of the Thirties, influenced by the example of the Soviet Union, had begun to believe in a highly centralised, planned, collectivist authority. Even those who condemned the lack of freedom in the Soviet Union tended to think that only through a similar society could socialism be introduced. It was popular in the Thirties to join the Communist Party — particularly if you were a student at Oxford or Cambridge. An influential generation moved in the direction of centralism, also foreseeing that the coming war could only be won through central planning. Among those who absorbed the fashionable thinking of the time was Dick Crossman, a future Labour Minister for Local Government.

It is important to understand such ideas and the co-relationship between local government and central government: only then can we grasp the problems that have developed in the age of growing centralisation. The argument put forward by the centralists is that, if central government is properly to control the social and economic basis of its citizens' life, there is little or no place for local government. It can be no more than a cog in the essential machinery of central government.

This has been primarily an argument not of Westminster politicians — many of whom have served in local government — but of Whitehall civil servants, most of whom despise local government. During the Labour Government of 1974-79, the civil service worked continually for the abolition of the Metropolitan Counties. This was partly a reaction to my advocacy, as Minister of Local Government and Planning, of regional government. The civil service saw it as a way of taking the impetus out of regionalism. Eventually it became an end in itself.

After Labour fell in 1979 the civil service continued to lobby to this end, and soon had their way. Powers that should, on abolition, have gone to the boroughs went instead to central government, thus furthering the cause of centralism and the power of those who work in Whitehall.

Mythology has it that the Thatcher Government wanted to abolish the Greater London Council and the Metropolitan Counties in order to rid itself of Ken Livingstone. The reality is that few had ever heard of Mr Livingstone when this policy was accepted by the Conservative administration.

The basic argument put forward by the civil servants was that local government had little function in an island as small as Britain: modern transport and communication had shrunk the country to the point where central government was adequate to handle all problems. This was closely related to the belief, popular with academics and others in the Sixties and Seventies, that in the age of national television regional and cultural variations were a thing of the past. Political variations were supposed to be a thing of the past as well, with voting patterns becoming uniform across the country.

The public argument was never pitched at this level. Instead the arguments put forward have been boosted by dubious economics. Central government is alleged to be more efficient and economical than local government, whose affairs must be tightly controlled and monitored. This premise is difficult to take seriously: the truth is that local government can be profligate or not profligate — it depends on the local authority. It is equally true that an elected local authority is in a better position to monitor local spending, and to respond to local pressures, than the civil servants in Whitehall.

Much of the 'irresponsibility' of local government, such a constant theme of those who wish further to limit its powers, is in fact a self-fulfilling prophecy. Take away responsibilities, treat local government as a naughty child, and inevitably it will not behave in a constructive manner. The much-publicised excesses of the Greater London Council in its dying days, its much-ridiculed 'women's committee' and other similar groupings, would certainly not have come about if the GLC had had a real job of work to do.

The truth is that the GLC at its creation only had one function worthy of an organisation of its size: housing. (It acquired transport when Barbara Castle insisted on the GLC taking over London Transport as a means of cutting Government expenditure). Once the GLC estates were handed over to the boroughs and London Transport returned to a quango, the GLC was left with a fire brigade, responsibility for historical buildings, and a few other bits and pieces. Under Ken Livingstone's enthusiastic leadership, it acquired numerous small tasks, none of which added up to very much. The budget also stretched to create a formidable publicity machine, which succeeded in making Livingstone a popular television performer, but did not convince many people that the GLC was doing anything very worthwhile, because it palpably was not. For those who wish to argue the case for stronger and more effective local government, the GLC is best ignored.

As late as July 1979 the Conservative Minister of the Environment, Michael Heseltine, told a conference of local government chief executives that 'an effectively functioning local democracy can monitor the activities of local councillors far better than civil servants in Marsham Street'. He might have added that local councillors are at least elected, whereas civil servants are only accountable to Ministers.

One uncomfortable truth is that Labour as well as Conservative Governments have been strongly influenced by civil service opposition to local government. When Labour came to power in 1964 it was Dick Crossman who became Minister of Housing and Local Government, instead of Michael Stewart, who had spent years immersing himself in the subject during the years of Opposition.

In Government Crossman was a sitting duck for his civil servants. He soon shared their impatience with local government, which did not suit his notion of socialism on the grand scale. In conversations with me he frequently expressed the view that local government was a nuisance and got in the way of good planning. He adopted enthusiastically the civil service idea of a Royal Commission on Local Government.

In the prevailing mood of the times, this commission, which produced what became known as the Redcliffe-Maud Report, could only come out in favour of larger units of local government, although it did, to its credit, also favour a real devolution of power. Reorganisation, when it eventually came, gave us the bigger units without the devolution. As it was implemented by civil servants and by politicians who shared most of their prejudices and ideals, one could not expect much else.

124

All this was part of the dream, floating like a mirage before so many civil servants and planners, of creating a 'rational' reorganisation of local government. When Aneurin Bevan looked at this idea after the Second World War he decided that it would crucify any Minister who attempted it, but others, less wise, who followed him, were not deterred.

Even before Redcliffe-Maud came Sir Keith Joseph's London Government Act of the early Sixties, which was to change the map of London. Bromley was brought in from Kent, Enfield from Middlesex, Richmond from Surrey, and, within London proper, a number of boroughs were jumbled together into larger units. The problem with such reorganisation, imposed from above, is that it really changes nothing. The poor borough of Deptford was decreed to be part of more prosperous Lewisham, but it has remained determinedly Deptford. Its rate of unemployment, even after two decades as Lewisham, is still where it was before: twice as high as the rest of the borough.

Many Deptford residents remember to this day where their Town Hall was. If they wanted help they could go to a Town Hall that was close by and talk to officers whom they knew or local councillors whom they had known since childhood. Today, Lewisham Town Hall is an expensive bus-ride away. It is large and imposing and forbidding. Staffing it, many Deptford citizens feel, are equally imposing local government officials, who, in the eyes of those citizens, have little knowledge of the problems that afflict their local area. A family allocated a council flat at the opposite side of Lewisham from Deptford often feels uprooted from all it cares about and knows.

The increase in size of the boroughs has meant an increase in bureaucracy. Elected councillors tend to reflect the melancholy truth that they are relatively powerless to influence a large-scale bureaucratic operation which is remote from local people and their needs. The problem is not solved by establishing scores of local offices: they simply create, or appear to create, more unfriendly offices full of unelected people with powers that seem to most local people to be excessive. Nor is the problem solved by setting up 'consultative committees', or co-opting local people on to council committees: this has no real effect on the unhealthy concentration of power. Like neighbourhood councils, they simply do not work.

There is, however, a case for large authorities. The vital

thing is that they must not be imposed by the destruction of small authorities, but out of decentralisation from central government. In the context of British politics this immediately raises the issue of devolution for Scotland and Wales, and whether there should be any form of devolution within England.

The idea of regional government for England had been favoured by the Redcliffe-Maud Report (in both the majority and minority reports), and by the time Labour returned to power in 1974 there seemed to be a fair wind behind the proposal. If some sort of Scottish devolution was to be implemented, some areas of England, especially the North, had a strong case for a degree of autonomy in economic planning. Ted Short, now Lord Glenamara, then Lord President of the Council and an MP from Newcastle upon Tyne, favoured devolution for the North that he knew so well. The civil servants did not.

They saw, correctly, that regional authorities would diminish the power of Whitehall departments. They were even reluctant to have regional authorities governed by unelected bodies under their control. Between one Whitehall department and another there was no agreement over regional boundaries: they were deemed to be an administrative matter of little importance. For a while the civil servants were forced to accept Economic Planning Councils, whose duty it was to plan economically for each region, but they made certain that the EPCs had no power and no authority.

I favoured elected EPCs, and produced a consultation Green Paper setting out the reasons why there should be English regions. Ted Short had responsibility for devolution, and my Green Paper was about to go to Cabinet Committee when the civil servants struck back. They persuaded the Prime Minister, Harold Wilson, to replace Gerry Fowler, the junior minister in the Cabinet Office responsible for devolution. Lord Crowther-Hunt was then given the job by Ted Short of 'looking at the dots and commas' of my Green Paper.

Gerry Fowler's removal was followed shortly afterwards by Anthony Crosland's move from Environment to the Foreign Office. Peter Shore, who had been a good administrator at the Department of Trade, replaced him. Shore came new to the Department of the Environment, which he knew little about, and like most new Ministers, was an obvious victim of civil servants' intrigues. Shore and Crowther-Hunt, egged on by the civil servants, unwittingly killed off my Green Paper. Soon, too, the creative side of planning — the regions, the new towns, the development of London docklands — had been downgraded.

After a time Peter Shore began to be dissatisfied with Whitehall's approach. The civil servants, ever obliging, then found a new approach for him, along which his energy and ability enabled him to gallop with great speed. This avenue was called 'organic change': it meant effectively that changes in local government would be few, far between, and irrelevant.

Further change, when it did come under the Thatcher Government, meant a further diminution of the power of local government, both through the abolition of what was left of the Greater London Council and the metropolitan counties and through lower grants and curbs on spending. Labour has been reminded again that centralised control, which may appear to offer opportunities for effective socialist planning, in practice diminishes the possibilities for progress.

This brings us back to the basic questions of democracy and of size. Britain is suffering from institutions that are too big — too big at borough level, too big at national level, and too big at the Common Market level. Boroughs are too far from the ordinary citizen, central government is too far from the boroughs and even from the regions, and Brussels is too far from almost everything.

Obviously the structure of local government in Britain cannot simply return to what it was before all the meddling; but some changes are needed. At the local level Britain needs something very like the old county borough: unitary authorities that deal with housing, with education, with social services, health, and sanitation. This is essential for efficiency. If a child is habitually playing truant, it is not simply an educational matter. It is a good idea if officers from the same authority can also look at the child's family background, which includes housing as well.

The next unit of government must be the regional authority. The shire counties should be abolished, since they can do little these days. Regional government must take over many of the powers currently residing in Whitehall. It must have the power to tax. It must be in charge of economic development and transport. Planning should be divided between the regional authority (at the structural level) and the county borough (at the day-to-day level).

If the political will can be found to create powerful regional government, the tide of centralisation would at last have been reversed. Regional authorities will be too big for Whitehall to subdue, yet so much nearer to local needs and priorities. Without reform in this direction, leading to a devolution of power, the long-running conflicts over local government and its relationship with central government can only drag on.

Chapter Ten

— ○○○○○ —

The Nation's Duty

An oft-quoted concept of Jeremy Bentham, 'the greatest happiness of the greatest number', has a superficial attraction for political economists. It implies that government has done its job if over 50 per cent of the population are advantaged by its policies.

Where Benthamism fails is in not addressing the problem of helping 100 per cent of the population. At various times during the twentieth century governments with a Benthamite philosophy have prided themselves on the prosperity of those with jobs while making life intolerable for those without. The Benthamite concept, at the end of the day, is that of 'the devil take the hindmost'. Its opposite is to see the nation as one family.

In a family those who are strong, healthy, and prosperous take responsibility for those of their kin who are too old or too young to cope, or who are sick or poor. One of the moral imperatives of socialism is to apply this principle to the nation, and ultimately to the world. It follows, therefore, that the Labour Party's social policy must give the fullest possible weight to this imperative.

It is a popular imperative with the population at large. People — even the very young — know that they will one day be old, that they or their families will need health care. Opinion

polls consistently show that people favour compassionate care
for those in need.

This sense of responsibility is not merely the result of living
in a civilised community where hospitals and unemployment
benefit are taken for granted. It is an instinct that has been
with man from the earliest times: man is a social animal whose
survival depends upon co-operation within the group in which
he lives. A selfish disregard for the condition of others will
ultimately threaten his own existence. Early societies had
difficulty in meeting this need, and this weakness led to those
societies' demise. Advanced societies, through more sophistic-
ated means of wealth creation and distribution, have a better
chance of achieving the ideal. To strive for any less is a
betrayal of civilisation and humanity. The basic responsibility
of a civilised community breaks down into the provision of a
number of basic services for all its members.

It must provide suitable accommodation for every family
and individual. It was Cicero who said: 'A man's dignity is
enhanced by his home.' For a middle-class Roman lawyer — or
a middle-class British lawyer today — this could be taken to
mean that the family home was a symbol of status. But his
remark has a wider truth: there is no dignity in being homeless,
in being one of the thousands who sleep rough every night
even in such a wealthy city as London.

For too long the provision of homes has been the subject of
two conflicting philosophies. One is that the problem should be
left to laissez-faire economics: the other is that it can be solved,
at least in the large conurbations, by the local authority
building and renting out huge estates.

In recent years, under Thatcherite Conservative Governments, the first philosophy has gained at the expense of the
second. In practical terms this means that tax relief on
mortgages has increased, while subsidies on council-house rents
have reduced. The result has been that very few houses have
been built that are affordable by the majority of people. Council
tenants have been allowed to buy their houses — and there is
nothing wrong with that — but funds realised by this
liquidation of local government assets have not been put back
into housing.

As a result, the number of available houses has shrunk
dramatically in recent years. Houses, like people, decay and
die. Part of the problem goes back to the Second World War,

when house-building stopped and much existing housing was destroyed. Social changes have also led to a greater demand for homes: families are smaller; bathrooms are a necessity, not a luxury; garages are needed to keep cars off the road.

The traditional British way of dealing with increasing housing demand is multiple occupation. Not for us the shanty towns that fringe Paris and Rome. More people are crammed into old houses. But a separate home ought not to be an ideal dream — it ought to be a reality for every family in the nation. And this reality should not mean a family being forced to live on the sixteenth floor of a tower block.

Tower blocks are the result of a financial miscalculation. For a long time it was assumed that the cost of providing flats was much less than that of providing independent houses. The reasoning was that land was the most expensive item in any urban housing budget, and that flats needed less land than houses, and would therefore be much cheaper.

This has proved to be wrong. Blocks of flats need empty sites around them to provide space and light and air for the flat dwellers. For civilised living there appear to be immutable laws of population density. Flats do not allow more people to be crammed on to a given area of land. As the old Labour Leader of the London County Council, Sir Isaac Hayward, used to point out, people want to live in houses. Some cities such as Glasgow have a tradition of tenement living, and here flats have proved more acceptable, but the same principles still apply. Glasgow has more parks than any other city in Europe to compensate for its crowded housing.

Homes do not exist in isolation, however much we all dream of shutting the world out when we go home at night. In my years as an MP running an advice service in Deptford, I found that as often as not those wanting a transfer to a different council house were not dissatisfied with the premises but with the loneliness, the harassment, and the pointless violence that occurs on large estates.

My generation was as much to blame for the fallacy of large estates as anyone. New housing seemed to us a matter of such urgency that the creation of large estates, of system-built construction to avoid the shortage of skilled labour, was unavoidable. I still believe it was better for people to have a council flat than no home at all — but the wisdom of Sir Isaac Hayward's comments becomes more clear as the years go by.

Thanks to past failures, the basic dilemma remains. Left to market forces, our people will not be housed. Yet the majority of people do not want to be beholden to a local authority for a home. With the best will in the world, a local authority in a major conurbation, with its size and inevitable bureaucracy, is not the best landlord. People wish to have a choice of whether they buy or rent their homes; they do not wish to live in large, crowded, and impersonal estates, and they need to be close to available jobs.

The problems of cities go deeper than just housing. Many have become too heavily populated to support the civilised existence of those who live in them: the problem is one of scale. Homes are needed, jobs for those of working age, schools and universities for the young, and facilities for the elderly, including such elementary things as shops within easy walking distance. In the past, because industrial processes were often noisy, smoky, and smelly, industry was placed away from the centres of population. Many modern industries are quiet and hygienic, yet still they are normally segregated from housing — although there is every reason why employment, housing, schools, shops, health-care centres, and parks should be brought together in the same environment.

The creation of such environments would lead to a radical decline in the population of the major cities. The post-war planners who designed the new towns understood this: it was the policy and the driving force of the new towns movement. The new towns also set out to provide a choice of renting or buying a home — either a house or a flat — and to create a leisure environment which made people happy to live where they were. It has become fashionable in some circles to deplore the new towns, to sneer at their 'suburban' environment, and to suggest that they take resources away from the inner cities. But those who make these gibes usually do so from a position of comfort, and they do not understand that the new industries that sustain the new towns could not be located in any inner city without massive reconstruction.

There is a limit both to how far a new town can grow and to the amount of land available to build new conurbations on this model. What is needed in future are clusters of villages surrounding the existing new towns, connected to them by good road systems at ten or fifteen miles distance. Each village should be large enough to provide minimum facilities and some employment, while providing swift access by car or bus to factories and offices of the new towns.

In areas where old industrial villages are in decline — the mining and steel-manufacturing areas of Wales, the North East, Scotland — an adjacent new town can provide an economic boost felt for miles around. Young people need no longer desert their dying village in search of work, but can stay on with their elders in a revived community.

But for such a policy to have any real impact requires government financing on a very large scale indeed. It also demands the setting up of new development corporations. Local authorities, which are the only alternative, are frankly not good developers. They are too bureaucratic, too timid, too unimaginative. The long history of Coin Street, on the South Bank of the Thames near the Royal Festival Hall, is a case in point: a decaying area of central London, where land is so desperately needed, was left neglected for years and years as local government argued over what to do with it. A development corporation, given the powers, would have had homes and industries rising on the site within a couple of years. This was the policy that I sought for London docklands when I was Minister for Planning — when I left the Department the idea lapsed until the civil servants resurrected it for Michael Heseltine, who put it into effect with a number of modifications.

Such is the success of development corporations that even the local authority co-optees often become infected with enthusiasm and support the corporation in its occasional disputes with the local authority.

Once a development corporation has done its job, and the new environment has been created, it should be returned to the people. I inaugurated the policy of returning the rented housing stock from the development corporations to the local authorities. I would have given all the assets — including corporation-owned commercial and industrial properties — to the local authorities. The Treasury blocked me.

The Treasury has never been sufficiently interested in people, only in money. The best that can be said in the Treasury's favour is that it is impartial — its officials are equally brutal to all those who need financing. Conservative Governments are more partial in their meanness: their cuts in rate support grants to local authorities have compounded the Treasury's meanness. They have set out deliberately to deny local authorities the resources needed to fund housing programmes.

This, in turn, has given housing authorities a perfect alibi — any defect in administration and management can be blamed on the lack of central government resources. Too often during my attendance at advice services — and other inner city MPs will have had the same experience — I have had to plead on behalf of constituents for the most elementary repairs to be done. Local housing authorities are apparently willing to accept conditions in publicly-owned property that no environmental health officer would permit in the private rented sector. Homes are often left empty far too long because the system of allocation and of doing repairs is bureaucratic and bungling.

Management is, of course, easier in a new town where the housing stock is modern and tower blocks are infrequent. Large housing estates and old terraced housing do present enormous problems of management and repair. Local councillors listen to the tenants' problems and frustrations, but often can do little for them. Housing management is something that ambitious people in local government avoid, which leads to highly variable standards. All too often the problems are so intractable that the will to tackle them disappears.

Unemployment and deprivation make matters worse. Social services are now the responsibility of the district councils in the conurbations, and of the county councils in country areas. Cohesion and a sense of purpose is lacking. Social workers, often equipped with little more than a sense of vocation and muddled academic qualifications, are too often not able to do their job in a realistic and consistent way.

It is bad enough that young people in their twenties are supposed to be advising middle-aged families. It is infinitely worse when their knowledge of the local community itself is defective, or is forced to fit book-learned stereotypes or ideological preconceptions.

If a black child is to be fostered, ought it inevitably and immutably to be fostered by a black family? Even to consider the question one must first define what is a black family. Is it a family that originates from one of the Caribbean Islands, with their varying traditions? Or are its origins in Africa, in Nigeria or Kenya perhaps, with quite different civilisations and cultures? Or can the term 'black' encompass people from the Indian sub-continent or from the Far East?

The more one delves into the question of defining people by their skin colour, the more nonsensical and destructive it becomes. The social services are there to deal with all British citizens, regardless of colour, race, creed, or ethnic origins. Trying to match colour with colour is something you do when decorating a room, not when you are dealing with human lives and families. Preoccupation with colour — like a preoccupation with the belief that natural mothers have a right to raise their own children regardless of how they treat them — can only create tragic blind spots. Consistent guidelines are needed, but not of this sort. They must be elemental: that a child in danger must be seen and examined regularly; that the child is the client, not the parents or step-parents.

The most fundamental failure of all is the inability to see the social services as part of a unified pattern — a pattern of housing, health, and education, all of them interlocked. Where deprivation exists in one section of these areas it is safe to assume that it exists in others as well. Bad housing, truancy, assaults on wives and children, bad educational standards — all come together, and need to be tackled in a unified way. Putting them in separate compartments increases the number of problems; it does not help to solve them.

Central government does not provide the lead it should. For many years the Ministry of Health used to concern itself with health, housing, and local government. They were considered to be linked. This was before the days of the big ministries. Then only the desire to prevent the department from expanding too much prevented education from being included as well, which it logically should have been, since local authorities control education.

One result of having giant ministries, with joint departments, is that health has become a junior partner national insurance — although there is no practical connection between the two — with no specific Health Minister in the Cabinet. The Secretary of State must speak up for both health and social security, and the greatest financial pressure on him today is to provide money for the unemployed.

Local government has been put into the Department of the Environment, and there it is handled by a Minister of State. Again there is no direct representation in the Cabinet. New towns and the construction industry fall to Parliamentary Under

Secretaries, with housing now a sinecure. With so many shepherds, it is small wonder that the sheep have become the prey of wolves.

At a time when technological advances in health care are coming with unprecedented speed, the National Health Service has lost its way. At the final analysis, health care is about the treatment of individuals with individual problems. The means of tackling these problems can be broken down into three elements: the medical and technical resources essential to the curing process; the medical staff to prescribe and administer them; and the will and mental stamina of the patient. The last element is perhaps the most important of all.

Large hospitals built miles from the areas where many of their patients live may be good value for money for governments, convenient for administrators, and useful for consultants — but they deal an often fatal blow to the patients' own ability to help in the cure. With a local hospital, friends, neighbours, and family can easily visit a patient, and it can be a small and friendly place; a large hospital is a long bus journey away and a daunting institution.

I remember visiting such a large hospital when I was the Opposition Spokesman for Health. I was assured by consultants and staff alike that it was a wonderful hospital. It was modern, clean, bright, and the patients had no complaints. The nurses did, however, have one minor complaint — it was a long way to the nearest town and the bus services were inadequate. They seemed quite put out when I suggested that these disadvantages were even worse for patients who looked forward to regular visits from their friends and relatives.

The probability is that the day of the big hospital, like the day of the tower block, is limited. The tower block was supposed to be economical, but has turned out not to be; the same truth is likely to be discovered of the large hospitals. Modern technology — through advances in pharmacology and computerised diagnostic devices and information services — is increasingly bringing the benefits of the best health care within the reach of the local group practice or health clinic.

The movement towards community health care is already well under way, but in practical terms little has so far been done. Apologists for the Conservative Government argue that the National Health Service is now better funded than ever before: this argument ignores the real and changing needs of the population. As people live longer, the demands on the NHS have increased far beyond the resources available. Old people are being forced 'back into the community' for help — a community that at present has neither the resources nor the willingness to cope.

Give it the resources, and the willingness will come. The community, like all families, wants to look after its own. But deprive the community of the resources necessary, and the result is bad health care, increased misery, and the final destruction of the National Health Service. Institutions that ought to be devoted to the welfare of the old and the sick, run by people who believe there should be more not less community care, are forced to accept lower standards.

A good home and freedom from avoidable illness should be the birthright of every citizen. Some think that another birthright should be the 'right to work'. But this assertion ignores the fact that for a very large number of people work, because of the particular job they are doing, is boring and monotonous — an unpleasant necessity to be got through before real living can begin. When people speak of the right to work they really mean the right to sufficient funds to enjoy a good standard of living — nobody, after all, talks of a right to work for a baby or a person of ninety.

The real evils of unemployment must be clearly stated: it condemns people to a standard of living far lower than that enjoyed by the majority of people in work; and life on the dole can be even more boring and unpleasant than being in work. Nobody has ever talked of the deprivation of aristocrats of previous generations who had no need to work. Their quality of life was enhanced, not diminished, by boundless leisure because they had the funds and the education to enjoy it.

Education is all important. Today, in an age when scientific advance appears to be all-pervasive and unstoppable, it is argued that machines and micro-processors will take the place of human beings and make most workers redundant. It may be so, although similar prophecies during the first industrial revolution did not prove accurate: after great upheavals and suffering, there were more jobs and more prosperity than before.

But whatever happens — whether we return to full employment or whether modern industrial society has to reconcile itself to at least one-fifth of its adult population having no work — our education system and the structure of our society must prepare and support people in getting the best benefit they can from leisure.

When I was a boy in the Thirties Depression I knew an unemployed Welsh miner who, having read Karl Marx in English in the public library, taught himself German in order to read Marx in the original. Finding he was a very competent linguist, he went on to teach himself French and Italian. Similarly, in the Seventies my law firm gave articles to a young woman who, in a relatively short space of time, passed 'O' levels, 'A' levels, and a law degree by studying in the evenings after a day's hard work as an extremely efficient secretary. Both cases are great achievements of will and intelligence — but also show the value of educational facilities to those both unemployed and in work.

Arguably the greatest achievement of the 1964-70 Labour Governments was the creation of the Open University. Thousands have now graduated from it. Without the persistence of Harold Wilson as Prime Minister in putting into effect his original idea of a 'University of the Air', and the brilliance of Jennie Lee's imagination and administrative ability, it would never have seen the light of day.

Not everybody wants to read Karl Marx in German; not everybody wants to become a lawyer; not everybody wants to go to the theatre or the opera; most people enjoy paintings, but not everybody wishes to become a critic of the arts. It is just as important that a civilised community gives its citizens the opportunity to enjoy spectator sports, the gentle art of conversation, or the sheer pleasure of doing nothing. 'What is this life, if full of care,/We have no time to stand and stare,' wrote W. H. Davies. He was writing of a leisure that was as valuable as any other.

The enjoyment of standing and staring is as much a part of what a civilised community owes to its citizens as the finest health service or the best housing. The important thing is not to confuse the standing and staring of unemployment with the standing and staring of leisure.

Chapter Eleven

—————————— ∘∘◯∘∘ ——————————

'The Capitalist Press'

The printed and electronic mass media — newspapers, periodicals, books, radio, and television — are major and growing industries both nationally and internationally. Rapid changes over the last decade have brought them under increased public scrutiny, but no nearer to any effective form of public control. Multinational communications conglomerates such as Rupert Murdoch's News International have arisen, with an unprecedented influence over the media in several continents.

The Labour Party's concern with these developments is heightened by two factors. First, the ownership of newspapers remains predominantly in the hands of those who support right-wing parties such as the Conservative Party. Britain's largest-circulation tabloid, the *Sun*, and the broadsheet that is traditionally the most influential, *The Times*, are both owned by News International, as are the *Sunday Times* and the *News of the World*. The *Daily Telegraph*, the *Daily Mail*, the *Daily Express*, and their Sunday equivalents are similarly committed to the Conservative Party, although the balance has moved slightly to the centre with the coming of *The Independent*.

Secondly, Labour is influenced by the experiences of the many trade union members who work in the industry. New technology has allowed newspapers to be produced with less labour at lower cost: the efforts of the print unions to resist these changes, and the efforts of management to impose them, have led to much conflict and bitterness. Newspaper publishing is not, of course, the first industry to go through such an upheaval — in fact it is one of the last — but the newspaper crisis, once it reached Fleet Street, has been better publicised nationally than any other. Fleet Street loves to write about itself; it is often less conscientious when it comes to reporting the problems of other industries.

These factors have generated a formidable dislike of 'the media' within the Labour Party. The media has become a popular issue for those to whom politics is a matter of marching down streets waving banners. This is particularly true in London, where a high proportion of left-wing activists, whether in the Labour Party or in fringe parties outside it, either work in the communications industry (within which one can include teaching) or in local government, where their own activities have been a favourite target for Conservative newspapers, and who consequently hate the press.

Such a popular cause is naturally a cause to be exploited. Trotskyite groups jump on the bandwagon, joining in every march or picket, expressing their 'solidarity' through rhetoric and lapel badges. Politicians within the Labour Party who wish to court hard Left support gladly join the bandwagon, incorporating a ritual denunciation of 'the media' in their speeches.

It is right and proper that people in the Labour Party should be concerned about the future of this industry, and with the whole issue of mass communications. The problem is that this concern expresses itself in a confused and irrational way, which tends to preclude constructive thought. Dislike of the ownership structure of the newspaper industry gets confused with a distrust of individual journalists, who have at times been subjected to extraordinary vilification. It is, of course, easier to hate an individual, or a small group of people, than to think constructively — although some journalists are certainly not the fearless seekers after truth they like to think they are.

This problem reached its peak during the 1984-85 miners' strike, when the National Union of Journalists, having offered to help the National Union of Mineworkers with its press relations, later found some of its members referred to by Arthur Scargill as 'liars', 'vermin', and 'piranha fish'. The NUJ does, admittedly, set a bad example itself: it is the only union whose delegates stand up and attack their own members at the annual Trades Union Congress.

This problem, of instinctive hostility towards the press, of condemning proprietors and journalists equally, is unfortunately not confined to the quasi-revolutionaries of the hard Left. Michael Foot was himself a journalist, yet his period as Leader of the Labour Party was marked by increasingly bad relations with the press. During the 1983 General Election campaign, he refused to write an article for the *Daily Mail*, even though it was a chance to put the Labour case to a million *Mail* readers. Instead, Foot's assistant, the former *Tribune* editor Dick Clements, proposed that alongside articles from Margaret Thatcher, David Steel, and Roy Jenkins, the *Mail* should reproduce the front page it had published during the 1979 general election campaign, entitled 'Ten Labour Lies'. A caption would say how disgraceful this sort of journalism was. The *Mail* rejected this idea, and instead cobbled together a Michael Foot article out of several Foot speeches. It read rather well.

Such a negative attitude towards the press leaves a political party with nowhere to go. In a mass democracy a party seeking mass support must use the mass media. Efforts to escape from this always prove futile. Michael Foot thought he had found an escape route in 1983, when he decided to, or was persuaded to, embark on a punishing schedule of meetings up and down the country. The theory was to appeal to the electorate directly, over the heads of the media. Half a minute with a pocket calculator would have revealed the nonsense of this approach. Even supposing it was possible to address 5,000 voters a day at meetings, by the end of a three-week campaign one could address barely 100,000. The electorate in England, Scotland, and Wales in 1983 was 41,147,122 — and anyone with any knowledge of social habits in Britain today will know that only a tiny per cent of them ever go to political meetings, even at election time. Of those who do, the majority are politically committed people who have already made up their minds how they intend to vote.

The folly of Labour's 1983 attitude was made even worse by a sheer lack of detailed application. Public meetings can, with a modicum of planning, make good television: care must be taken to give the cameras a good position; the director must be given a script in advance, and advised on what passages have a likely news value; the speaker will deliver these passages with a muted style suitable for living-room viewing. Harold Wilson did this as a matter of course; but by 1983 such elementary skills seemed to be beyond the Labour Party, its Leader's office, and its press office.

The attitude of the press office was especially negative. An extremely helpful offer from the Mirror Group Newspapers, to lend the Labour Party journalists for the duration of the campaign, was, as I have already noted, ignored. A group of experienced freelance press officers was hired, given an office with a bank of telephones, and then also ignored. They were given no information. They were expected to answer telephone queries, seek out the answers from the appropriate Labour Party official, then 'phone the enquirer back. At least, they assumed that was what was expected — they never really knew. The idea that Labour Party press officers might play a creative role, initiating contacts with the media and offering them stories of mutual benefit to the media and the party, was viewed with horror. Press officers were, after all, journalists themselves, and could not really be trusted.

Fear is the basis of this hostility. It is a fear that leads people to feel that all contacts with the press are bound to be damaging, and should therefore be minimised. From this has emerged the belief that, if you say nothing to the press, then the press has no right to say anything about you. In Trotskyites and others of that ilk this attitude makes some sense: it corresponds to their fantasies of future power, when the media will no doubt have to print verbatim any statements from the Central Committee, and say nothing until such a statement is released.

In the 1982 Labour Party Young Socialist Conference this fantasy came into contact with reality: the Militant-dominated executive demanded that they have the right to vet all copy from the *Daily Mail* reporter covering the conference. The Labour Party press officer present, Jim Innes, naturally refused to attempt to implement this decision. He left the Conference, and later resigned from the Party's employ when the NEC, voting absent-mindedly on Left-Right lines, failed to support him. It was a sad and shameful episode.

Labour successes with the media tend to come about in spite of the Party, not because of it. It follows that those Labour politicians who have been most successful with the media have generally been mavericks. Tony Benn and Ken Livingstone are two prime examples.

Tony Benn is himself a journalist, which explains both his skill with the media, and his obsession with it. Like Livingstone, he has frequently been able to have it both ways: he has received wide media coverage for his views, while gaining the status of a martyr within the Left as one abused by the media. But he has always understood that a radical politician cannot be timid of the media — on the contrary, he must learn to thrive on controversy. Like a boxer, he cannot win unless he is willing to climb into the ring. Bruises are a price he must be willing to pay.

Livingstone is not a journalist, and after he became leader of the Greater London Council his handling of the press was at first inept. But he did not let his bad experiences drive him into his shell. A good press officer, Veronica Crichton, taught him the basics of handling the media, and he continued to maintain a high profile. Eventually the press began to find virtues in him. As Gore Vidal once said of Norman Mailer, if you spend thirty years insisting you are the greatest living American writer, people will start believing you. Ken Livingstone is a more modest example of this principle in action. What were (and are) highly dubious propositions — that Ken Livingstone was an original thinker, that he had done things for London that no previous politicians had done, that he was a future leader of the Labour Party — began to be taken seriously.

Contrast this with two examples of the Labour Party's official handling of the media, both of which I saw at first hand as the Labour spokesman involved. Both illustrate the truth that one must never run away from the media.

The first happened during the 1979 General Election campaign. One of the Labour Government's successes in the year before that Election had been to force a price freeze on the EEC's Common Agricultural Policy and to resist attempts to push through a Common Fisheries Policy that would have harmed the British fishing industry. It was a success noted by the Conservatives: a commitment to maintain the price freeze was included in their election manifesto, and during the campaign itself their Party leader, Margaret Thatcher, told a meeting in Aberdeen that the Tories would be 'as tough as John Silkin' in future EEC negotiations.

But for the Labour Party the issue of the EEC was deemed to be too dangerous: the Party leadership was divided on the issue, with such powerful voices as Denis Healey and David Owen opposing the majority within the Labour Party who were in favour of withdrawal from the EEC. The EEC referendum of 1975 had gone two-to-one against withdrawal, which lent further weight to those who argued that the issue should be buried. They won the day despite the palpable nonsense of a party of government being both shy about its past achievements and coy about its future intentions. On my own initiative I spent a week of the campaign speaking in marginal seats where the fishing industry was important — Aberdeen, East Lothian, South Shields, Hull, Grimsby — but this was no substitute for the Labour Party using all its resources to push the issue.

The second example involved the 1983 General Election and the issue of defence. Again the party was divided, between those who favoured unilateral nuclear disarmament and those who did not, and again the official response was to try to bury the issue. Opinion polls seemed to support this tactic, since they showed that Labour's defence policies were not popular. But they also showed that the Party's defence policies were widely misunderstood. The positive way forward would have been to put resources into rectifying this ignorance. Again, the negative path was chosen. The result was to draw attention to the issue of defence even more. The media, quite legitimately, sought clarification of Labour's policies, and were far from happy with the answers they got. Once Labour was committed to playing the issue down, it could only appear defensive and furtive. If Labour appeared to have no faith in its defence policies, how could it expect the electorate to have any?

Yet only a few months before the Labour Party had produced a highly successful party political broadcast on defence, in which I and my then deputy defence spokesman, Denzil Davies, sought to explain policies. The response from the public was very good, and it caused concern in Conservative Central Office — a concern that showed itself during the election campaign, when the Secretary of State for Defence, Michael Heseltine, launched a lengthy Conservative document that attempted to demolish Labour's defence policy in great detail (the Labour Party deflected this onslaught only through a brilliant piece of opportunism by Francis Beckett, one of the freelance press officers working for the Party, who rejuvenated a somewhat stale report from NEDO on the state of the British economy — it grabbed the headlines that weekend, in place of Heseltine's blunderbuss).

The Labour Party Leader, Michael Foot, came under enormous pressure. If Labour were not to hold a press conference on defence — which it did not — then the media naturally expected clarification from him. He was a founder of the Campaign for Nuclear Disarmament, he was a passionate advocate of unilateral nuclear disarmament, and talked of the horrors of nuclear war in all his speeches during the 1983 election campaign. But he was left dangerously vulnerable by his Party's failure to project its commitment to strong conventional defence. Questioned on television by interrogators such as Brian Walden, he could only twist and turn.

Defence was doubly important in 1983 because it was the first general election to follow the Falklands War. Labour had supported the use of armed forces to expel the Argentine invaders, since they were a fascist regime invading a country that did not want them. But it was Margaret Thatcher who naturally got most of the credit for pursuing the war to its successful conclusion. But Mrs Thatcher was vulnerable on two counts: her Government had allowed the war to break out; and during the war many Welsh Guards had died apparently unnecessarily in the tragedy at Bluff Cove.

The issue of whether or not the Falklands War could have been avoided raised many questions about Conservative defence policy: was it really desirable to have a massive nuclear deterrent in Europe if it had to be paid for at the expense of the conventional naval forces needed to deter an attack on the Falklands, or any other British dependency that we were obliged, under international law, to defend? It was evidence to support Labour's argument that the nuclear deterrent did not satisfy Britain's real defence obligations.

But it was never allowed to be used. Instead the electorate was subjected to an unopposed Conservative onslaught on Labour's defence policy, which was to damage the Party's credibility beyond repair by polling day.

From this it should be obvious that policy cannot be divorced from publicity, any more than electioneering can be divorced from the media. Mavericks such as Tony Benn and Ken Livingstone have grasped this point; the official Party machine has not, and in this failure it has progressively weakened itself. With the move of Labour Party headquarters to Walworth Road, real politics gave way to office politics: an increasingly introspective central bureaucracy earned the irritation and even contempt of both Labour politicians and Labour Party members in the country.

For Labour to succeed with its press relations three things are required: the will, the strategy, and the tactics. The will must come from the very top of the Party. The NEC must decide to employ press officers of the very highest quality. It must pay them adequately, respect their professional judgement, and trust them to get on with the job. This is still not happening: since 1983 far more attention has been paid to the visual presentation of the Party, but journalists are still not trusted.

Journalists must be trusted, and by all heads of departments at Walworth Road. Press officers cannot be kept in ignorance of what is going on: they must be part of the decision-making at every level. Only then will they be sufficiently knowledgeable to go forth and play a creative role in projecting the Labour Party, both trusted by others and trusting in their own judgement.

Strategy is largely a matter of resources. The Labour Party in recent years, with its limited financial resources, has undoubtedly got the balance wrong between policy-making and communication, and between the centre and the regions. Resources have been allocated less through a rational assessment of need than through empire-building and horse-trading among departmental heads. The Labour Party needs to spend more on communications and more in the regions.

Communication with members of the Labour Party is a vital part of the overall publicity strategy. After 1971, with the creation of *Labour Weekly*, the Labour Party had all its eggs in one basket — before then there was a range of Labour publications. It was felt that a weekly journal could fill the function of the earlier specialised publications — such as *Labour Organiser*, aimed at Party agents, whether full-time or part-time — while gaining the party both prestige and income by selling to the general public.

On every count it failed. As an information tool for party workers it has been of little use. Far from adding to the prestige of the Party, it has become a haven for journalism that is dull, mediocre, and partisan, reflecting fashionable sectarian views rather than the broader spectrum of the Labour Party. Far from making money for the Party, it has survived only through being heavily subsidised from Party funds. The will to make it a healthy part of the Labour machine has never been there: rather than appoint a good publisher and business manager, and insist that *Labour Weekly* be financially independent, the NEC insists on maintaining direct control. Executive members are thus making decisions on pricing and other aspects of management policy of which they have little knowledge.

Indeed rather than face the problems of *Labour Weekly*, the NEC in 1981 decided to compound them by setting up another journal, *New Socialist*. It was, in theory, to be a bi-monthly 'theoretical journal'. It became, in practice, a house journal for the entryists. Far from giving us anything new and theoretical on socialism, it became the purveyor of some of the stalest orthodoxies to be found in the larder of the hard Left.

In more recent times it has put some of the loonier aspects of the entryist philosophy of catering for minorities between glossy covers: socialist vegetarianism and suchlike. It is difficult to see what connection it has with the Labour Party, apart from sharing its premises. But those who run it have at least shown some vigour in promoting it. It became a monthly in 1986, and plans were considered to float it off as an independent publication. This would undoubtedly be the best course, for editorially it has never been anything else.

Yet another new publication came into being in 1986: *Labour Party News*, a glossy newsletter aimed at all party members. It is too early to judge whether it will be a success and a constructive influence on the Party.

The truly independent Left press is another important aspect of Labour Party communications: journals such as the *New Statesman* and *Tribune* have no formal links with the Party, but they have been founded and run by Labour Party people, and at their peak have been extremely influential. When Labour came to power in 1964 the *New Statesman* had a circulation of around 100,000, and *Tribune* one of over 20,000. Both have declined sharply since then.

The *New Statesman* was very much a product of Fabian socialism, of the left-wing literary intellectual. It was tradition-ally read as much for the review section at the back as for the politics at the front. *Tribune* was always a less popular and more idiosyncratic journal, further to the left and lacking the resources to build a large circulation. The *New Statesman* benefited from the continuity of Kingsley Martin's editorship over three decades; *Tribune*'s rise and fall has been more abrupt. Nye Bevan made it a great political newspaper during his period of editorship in the Second World War, when he was leading the campaign for a second front to be opened up in Europe, and it had another peak in the Fifties, when Michael Foot was in charge: the issue then was nuclear disarmament.

Under Dick Clements' twenty-year editorship, which ended in 1982, *Tribune* declined steadily in circulation, but remained an influential journal of the Left. It also strengthened its links with the broader Labour movement by sustaining itself on advertising from the trade unions. This was an important development, one that encouraged the trade unions to become more aware of the need to communicate.

Although most trade union advertising in the Left press remains, to put it politely, narrow in its appeal ('May Day Greetings from the National Union of Mineworkers') it has been a step towards the sort of professional and imaginative campaigns that trade unions, particularly those in the public sector, have mounted in recent years. Nineteen eighty-six actually saw Margaret Thatcher and the Conservatives borrowing a slogan, 'Put People First', previously used by the National and Local Government Officers' Association in a campaign against privatisation.

But advertising campaigns, important as they may be to highlight particular issues, are no substitute for the sustained influence of political journals, which can help to mould the ideas of generations of readers. The decline of the *New Statesman* and *Tribune* is a serious matter, and became even more so in 1982 when a new editor of *Tribune*, Chris Mullin, took over from Dick Clements and began to turn it into a journal of the sectarian Left. It became, in effect, a journal to promote Tony Benn within the Labour Party, and since Benn had missed his great chance to be a future Leader of the Party, by failing to win the Deputy Leadership contest in 1981, it became a bitter and destructive journal.

Its new hallmarks were personal abuse and the use of political journalism as a weapon to achieve narrow political ends. When the Benn faction wanted to take control of the

Campaign for Labour Party Democracy, *Tribune* became a recruiting sergeant for this battle. Far from encouraging people to think, *Tribune* became one of those political journals — *Militant*, *Socialist Worker*, and *Labour Briefing* are others — that encourage people not to think. Readers are there to learn the line and vote for the slate.

Chris Mullin also hoped to raise money to promote *Tribune* through making the paper over to a new friendly society. There was no consultation at all with the existing shareholders, and — even more worrying — there was no guarantee that the friendly society would be owned and controlled by Labour Party members. Advertisements offering shares in the friendly society were, in fact, placed in a journal published by the International Marxist Group. When asked about this by a journalist, Chris Mullin said he would be happy to sell shares to members of the Conservative Party. The connection between ownership and control seemed not to have occurred to him.

I was appalled that this could happen to *Tribune*: so too were Nye Bevan's widow, Jennie Lee, Nye's former Parliamentary Private Secretary, Donald Bruce, and my friend the Labour MP Russell Kerr. They were shareholders in *Tribune*, and were determined to steer it back to its old course. They used their votes to put Donald Bruce and me on the board of Tribune Publications Limited as a first step. This action brought a torrent of abuse, directed mainly at me. I had, it seemed, staged a 'take-over' and was a threat to 'the freedom of the press'.

The real take-over came a few weeks later. At a board meeting held at short notice two days before Christmas, those present — most of whom were worker-directors — voted to give the staff a majority shareholding in the company. They announced that they would go ahead with the friendly society scheme. They assumed that Donald, Jennie, and I would just admit defeat and go away. We did not, but it took us almost three years to settle the dispute.

I believe independent Labour journals can be important for several reasons. They can be a forum for fresh ideas and thinking — vital for a party that is still recovering from the traumas inflicted upon it by Bennery and Trotskyism, both of which tried to stifle originality and realism. There is no doubt that Thatcherite Conservatism gained much of its vigour from the work of independent research bodies set up to develop ideas free of the constraints of the official Conservative research office. Labour has lacked such bodies: a journal like *Tribune* could fill this gap. It did so in the past.

Many of George Orwell's greatest essays were written for *Tribune*. Michael Foot's articles on nuclear disarmament in the Fifties led to the creation of CND. More recently Walter Kendall's articles challenging the Militant Tendency to give honest answers to questions about their aims and organisation came when most on the Left of the Party were still inclined to be indulgent towards Militant.

It was Orwell who complained of the intellectual's habit of importing his ideologies from abroad, rather than using his self-proclaimed intellectual powers to work one out for himself. Few on the Left today import their political beliefs from Moscow, which was what Orwell was complaining about, but importing Euro-Communism from Rome (as does the Communist Party's *Marxism Today*) or Trotskyism from a Mexican tomb is if anything even sillier. All are inimical to the creativity that the Left should be stimulating.

This creativity should not take the form of spawning hordes of would-be Orwells. There is no shortage as it is of universal experts writing for the Left press, usually dedicated to trying to prove that the Labour Party Leadership is both wrong on everything and betraying the Left. The Left press could do with a few more genuine experts, well versed in specific areas of industry or home or foreign affairs, and able to impart their knowledge to a non-specialist audience. There is in the Left press a lamentable lack of fresh information, thought, and ideas for the reader to get his teeth into.

But gathering fresh information is a time-consuming and expensive business. Good practitioners at it are rightly very well paid. Small, impoverished journals of the Left, with tiny, poorly-paid staffs are at a great disadvantage.

When I first joined the board of *Tribune* I was shocked at the low pay of staff, which the trade unions, both inside and outside the journal, were prepared to turn a blind eye to. This meant that the staff were either young and inexperienced, and likely to find work elsewhere as soon as possible, or much older and with a spouse to support them. This effectively precluded the employment of the very persons any successful newspaper needs: professionals in their prime.

The only way to solve this problem is to make journals such

as *Tribune* much more profitable. They need to achieve much bigger circulations and advertising revenue. That means that the much-needed creativity must not stop at journalists: managerial, promotional, circulation, and advertising staff must be of very high quality.

The encouragement of such talent must create a valuable resource for the Labour Party as a whole, most obviously in the field of publicity and press relations.

The impact of television on newspapers is still not fully appreciated, even by professionals in this field. The number of people who use newspapers as their primary source of news is now very small. This has pushed newspapers in two directions: the popular papers have become an adjunct of show business — television, popular music, and football are their main concerns — while the more serious papers have shifted their emphasis from straight news-reporting to comment. The political columnists of *The Times* and the *Guardian* will no doubt be deeply offended to be classified as the up-market version of the pop columnists of the *Sun* and the *Mirror*, but it is close to the truth.

The role of the Saturday newspaper has changed even more than that of the Monday to Friday editions. Minimal coverage is now given to Friday's business in Parliament; great space is allocated instead to entertainment guides to the weekend. The days when major political speeches were given on a Friday evening to get maximum coverage at the weekend have long gone. Friday debates have also been devalued by neglect. They tend, of course, to be non-controversial in party political terms, because many out-of-London MPs need to travel back to their constituencies on Friday, but they can be of major importance. I can remember two examples from when I was Labour Spokesman on Industry: a debate on the Finniston Report on the training of engineers; and a debate on new technology. In both cases the press gallery was virtually empty, despite the clear national importance of the subjects under debate.

In spite of new developments in printing, or perhaps because of them, print deadlines have got earlier, not later. Early editions of Sunday newspapers will be heading for Scotland on Saturday morning, which means that to get a story in the Sunday papers one has to tip them off on Thursday and give them the details no later than Friday.

With fewer column-inches of news space available, the need

to give advance copy to journalists is growing. In the past, wind-up speeches delivered between 9 and 10 o'clock in the evening were often covered in the later editions of the next morning's papers. Now these speeches are usually only covered, and then rarely, by radio and television.

The rise of the Parliamentary sketch writers, one result of the decline of straight news reporting, has had a wider impact than may appear obvious.

A really amusing Parliamentary sketch requires leisure and preparation in its composition. The witty remarks are thought up well in advance. The sketch writer is aided by the notice of statements and private notice questions, whose content in recent years has often come to be known both to the press and Members of Parliament in advance. The results are that the sketches are more polished, but their subject matter has become much more limited. Ministerial statements and answers to private notice questions now get the maximum publicity but major debates which in the past were often brought to life through the lively pen of the sketch writer are hardly ever now described.

Question Time is the ideal subject: it comes early in the day and is predictable. Prime Minister's questions come every Tuesday and Thursday, while other Ministers are questioned every three weeks on a rota basis. There is almost always a statement on the next week's business from the Leader of the House on Thursdays, but that is another regular date for sketch writers.

Although Parliamentary sketches appear only in the more serious papers, their influence in the press gallery extends to the popular papers as well. Question Time is seen as more important than the debates that follow, unless the debate is both crucial and dramatic. Seldom is anything that happens in the House after 6 pm covered in any depth.

For the regional and local press the problems of deadlines is even worse. The slightly silly situation arises where something on breakfast television, put out an hour or two later by the Press Association, can emerge again as a big story in the regional press the following day.

For a party in Opposition, there are added problems. The Whitehall machine has formidable advantages over a party machine, even an effective one. In practice, the Labour Party press office these days has virtually no contact with most of the Shadow Cabinet, with the exception of the Leader's office. This will have to change. The existing disadvantages of Opposition cannot go on being compounded by indifference.

Governments have obvious ways of influencing media coverage in its favour, such as inviting journalists to travel to look at defence equipment at the taxpayer's expense. But the less obvious ways are more insidious and unfair.

Supposing the Government wishes to make a statement in the House or publish a White Paper. It can tip off friendly journalists, while not being obliged to inform the House, or the Opposition, until noon of the day when the statement is to be made. If the Opposition is lucky it will pick up a clear hint in the newspapers or from gossip that something is afoot, but this cannot be relied upon.

The statement will come at about 3.30 pm. The Opposition will only receive an advance copy about half an hour before it is due to be delivered. The Opposition spokesman will then go into an all-too-brief conclave in the Whips' office, usually with junior spokesmen, and possibly an adviser and the Opposition spokesman in the Lords. The statement will be delivered more or less simultaneously in both Houses, so clearly the Opposition must respond in similar fashion in both Houses.

A statement of great importance may be made in Parliament; but before the Opposition and backbench MPs have had time to comment journalists will often be leaving for a press conference at the Ministry, to which the Minister will be whisked by limousine once he has made his statement to the House. Instead of taking the statement down in shorthand, other journalists will be reading a copy of the statement in a Ministry conference room, waiting for the Minister to arrive and give them his undivided attention; these journalists will not have time to approach the Opposition for comment before writing their stories. The Minister will also be able to talk to television cameras and radio microphones within minutes of speaking to the House.

It is all too easy for journalists to accept this ministerial spoon-feeding and cover only the Government's point of view. The Opposition, in contrast, will have had no time to put its views in writing or book rooms for press conferences. The Opposition spokesman will have to rely upon talking to journalists in the Members' lobby while his assistant is hastily drafting a press release and putting it out through the Press

Association — plus, of course, whatever impact he has made in the House.

Here radio is, of course, the principal medium involved. The coming of radio to Parliament has undoubtedly been a great benefit: it gives the public a chance to make up its own mind about issues, free of both the comment that dominates the press or the extreme selectivity — itself a form of comment — that characterises television. Sometimes radio has caused the public to make up its mind in a way that has not been favourable to the Labour Party: Michael Foot's performances at the dispatch box against Margaret Thatcher were a major factor undermining his credibility as a future Prime Minister. But it remains a fairer and more neutral medium than television. Experience of televising the House of Lords has shown the extent to which it favours the performer over the more self-effacing politician.

The lobby system in Parliament, whereby journalists receive off-the-record briefings, has been much criticised, particularly by those with no experience of it. From the outside it looks suspicious. Lobby journalists have been attacked as having a parasitic relationship with the politicians who brief them, of being tame poodles not prepared to write the unvarnished truth. The accurate word is not 'parasitic' but 'symbiotic'. Politicians and journalists do have a close relationship under the lobby system, but it is one that depends on honesty and trust on both sides; no one side can exploit the other.

It is not the lobby system that gives the Government of the day its power. The journalists get to know the politicians very well, and are able to put across their views accurately and perceptively. The other word used to attack this relationship is 'cosy'. This misconception stems from the idea that British politics is steeped in gross wrong-doing, that it is the task of journalists everywhere to root it out, and that the lobby is part of some sort of cover-up. It is not: the lobby is a useful relationship which enables the public to receive a certain type of generally reliable intelligence on the way the country is being run. It is not intended to stifle investigative journalism, nor could it even if it wanted to.

As a pact between politicians and journalists it does, of course, curb any tendency to 'publish and be damned'.

People who think that the Palace of Westminster is an instinctively secretive place should look at the rapid rise of the

Select Committee system. Open to all journalists, not just to those with Parliamentary credentials, meeting in the morning, thus overcoming the problem of deadlines, they have been a significant step forward towards open and effective government. Bill committees are similarly open to all journalists, allowing those with specialised interests, in particular, to follow the development of a Bill in great detail.

I remember when I was Chief Whip a journalist came to me, having picked up a story on the economy. I confirmed the story, suppressing nothing, but told him that if it was published it would damage the pound. He did not publish.

Openness with journalists was always the best policy in my experience. During the so-called 'Winter of Discontent' in 1978-79, the lorry drivers' strike raised much concern about food supplies. As Minister of Agriculture, Fisheries and Food, I held daily press conferences, seven days a week, and told the press exactly what the situation was. I also met daily with the lorry drivers' union, the TGWU, to ensure that essential supplies were not blocked. This open relationship on both sides helped when one TGWU district office, in Hull, failed to pass on to its members instructions from Transport House on the release of essential supplies from the docks. I went on local radio and was able to talk directly to TGWU members, who responded positively.

A similar openness with the media was my policy during farm-price negotiations in Brussels. I was fortunate in having the best and most professional press officer in Whitehall, Terry Dawes. He had worked with both Labour and Conservative administrations with enthusiasm, and knew the press and their demands very well. He was trusted and respected by the Brussels press corps.

This was vital because press briefings in Brussels did not just have their impact on the information that reached the British public, but influenced Ministers from other countries, who would have the British position relayed to them through journalists from their own countries.

In both Brussels and Luxembourg it was virtually impossible to get out of the building without encountering the press. All Ministers took a positive approach to this: there was often an unseemly rush to grab one of the available conference rooms for a hastily-convened press conference. Even during short breaks in negotiations the press were not forgotten. Ministerial press officers and advisers were with the press continually, both spelling out their national position and picking up intelligence of what other negotiating teams were up to.

As the British Minister involved, I always felt it was my duty to tell the British public all that I could, especially since the policy I was pursuing was a highly controversial one, and was bitterly attacked by many in Britain and even more abroad. I believed what I was doing was right, and I explained why. Those acrimonious all-night negotiations became popular with radio and television, attracted by the controversy, so I was able to take full advantage of their presence. The result was a very positive one for the Labour Party, with the Conservatives being forced into trying to steal Labour's clothes in the 1979 General Election campaign.

It is all too easy to think in terms of the national press and to ignore the local press. Yet in the end democracy requires that every citizen should be able to be aware of what is being done in the name of the people in their own locality. The local press has more than a right to report the actions of the council in whose area it operates — it has a duty to do so. It was for that reason that when I led for the Labour Party in the committee stage of the Local Government Act my colleagues and I insisted on the right of the press to attend every meeting of a local authority.

Opening up new avenues of communication with the media can only be good for the Labour Party.

Part Three

———————— ○○◯○○ ————————

Foreign Affairs

Chapter Twelve

────────── ∘∘⭕∘∘ ──────────

The World About Us

Nobody who grew up in a Labour family in Britain during the Thirties could avoid the impact of foreign affairs. Like the generation growing up in the Eighties, we could see unemployment and bad economic conditions all around us. But the Thirties were also heavy with the rise of fascism, and the inevitability — so it seemed to many of my generation — of world war.

The die was cast with the Japanese invasion of Manchuria in 1931. As the decade progressed the *News Chronicle* was able to point out that Manchuria, Abyssinia (invaded by Mussolini in 1935), the Rhineland (occupied by Hitler in 1936), and the fascist rebellion in Spain spelt out the ominous acronym MARS. My generation had no doubt what its destiny would be. Every new fascist aggression made a second world war inevitable.

There were compensations. We greeted the election of Franklin Roosevelt in the United States with intense relief. We looked to the Soviet Union as a potential ally in the fight that would one day come. We applauded the fight — real or mythical — of Chiang Kai-shek's forces against the Japanese. Yet all the while we saw Britain's Conservative Government make one humiliating gesture of appeasement after another to the worldwide aggressors.

For the generation of our parents, the events of the Thirties were not so clear-cut. They had been through the bloodiest war in history. Many of them accepted the old and honourable tradition of quasi-religious pacifism with which British socialism had always been associated.

Ramsay MacDonald was of this tradition, and even more so his successor as Labour Party Leader, George Lansbury. It was the pacifist tradition that led Lansbury to visit Hitler in 1937 — Clement Attlee had already replaced him as Leader — with the idea of converting him to his own view of peaceful co-existence.

Today, the contradictions of this position are obvious. In the Thirties they were blurred. My father certainly wondered how the Labour Party could be strongly opposed to fascism and aggression and yet support the 'peace ballot' of 1936, which seemed to favour a refusal to take up arms against anybody.

Labour's opponents certainly asked the question. The Party's response was muted. It could only say that the League of Nations should fight aggression with economic sanctions, and, if they failed, should be prepared to take military action.

This begged the question. Clearly military action by the League could only be possible if the democracies rearmed. The League was, in any case, falling apart. The United States had never joined; Germany and Japan walked out in 1933; Italy followed in 1937; the decision of the Soviet Union to join in 1934 made little difference. The League had clearly ceased to be an instrument that could achieve anything. Its final degrading performance in 1939, when it refused to condemn Germany for starting the Second World War, but instead condemned Russia for invading Finland, only added to the confusion.

When the Second World War ended in 1945 I was a young Royal Navy officer in the Pacific. I was struck not only by the fact that the war had ended, after fourteen years, in the same region in which it had begun, but also by the fact that my generation, young at the time of the Manchurian invasion, had had to expiate the follies and mistakes of previous generations. But, like the rest of my generation, I was confident that by conquering my generation's MARS we had put an end to war for all time.

'We have taken part in what I believe is the last carrier-borne raid in history,' I wrote to my parents on August 9, 1945 — the day after the second atomic bomb had fallen on Nagasaki. I viewed the future with an optimism that bordered on certainty. These feelings I shared with others in my ship.

'I think that everyone is certain that we are on the verge of a new industrial revolution — one that will change the whole concept of power. Already people in the wardrooms and on the messdecks are saying that things like the Australian problem of soil erosion could be remedied by the judicial use of atomic power, while the energy released by atomic disintegration if properly controlled will kill petrol and steam as sources of power . . .'

Such optimism, after the fourteen-year fight against fascism, was widely shared. My comrades and I had a keen sense of priorities. We believed that the nations that had defeated fascism must evolve into a United Nations that kept the peace; that atomic weapons must be under United Nations control; and that atomic energy must be put to use for peaceful purposes.

The peace that followed the Second World War, like the peace that followed the First, was destined to be one of disillusionment. Once again, yesterday's allies split apart, and after that began the process of making new wars through surrogate countries from Korea to Latin America. The United Nations acted more firmly and with greater effect than the League of Nations had before it — the United States and the Soviet Union were members, and its authority was much more established — but even the UN seemed to prefer resolutions to solutions.

As the scientists had prophesied, the making of nuclear weapons became cheaper and technically easier as time went by. Optimism over nuclear power proved unfounded. The great Soviet physicist, Peter Kapitza, once defended nuclear power by saying that 'to talk of atomic energy in terms of the atomic bomb was like talking of electricity in terms of the electric chair'. Unfortunately, in most industrialised countries — Canada is the noble exception — it has become intrinsically linked with the production of plutonium suitable for weapons.

Nuclear weapons became cheaper, but nuclear power proved too expensive and too inflexible — and possibly too dangerous — to play the role in energy production most envisaged for it. The need for portable energy in an increasingly populous world has made the demand for oil greater than ever, and consequently a greater source of international friction than it has ever been.

After allowance is made for technological change, the world's problems as it approaches the twenty-first century are not fundamentally different from the problems that faced it at the beginning of the twentieth century. Misuse of political power, misuse of resources, poverty and preventable diseases are still the enemies of the sort of worldwide order about which socialists dream.

The Labour Party has always liked to believe that it is possible to have a socialist foreign policy. But what is socialism? It is a belief in the popular ownership and control of the means of production, distribution, and exchange. It is not a theory of international relations. The phrase 'socialist foreign policy', to old-style communists, was a euphemism for supporting the Soviet Union. To attempt to apply it to democratic socialism is hopeless. Do we trade with West Germany when the Social Democrats are in power, but not when the Christian Democrats are in coalition with the Liberals?

In 1983, *Tribune* ran the immortal headline: 'Send Kinnock to Nicaragua.' It was not at that time suggesting exile, merely a show of 'solidarity' with the Nicaraguan Government. My dictionary tells me that 'solidarity' means 'holding together, mutual dependence, community of interests, feelings, action'.

The problem is that Britain and Nicaragua are not mutually dependent; they have few interests in common; they can take no common action; they cannot hold together because they have never been together. All that is left is feelings. Feelings are important, but to reduce socialism to feelings is to turn it into an anaemic quasi-religion. Socialism is a materialist and rationalist philosophy, a strategy for changing society. Waffle about 'socialist foreign policy' is profoundly unsocialist, and even an obstacle to the sort of international order that might make domestic socialism less vulnerable.

The Labour Party's foreign policy, throughout its history, has always been a reaction to events, with no identifiable set of principles beyond a belief in the brotherhood of man. This belief has always been easy to equate with individual crusades. Home rule for Ireland and home rule for India were relatively simple concepts: clearly both the Irish and the Indians wished to have their own government.

The problems arise when such individual cases are projected into general principles. If home rule was right for Ireland and

India, why not for every British-held territory? The problems of individual territories were ignored. Many colonies were artificial creations of the nineteenth century, set up regardless of local tribal, cultural, or religious divisions. Unlike Ireland and India, many of them lacked experienced administrators and effective communications.

George Orwell spelt out the problem ruthlessly when he wrote *The Lion and the Unicorn* in 1940. The details have changed, but the principles remain the same. 'To a Labour Government in power, three imperial policies would have been open. One was to continue administering the Empire exactly as before, which meant dropping all pretensions to socialism. Another was to set the subject people "free", which meant in practice handing them over to Japan, Italy and other predatory powers . . . The third was to develop a positive imperial policy, and aim at transforming the Empire into a federation of socialist states, like a looser and freer version of the Union of Soviet Republics.'

Even India, he pointed out, could not defend itself. 'What we must offer India is not "freedom", which, as I have said earlier, is impossible, but alliance, partnership — in word, equality . . . What India needs is the power to work out its own constitution without British interference, but in some kind of partnership that ensures its military protection and technical advice.'

This, he said, could only happen under a socialist government in Britain — but he was highly sceptical of a Labour Government's ability to do this. It was the party of the trade unions, parochial in outlook, 'with little interest in imperial affairs and no contacts among the men who actually held the Empire together'.

The Labour Party was inevitably born into the anti-imperialist 'Little England' camp. In the nineteenth century there were demonstrations in Trafalgar Square opposing the war against the Maoris in New Zealand and against the suppression of the Jamaican uprising. By the turn of the century British socialists and trade unionists were standing shoulder to shoulder with Lloyd George and the pro-Boer faction over the South African war.

It was Bernard Shaw who took the common-sense view — an unpopular one among socialists — that the British Empire at its worst was better than the Afrikaaners at their best. The anti-Boer feelings in the Labour Party, which ought to have been there from the beginning, have only emerged in the last thirty years.

The Labour Party's failure to develop an informed and positive foreign policy, and its consequent reliance upon reacting to events, have led it into many similar traps. Fighting the excesses of British imperialism often blinded the Party to the fact that things could be worse abroad. Confronted with the arms race in Europe before 1914, most Labour leaders denied that there was any such thing as German militarism. When Hitler came to power Labour leaders made the point, and kept making it long after it had become academic, that the Treaty of Versailles had been unjust to the German Republic.

A faint, pathetic echo of this mentality could be seen during the Falklands War of 1982. The NEC had correctly assessed the fascist nature of the Argentinian military junta. It had foreseen that the junta might well threaten the Falklands Islands, and that their military defence was therefore essential.

But when the junta invaded the Falklands many on the hard Left of the Labour Party saw not the aggression of fascism against a free people, but a relic of British imperialism in the South Atlantic that must be repudiated. In their scramble to overturn the Labour Party's anti-fascist policy and tradition, the pro-Argentinian faction within the Party did their best to ensure that the defeat of the invasion should not be heralded as a victory over fascism but a victory for Margaret Thatcher.

I wish Tony Benn and Tam Dalyell and other supporters of Argentina's claim to the 'Malvinas' had been in my ship in the Pacific during the Second World War. Our generation, as it fought fascism, grew up with an understanding of the influence of history on current affairs. In the last year of that war I recall a brains trust that was broadcast over the ship's radio. My best friend aboard was a red-bearded lieutenant-commander called Kenneth Robinson, who was a staunch socialist. He later introduced me to the House of Commons when I won my by-election in 1963, and became Minister of Health in the 1964 Labour Government.

Kenneth Robinson and I were able to work out one or two questions to put to the brains trust, including a quotation from the poet Heine: 'The only thing we learn from history is that we learn nothing from history.' It was a message we both opposed, and a successful means of allowing Kenneth to give the whole ship ten minutes of undiluted Labour propaganda. It was, not surprisingly, the last brains trust we were ever allowed.

Britain's Empire is now nearly gone in Europe. Only Gibraltar remains to remind us that we once looked upon the Mediterranean as a British lake. It is important that we as a country — and as a Party — do not fall into the trap of rigid anti-colonialism over Gibraltar. The Gibraltarians know they cannot survive alone as an independent nation. They prefer the established and working relationship with Britain to an uncertain one with Spain, a country so recently fascist and still dedicated to claiming Gibraltar regardless of the wishes of its citizens.

A Spain that cannot tolerate a British-aligned Gibraltar is a country with a flaw in its democratic mentality — and a country deeply hypocritical, since it still maintains its own colonial enclaves on the Moroccan coast.

But certainly it is true that people who wish to govern themselves should have a right to do so; that is the simple principal upon which decolonialisation rests. It is irrelevant whether the colonising power thinks that those who demand independence will govern their country well or badly — the obligation is to help in a spirit of partnership and equality.

The Labour Governments of 1945-51 under Clement Attlee have rightly been praised for so resolutely beginning the process of turning Empire into Commonwealth. Not since the Swiss turned their back on the prospect of becoming a great European power in the fifteenth century had any nation voluntarily — as far as that word is ever applicable to the actions of nations — relinquished power.

But in decolonialisation there must be safeguards, as Orwell understood. The example of India, by far the largest colony to be freed, shows the dangers. The Government of India Act of 1935, setting up elected provincial parliaments, was a first cautious step towards self-government, but it led to intense rivalry between the Indian Congress movement and the Muslim League. The League, in a position of weakness, asked for coalition administrations in those provinces where both factions were strong. Congress, confident in its power and its aims, refused.

This conflict was not resolved when the Attlee Government set a timetable for Indian independence after the Second World

War. Nehru and Gandhi desperately wanted a unified India. Gandhi even suggested that the Hindu majority should relinquish power to the Muslim minority in order to persuade them that unity was the best way. But by then thousands had been killed in factional fighting. The last Viceroy, Mountbatten, aided by pragmatists within the Congress leadership, pushed through the partition of India.

In theory the Labour Government's position was that no Indian state — there were over 600 of them — should be coerced into joining a united India against its will. In reality, the Government, by setting a deadline for independence, made this ideal impossible to achieve. Those provinces and states that did not acquiesce, such as Muslim Hyderabad in the south, were occupied by government troops and crossed off the map. In northern Kashmir a conflict of interest between the Hindu Maharajah and his Muslim citizens created a conflict that is still unresolved forty years later.

In all, over six million Indians became refugees, and the new state of Muslim Pakistan was divided geographically and politically from the beginning into East and West. Within seven years of the Indian Independence Act being passed in Westminster, a new Bangladeshi independence movement had sprung up in East Pakistan. Civil war sent ten million refugees fleeing into India. It was Indian troops who granted independence to Bangladesh — an independence that has proved turbulent and often bloody.

Less haste, a commitment to unity, perhaps within the federal framework that was discussed in the Twenties and Thirties, would clearly have held a better prospect for peace.

The decolonialisation of Palestine, also in 1948, led to even unhappier results. The rapid British retreat from Palestine left a Jewish state that could only survive by force of arms. It is understandable that Britain, tired after six years of world war, should withdraw from a growing conflict that was costing British lives, but the long-term result of this expediency has been forty years of dangerous instability in the Middle East.

In other former colonies the growth of one-party states, created in order to impose unity on a territory that is racially or tribally divided, has caused untold suffering. Africa, conquered towards the end of the European colonial period, was effectively franchised out to commercial trading companies — or, in the case of the Congo, became the personal property of a Belgian king whose sole interest was in paying off his debts. Such nations were launched into independence with little realistic preparation. Of former British territories, Nigeria has suffered a prolonged civil war; Uganda the murderous activities of Idi Amin and Milton Obote; and even Zimbabwe, liberated finally in the Eighties, has suffered tribal bloodshed.

As for South Africa, Bernard Shaw's strictures against the Boers, looked at eight decades later, suffer only from being an underestimate.

Britain cannot unscramble the past, nor can Labour rely upon a foreign policy labelled 'socialist' but offering no more than goodwill and rhetoric. Hard options must be looked at if the mistakes of the past are not to be repeated in different forms.

Britain has at least four distinct options, leaving aside those — such as alignment with the Soviet bloc, or military adventurism — that are clearly incompatible with public opinion or common sense.

Of the four, neutrality on the Swiss or Swedish model has much to commend it. Both Switzerland and Sweden are prosperous and are doughty defenders of their independence. But to follow that road is to turn away from the history, associations, and responsibilities that have spread the best of British qualities without the world.

The remaining three options are therefore more likely. Britain currently adheres to all three, with varying degrees of enthusiasm and doubt. They involve supporting Atlanticism, or the Europe that centres on Brussels, or the Commonwealth. All have emerged out of Britain's past; whether they will be part of her future is more contentious.

Atlanticism is a continuation of the Anglo-American alliance formed to fight fascism in Europe and Asia, but now turned against the old ally, the Soviet Union. The European Community is a Franco-German economic alliance, brought into being with American patronage, which Britain joined only belatedly. The Commonwealth is a combination of those countries of the British Empire that chose to remain associated with Britain and each other. Some continue to recognise the Queen as Head of State; others adhere to the Commonwealth as a looser grouping of nations sharing common ideals and interests.

Atlanticism makes sense, and would no doubt survive,

insofar as Britain and the United States have a shared interest in transatlantic trade. The Royal Navy has a traditional role, dating back to colonial times, of protecting the Eastern seaboard of the USA. The US Navy helped to protect British convoys in the Atlantic even before America entered the Second World War: it was in her own interests to keep these sea-lanes open. This reality will never change.

What is more doubtful is America's present commitment to Western Europe. The present East-West tensions of the Cold War must eventually die away, and with it the reasons for the American presence in Europe. The real Cold War is anyway fought in the Middle East and the Third World — Europe has long ceased to hold the centre of the stage.

The Americans are far more aware of this than most Europeans. They would like to expand NATO into a global alliance, matching their own global military capabilities. Some Americans would like to take over the role that Britain once had of the policeman of the world. Despite America's immense economic and military power, this will never happen. The world is a much more self-aware place than it was in the heyday of the British Empire.

The British mistake is the reverse of the American one. Having ceased to have an Empire, we have now largely convinced ourselves that we have no global role. To the Foreign Office the Commonwealth is an irrelevance. In their blinkered mentality it was the Empire or nothing. They turned instead to 'Europe', convincing themselves that a new empire of British influence could be created around Brussels. It has not, and it will not be, for the European Community is essentially a partnership between France and Germany.

I talk of four options for Britain. In the eyes of the British Establishment there are two: Europe or a Britain 'alone'. This aloneness is never explained or defined, since it cannot be. It is a totally worthless and vacuous concept. Britain cannot be alone. Britain will continue to have common interests, maritime and cultural, with the United States and with the Commonwealth. That she is also European is a fact of geography, and is not dictated by the Rome Treaty. Her need to feed herself and to trade gives her a symbiotic relationship with nations around the world.

Through the Commonwealth Britain has a worldwide network of contacts with countries that share common political and cultural ideals — ideals that are not always lived up to, but which are still a beacon and a common bond.

The Commonwealth is represented in all the continents of the world, and is an active force for peace and stability in all of them. The poorer continents are often a cause for despair, but that will change. The years of post-colonial turmoil will pass — as they did in the United States and every other former colony that struggled to statehood — and national economies will begin to take off. Then, belatedly, the British Establishment will no doubt want to be part of this new prosperity.

But by then it may be too late. The Commonwealth will wither and die by the end of this century unless it is given new strength and purpose. Without its democratic beacon, the new wealth of the Third World may be directed into a new fascism and a new militarism, as happened when Germany, Italy, and Japan first became industrialised in their turn.

Chapter Thirteen

— ○○○○○ —

'Linked but not Comprised'

Marlene Dietrich once phoned her old friend Ernest Hemingway to ask his advice on whether she should take a particular film role. She did not really want the part, but felt that she should accept it rather than remain idle. The writer gave her what she gratefully described as a whole philosophy in one sentence: 'Never mistake movement for action.'

Britain's decision to enter the EEC was that very mistake. Those who favoured the decision and eventually achieved it deluded themselves into believing that it was an action that would solve Britain's growing economic problems. In reality, it was an evasion of these problems. In the Hemingway definition, it was movement, not action. It was also something of a panic reaction.

What had brought about the panic was the transformation of Empire into Commonwealth, the 'wind of change', in Harold Macmillan's phrase. For a generation that had been in charge of Britain since the Thirties, it shattered many assumptions that they had been born with.

For those whose power was commercial, the wind of change brought with it the unaccustomed prospect of having substantial investments in countries where Britain no longer had direct political control. For those of the civil service classes, it introduced the equally worrying prospect of what to do with a son who might have expected to join the colonial service, when there were no longer any colonies. What, indeed, was the continuing justification for Eton if Britain no longer needed viceroys for India, or the lesser public schools if governors and district commissioners were to be made redundant?

For a generation attuned to Empire the idea of Britain being 'alone' in the world seemed undesirable and dangerous. The fact that Britain was still a major world trading power, and would clearly remain so after decolonialisation, was swept aside. For the civil servants there was a clear vested interest in insisting that administrative control and profitable trading were inexorably linked — that trade follows the flag.

Their best bet for the future — their future — was the European Economic Community, the trading group established after the signing of the Treaty of Messina in 1955. It was a group of six Western European countries dedicated to establishing a customs union between themselves, collectively supporting their agricultural industries, and harmonising their various laws relating to industrial standards and subsidies, with the aim of achieving fair competition between their industries. The eventual aim was political co-operation, leading to political integration.

The ideas behind this Common Market go back to the nineteenth century. Political integration of different states following step-by-step from a customs union was inspired by the unification of Germany under Prussian domination. While Bismarck had rejected the idea of a 'Greater Germany', stretching in some people's minds from the Dutch coast to the Black Sea, such a grandiose idea continued to have a powerful appeal, both to German imperialists and to those outside Germany who were attracted by German power. As the Swedish and Austrian Empires came to an end, there were frustrated imperialists on the fringes of the new German Empire who looked to it as a substitute for their own past. Britons who felt the same way about the Common Market a half-century and more later were following a well-worn path.

Two world wars were fought to stop a German Empire being established by force. But in parallel with the naked violence of Prussian imperialism and Nazism there were calmer, apparently more reasonable, voices to be heard. Friedrich Naumann's book *Mitteleuropa*, published in Germany in 1917, became a best-seller both during and after the First World

171

War, and was translated into most European languages. Devoid of nationalistic bombast, it spoke of the benefits of combining the German and Austrian Empires. It provided a respectable face for German imperialism in the post-1918 world. Naumann was abetted by such intellectuals as General Karl Haushofer, a soldier-academic whose Institute for Geo-Politics in Munich poured out publications and students versed in the historic inevitability of European unification.

One who was receptive to such ideas was a half-Japanese Austro-Hungarian citizen named Count Coudenhove-Kalergi. This gentleman had woken one morning in 1918 to find himself a Czech, and was aggrieved. He decided to set about not only putting the old Empire back together but uniting the rest of Europe as well. He was a brilliant publicist, and gained the public support of politicians throughout Europe.

Such ideas were popular enough in the Twenties for the American magazine the *Saturday Evening Post* to commission Winston Churchill to write an article on the subject, which appeared in February 1930. Churchill at that time had much sympathy with the idea of European unity. After the Treaties of Versailles and Trianon — 'the apotheosis of nationalism' — Central and Eastern Europe had acquired 7,000 miles of new frontiers, with national economies protected by an astonishing variety of controls and tariffs and multiple exchange rates. The new nations were finding that independence could be uncomfortable.

It was a genuine concern for the economic problems of European nations that led to the Briand Plan for European Unity, aimed at economic co-operation, which gained international acceptance under the auspices of the League of Nations in 1931. It was a much looser federation than that envisaged by the pan-European zealots, and both Britain and the Soviet Union were signatories — Coudenhove-Kalergi's 'Europe', while embracing Mussolini's fascist Italy, was to exclude Britain and her Empire and the Soviet Union as well, which he saw as 'Asiatic'.

But this was a nationalistic concept of 'Europe' that Churchill warned against: 'In so far as the movement towards European unity expresses itself in the vast increase of wealth which would follow from it, by the ceaseless diminution of armies which would attend it, by ever increasing guarantees against the renewal of war, it bodes no ill for the rest of the world . . .

'But clearly there are limits, now assuredly to be reached in our lifetime, beyond which a United States of Europe might revive on a scale more terrible, the rivalries from which we have suffered in our lifetime. A day of fate and doom for men will dawn if ever the old quarrels of countries are superseded by the strife of continents; if Europe, Asia and America, living, coherent and potentially armed entities, come to watch one another through the eyes with which Germany, France, Russia, and Italy looked in the twentieth century. Conflicts of countries are, we trust, ended. They must not be succeeded by the antagonisms of continents.'

Britain, he argued, could never be part of such conflict; with her Empire around the globe, she had interests in every continent. On Britain's relationship with continental Europe he was clear: 'We have our dream and our own task. We are with Europe, but not of it. We are linked, but not comprised. We are interested and associated, but not absorbed. And should European statesmen address us in the words which were used of old — "Wouldest thou be spoken for to the king, or the captain of the host?" — we should reply, with the Shunammite woman: "I dwell among my own people."'

The Briand Plan was effectively destroyed by Hitler's rise to power in Germany. The Nazis had their own concept of 'Europe', and could exploit the ideals and rhetoric of pan-Europeanism. The concern and perception shown by Churchill was alien to them. Their favourite mad scientist, General Haushofer, wrote an essay in 1933 with a title that said it all: 'Small countries have no right to exist.'

'Survival of small states is a clear sign of world-political stagnation,' wrote the general. 'Absorption, on the other hand, indicates life and development. The far-reaching co-ordination of all German member states within, and the growing absorption of Austria into the Reich, the various Balkan federations, the unification of Yugoslavia and Turkey are all symptoms of world-political evolution . . .'

On the eve of the invasion of France in May 1940 an active general, Franz Halder, was to say: 'This war is as necessary as the one we fought in 1866. When it is over we will have the United States of Europe . . .' Neither Halder nor Haushofer was a conventional Nazi. Hitler later sent Halder to a concentration camp. Haushofer, a friend and backer of Coudenhove-Kalergi, was married to a Jew. They were deluded more than evil, as they surveyed with approval a German-united Europe with its own industrial and agricultural policies, even its own multi-national army, the Waffen SS, whose recruits were told that they were fighting for 'European' values against 'Asiatic' Bolshevism.

For those who opposed Hitler, his rise to power forced the emphasis of unification proposals sharply westward. The talk now was of uniting the West European democracies with the United States and the British Empire, to provide an economic and military force to defeat Nazism and fascism. From this emerged the doctrine of 'Atlanticism', which finds expression today in the North Atlantic Treaty Organisation — with Communism, not fascism, as the perceived enemy.

With the spread of Atlanticism came a growing belief in Washington that a Europe with the enemy defeated should be economically and politically united. Europe, in other words, should look rather more like the United States. Seeds sown over fifteen years by the pan-Europeanists began to take root, although they were opposed by President Roosevelt. Coudenhove-Kalergi, who spent the war years in the United States, was a precursor of McCarthyism in blaming this on Communist influence. 'Since the decline of Germany,' he wrote of the period of the end of the war, 'Stalin had become the chief antagonist of a United Europe. He had succeeded in detaching Roosevelt from the idea. Agents of the Soviet Union were now penetrating into the precincts of the White House and the State Department . . .'

One would have thought that agents who could manipulate the veteran Roosevelt would have no trouble with the novice Truman after Roosevelt's death. Yet when the State Department's plans for a united post-war Europe — which took increasingly definite form after 1942 — were put to the new President, his response was enthusiastic. With his conversion the idea of European unification was quickly propagated around the world by the *Reader's Digest*.

I have dealt with the pre-Second World War development of the idea of a United States of Europe because it is necessary to correct the distorted perspective given by the EEC's own

174

histories of itself, which say nothing about events before 1945 — except by harking back romantically to the Holy Roman Empire (the Charlemagne Prize is a large cash award that 'European statesmen' take turns in giving to each other). The official history of 'Europe' jumps from the Roman Empire to the Holy Roman Empire to the European Coal and Steel Community.

As with modern German history books that omit the rise of Nazism, the EEC draws a deliberately misleading picture of itself, designed to foster the illusion of freshness and spontaneity, of a movement born out of the defeat of Nazism and of post-war idealism. A speech given by Winston Churchill in Zurich in 1946 is today presented as if it were the first time for centuries that anybody had even thought of uniting Europe. The reality is that the EEC is firmly rooted in the nineteenth century, and is based largely on German ideas. Most of its structures are founded, in surprising detail, on ideas dating back to the First World War.

Churchill's Zurich speech was, of course, important. He spoke with enormous moral authority. He called for the creation of 'a kind of United States of Europe', a regional organisation that would not conflict with the world role of the United Nations. It would be comparable with the British Commonwealth. He praised the pre-war efforts of Briand and the League of Nations. He spoke of the need to punish those guilty of the Second World War, and then to end retribution.

'I am now going to say something that will astonish you. The first step in the recreation of the European family must be a partnership between France and Germany. In this way only can France recover the moral and cultural leadership of Europe. There can be no revival in Europe without a spiritually great France and a spiritually great Germany.

'The structure of the United States of Europe will be such as to make the material strength of a single state less important. Small nations will count as much as large ones and gain their honour by a contribution to the common cause . . .'

After warning of the danger of atomic war, Churchill went on to say:

'Our constant aim must be to build and fortify the strength of the United Nations organisation. Under and within that world structure we must create the European family in a regional structure called — it may be — the United States of Europe and the first practical step will be to form a Council of Europe.

'If at first all the States of Europe are not willing or able to join a union we must nevertheless combine those who will and those who can.'

It is a speech that could be analysed endlessly in the light of subsequent events. Several things are clear. Churchill was talking about collective security more than economic co-operation, and collective security under the auspices of the United Nations. He saw the Commonwealth as separate, with France taking the 'moral and cultural leadership' of the new alliance. In talking of a partnership between France and Germany he could claim to be the harbinger of the Common Market, but in all other respects he was envisaging something quite different, something that has never remotely come into being.

The actual course of post-war Western European 'unity' has been much more prosaic. The Council of Europe has never attained any significant power or influence. Plans to set up a European Coal and Steel Community succeeded in 1952; plans for a European Defence Community failed in 1954. It was the failure of the EDC that turned energies towards the setting up of the EEC, which came into being in 1958 following the Messina Conference of 1955 and the signing of the Treaty of Rome in 1957. Britain was initially not interested in joining, but by 1960 the Conservative Government had changed its mind. Informal talks over British entry began, and in July 1961 Harold Macmillan announced to the House of Commons that formal negotiations, assuming the EEC accepted the British approach, would begin.

'This is a political as well as an economic issue,' said Macmillan. 'Although the Treaty of Rome is concerned with economic matters it also has an important political objective, namely to promote unity and stability in Europe which is so essential a factor in the struggle for freedom. I believe it is both our duty and our interest to contribute towards that strength by securing the closest possible unity within Europe.

'At the same time, if a closer relationship between the United Kingdom and the countries of the European Economic Community were to disrupt the long-standing and historic ties between the United Kingdom and the other nations of the

Commonwealth the loss would be greater than the gain . . .

'No British Government could join the European Economic Community without prior negotiations with a view to meeting the needs of the Commonwealth countries, of our European Free Trade Association partners, and of British agriculture consistently with the broad principles and purposes which have inspired the concept of European unity and which are embodied in the Rome Treaty.'

It was a naive and inept approach, steeped in both ignorance and dishonesty. It set the tone, tragically, for all Britain's subsequent relations with the EEC, right up to the present day.

It glibly linked the EEC with 'freedom and progress through-out the world', yet made no attempt to substantiate this claim. It talked of EEC membership, rightly, as political as well as economic, but with its vague talk of 'closest possible unity' and 'broad principles and purposes' did not seem to grasp that the Treaty of Rome was a treaty with binding legal provisions. It expressed concern for British agriculture, but assumed that industry could look after itself — indeed, that it could flourish within the EEC market. It assumed, after a caveat about reaching agreement with Commonwealth countries that would become increasingly meaningless as the years went by, that Commonwealth and EEC ideals were not in conflict.

One man who was not fooled was President de Gaulle of France. He saw that the British were naive enough to think they could enter the EEC on their own terms, bringing the Commonwealth along as part of the deal — something that had never been envisaged in any attempt at European unification. De Gaulle, moreover, did not want a power as large as Britain to be added to the six-nation EEC.

'One cock and five hens is good — two cocks and four hens creates discord.' France ruled the roost — as Churchill thought she should, since Britain had a roost of her own — and wanted it to stay that way. Britain's entry was vetoed — the right of any member state to veto new applicants had been established to stop undemocratic countries, such as fascist Spain, from gaining entry. Edward Heath, Britain's chief negotiator, came home frustrated but oblivious to the full import of the veto. Macmillan's successor as Prime Minister, Sir Alec Douglas-Home, with an appropriate change from land to water fowl, described the issue as a 'dead duck'. For a dead duck, it showed remarkable powers of resurrection.

The Labour Party had for a decade opposed all steps towards European 'unity'. The undemocratic nature of the Coal and Steel Community had been attacked: it took power away from elected national governments and gave it to a far less accountable 'High Authority'. The plans for a defence community and the rearming of Germany were attacked as an intensification of the Cold War.

When the EEC came into being nobody opposed it more strongly than the Labour Party Leader, Hugh Gaitskell: to join, he said, would be to throw away a thousand years of British history. When he met the Frenchman Jean Monnet, one of the numerous 'fathers' of the EEC, he put to him detailed objections to Britain joining. 'But you must have faith,' said an impatient Monnet. 'I don't believe in faith; I believe in reason,' said Gaitskell. 'And you haven't shown me any.'

But with Gaitskell's death hostility gave way in the Sixties to a qualified acceptance of the idea of membership, providing the right terms could be negotiated. The Labour Party, in effect, abdicated this area of foreign policy to the Foreign Office. In 1967 the Wilson Government applied for membership, but again de Gaulle vetoed it. Most candidates in the 1970 General Election regarded the issue once more as a dead duck.

The 1970 General Election was followed by two important events. Heath, the most uncritical of pro-Marketeers, became Prime Minister, and de Gaulle died. The duck was alive and quacking. On the British political scene this was not particularly obvious, since both Front Benches agreed that the UK should apply for membership. As is normal when the two Front Benches are in agreement, debates were badly attended, ended without divisions, and contained many long and unmemorable speeches.

Yet there were a large number of Labour MPs who felt that entry into the Common Market would be a disaster for Britain, and I was one of them. The problem was making our voice heard properly within the Party. Some — including Peter Shore and Douglas Jay — felt the time was not ripe to press the issue. In January 1971, in a mood of utter frustration, I circulated a draft of an Early Day Motion to my fellow members of the Tribune Group: 'This House believes that entry into the European Economic Community on any terms is against the best interests of Britain.'

I agreed to an amendment that deleted 'any terms' and replaced it with 'terms so far offered'. I did not myself believe any terms could be acceptable, but the amendment had the advantage of broadening the potential support for the motion. It went on the Order Paper that night, and over a hundred MPs signed it. Within a week or so we had enough signatures to show that the majority of the Parliamentary Labour Party were opposed to EEC membership. After much equivocation Harold Wilson and the Shadow Cabinet agreed to reject the terms. The Heath Government forced British membership through Parliament, the PLP opposed it with the full rigours of a three-line Whip, although many Labour MPs rebelled or abstained.

But while the majority of the PLP and the NEC opposed membership, and the majority of Party members in the country felt even more strongly on the subject, the Shadow Cabinet was narrowly in favour of entry. This created a problem for Harold Wilson, who put unity above all else. His tactic for solving this problem was to adopt an idea put forward by Tony Benn: a national referendum on EEC membership when Labour returned to power.

Labour duly returned to power in 1974, and the Cabinet agreed to a referendum the following year. The anti-Marketeers in the Cabinet — there were six of us — were given complete freedom to campaign against membership. Harold Wilson was wise enough to know that unity would only be maintained through tolerance of other opinions. Wilson himself was now firmly in favour of entry, although he was not saying so publicly.

He calculated all along that he would get his way. All the Government propaganda outlets were preparing for a devastating pro-Market chorus. All the departmental information officers were briefed to give the message. A special unit was set up to give 'factual' answers to public enquiries on the EEC — in practice it was a propaganda unit. The Government was able to send its own referendum leaflet to every household in the country, along with the leaflets from the 'official' pro- and anti-campaigns.

The pro-Market campaigners were well funded by their friends in the City of London, who enabled them to hire the best public relations and advertising help. Help also came directly from the EEC. Both campaigns received £180,000 from the Government, and the anti-Marketeers, with no other significant source of funding, made the unfortunate discovery that such a sum of money was totally inadequate for running a national campaign. Simple matters such as booking advertising sites often proved impossible: they were already booked by commercial advertisers who had arranged to hand over the sites to 'Britain in Europe' for the three weeks before polling day. The tactics used by the pro-Marketeers were blatant and effective. For working-class voters there were posters of happy schoolchildren with the slogan 'Jobs for the boys'. If Britain were to leave the EEC, the pro-Marketeers said, unemployment could go as high as two million. Lord Stokes, chairman of Britain's largest car manufacturer, British Leyland, talked of the vast potential for exports inside the EEC. For Conservative voters, the EEC was presented as a bulwark against Communism. The fall of Saigon only days before the vote gave a boost to this line of propaganda.

The result was overwhelmingly for staying in — so overwhelming that Tony Benn said, 'The electorate has spoken; we must tremble at their voice.'

When I was appointed Minister for Agriculture, Fisheries and Food in the following year, I was asked at a press conference how I, as a prominent anti-Marketeer, could reconcile my political beliefs with dealing with the aspect of the British economy most closely regulated from Brussels. I said that my views had not changed and that I would be going to Brussels to represent Britain. I thought than an anti-Marketeer might be able to do a better job than somebody who was fanatically pro-Market.

So far my opposition to the EEC had been theoretical: it was concerned with the law and constitution of the EEC and of my own country, and with the erosion of ties with the Commonwealth. In Luxembourg for my first meeting of the Agricultural Council, I started to gain practical experience.

The EEC consists of four main bodies that interact with each other. The Commission is an international civil service with the task of initiating new common policies and administering and monitoring those that exist. The Council consists of national governments coming together. It, in theory, has the final say in almost everything. The EEC Assembly — which now by statute we have to call the 'European Parliament' — has the power to dismiss the Commission and block the EEC budget. It has been directly elected since 1979, and has since then been actively engaged in seeking powers of detailed control over everything that happens in the EEC. The European Court decrees what is legal under the Treaty of Rome and the EEC's numerous laws — which are usually called regulations or directives.

There is also something called the Economic and Social Committee, which has a large enough membership really to be a second assembly. It would cause offence to call it the EEC's Fascist Grand Council, but it is an historically accurate comparison. It is corporatist in the political sense, bringing together the 'corporations' of the member states — industry, agriculture, the trade unions, the professions — and lets them mull over EEC policy. Nobody takes much notice of it, or can quite remember why this committee ever came into being. It is typical that even now nobody dares to contemplate abolishing such a useless and costly institution.

I came up against the difference between theory and reality when I attended my first Council meeting in Brussels. I had been told that one of the things that the Common Market was supposed to have swept away was the protectionist practices of the Thirties, including multiple exchange rates, with different rates applying to different commodities. I found instead that the Common Agricultural Policy is a highly protectionist system which uses a labyrinth of 'green' exchange rates, varying from country to country and from commodity to commodity, and often differing considerably from the regular exchange rates which apply to other industries.

The CAP was intended, inter alia, to bring a degree of stability to agricultural prices — in other words, protection — at a time when normal exchange rates were fluctuating considerably. When a national currency went up, making exports less profitable, a subsidy was paid; when a currency was going down, the reverse happened. Essentially it was a system that favoured a big exporter with a strong currency, West Germany, which got good prices and a big importer with a weak currency, Britain, which got cheaper food.

At my first meeting came a demand from the Agricultural Commissioner, a Dutchman named Pierre Lardinois, that Britain devalue the Green Pound by about 3 per cent. I opposed it because of the rise in British food prices that a devaluation would have involved.

Around the table in Luxembourg the national delegations sat in alphabetical order. The procedure was for the Commissioner to make his demand, and then for the delegations to respond in turn. I say 'delegations', not 'Ministers', for — to my great surprise — civil servants were present and allowed to speak. Although a quorum of Ministers was necessary before a meeting could start, top civil servants had a kind of honorary ministerial status. It had the obvious advantage of bringing more expertise to the table, which was particularly valuable if one was arguing from a minority position.

But the disadvantage of having civil servants acting as locum ministers is that some of them tend to believe that they are real ministers. The British agricultural delegation had been for many years effectively run — despite a political change of government — by a Second Permanent Secretary who, having told his political master that he might spend the rest of the day in the bar or delegation room, would take over the heat and burden of the day himself. The other delegations regarded him as the real minister.

But life became more difficult for the real Minister during 'super-restricted sessions', which Ministers only are allowed to attend — he was often totally unaware of the position taken by his civil servant. I was fortunate, after a while, to have as my civil service adviser a brilliant man, Sir Brian Hayes, with no illusions of political grandeur. He never tried to assume the political position. My private secretary Richard Packer and my chief information officer Terry Dawes and my adviser Ann Carlton completed a team that was better than that of any of the other nations represented on the Council.

The chief function of 'super-restricted sessions' is to coerce a minority. The voting system ensured that opposition has to be active. Silence — or absence — can be counted as approval. If you were in a minority of one in a super-restricted session, you dared not leave the room. If you were a member of a comfortable majority, there were no problems: the bar was on the same floor, as, indeed, were the lavatories. Having relieved and refreshed himself, a member of a comfortable majority could then go downstairs to the press bar and give his account of what was going on upstairs to the press corps.

British Ministers, because of Britain's different agricultural situation — a result of history — often found themselves in a minority of one. Stripped of their advisers, forced to sit for hours at a stretch, and unable to communicate with the British media, their task was an unhappy one.

During the most vital negotiations — the price-fixing within the Agricultural Council, deciding on national quotas and conservation measures within the Fisheries Council — Council sessions inevitably became protracted. The all-night sittings, which British MPs experience periodically and with great reluctance, are an integral part of the Brussels scene during these annual bargaining sessions.

In the House of Commons, all-night sittings last for just one afternoon and a night; in Brussels they go on and on until either a decision or a deadlock is reached. Deadlock occurs if dissenting Ministers have enough willpower and physical stamina to conquer their weariness and fight on. In time, what may appear to be an unchallengeable majority against them may itself be eroded by weariness.

The other great ally of dissenting Ministers is the unavoidable engagements of the other Ministers, who may be needed in their respective capitals for Cabinet meetings or other important assignments. Then a super-restricted session must give way to a restricted or even an unrestricted session. The dissenting Ministers can then hand over the negotiations, however briefly, to somebody else.

Such protracted negotiations have been institutionalised in Brussels. The press know at exactly what time they should turn up. The nocturnal whisky for Ministers arrives at a set time — usually 9 pm — in anticipation of the long hours of conflict to come.

The luckiest Ministers in these endurance tests are those from small countries: Ireland, Denmark, Belgium, the Netherlands, Luxembourg. Whatever they gain from negotiations will not be too much of a burden on the Community's finances, so they can hold out for better treatment than they really deserve. In a matter of minutes a suitable bribe can be negotiated.

Once a decision was reached, it was the rule that the President of the Council — provided by each country in turn for a six-month period — would give the summing up. This was taken as the authentic record of the decision, unless challenged immediately. A Minister in a minority who had achieved any sort of victory had to listen closely, and, if necessary, as politely as possible say that he disagreed with the summing up. This could be difficult in the early hours of the morning, after an interminable session, with the interpreters getting slower and slower. A vital moment could easily pass without a necessary protest being made.

No translation is perfect. In one Council meeting a Dutch Minister, a Shakespeare fan, spoke in English when he said, 'There is something rotten in the state of Denmark.' The Danish delegation got into an understandable huff although no real insult had been intended to the Danes.

All these problems hit me very forcibly during my first visit to Luxembourg. I survived because my adversaries were not used to total opposition. It is another EEC tradition — and a tradition of Continental politics in general — that minorities accept majority decisions. You might resist to the last possible moment, but then you accept the majority view. The resistance had been used previously as a tactic, to extract every possible concession, after which the usual procedure was to 'rally to the majority'. I heard that phrase so often in Brussels I came to believe it was carved on the tombstone of every European politician — 'I rallied to the majority.'

The British approach to negotiations is very different. A French Minister of Agriculture was not entirely joking when he said about me: 'The trouble with Mr Silkin is that when he says "no" he means "no".'

The French tended, however, to be an exception to the rule of 'rallying to the majority'. It was they, under de Gaulle, who invented the Luxembourg Compromise, which allowed a member state to veto any decision that it judged to be not in the national interest. You do not actually use the word 'veto'. You tell the President that there appears to be much more to discuss on the question, which involves a vital interest for your country, and ask that the debate should continue. In my time, the Germans always opposed the veto, mainly because they were strong enough to get their way by majority voting on practically everything. (Recently, to everybody's surprise, they have in fact employed the veto).

The French, until de Gaulle's policy was heavily modified by President Mitterrand, had a policy of backing any other country that wanted to use the veto, in order to keep the principle alive. They were particularly adept at using the principle of 'linkage' — of using opposition in quite unrelated fields to force a concession. It was fear of linkage between

184

fisheries and the Joint European Torus (JET) nuclear fusion project that caused Tony Benn to request me to make concessions on fisheries.

The EEC decision-making system causes increasing uniformity — which is clearly desirable if you place the political unification of Western Europe above all else, but not if you think diversity and democracy are higher priorities. The system has been strengthened still further since 1979, partly through the weakness of Conservative Governments, who have allowed the veto option to be eroded during the annual farm-price review, and partly by the French, weakening their stance on use of the veto. This policy has been codified under the European Act passed by national Parliaments in 1986. It is now virtually impossible for one member state to defend its individual national interests on the Council of Ministers. This means, in practice, that Ministers will 'rally to the majority' rather than appear weak and defeated.

For Britain this is uniquely bad. In the two areas I had to deal with — agriculture and fisheries — our national resources and interests are markedly different from those of any other EEC state. Increasing pressure for uniformity could — and has — only damaged us further.

This pressure is built into the whole constitutional system. The division of responsibilities has seen to that. The founding fathers of the Community gave to the Commission the right to propose changes and gave to the Ministers the right to reject the Commission's proposals. In theory this created an equality between the Commission, the international civil service of the Community, and the politicians.

The powers and status of the unelected Commission are too strong in relation to the status and power of elected Ministers. Furthermore, the Commission, because of its continuity, is able to exercise greater power than Ministers who come and go with changes of Government.

The strength of the Commissioners is reflected in their self-confidence. Just as some civil servants in the national delegations see themselves as surrogate Ministers, Commissioners quite correctly see themselves as the real legislators of the European Community. Whatever they propose, they will always have allies, which is not true of national delegations. Sometimes their allies will be in the European Parliament, from where pressure can be applied to national governments.

More frequently the allies will be one or two national delegations, bribed with the promise of special benefits.

Commissioners pay a price in personal terms for this power — a price in emotional involvement. National civil servants, working in the capitals of the democracies, have everything to gain from being impartial and professional in carrying out their Ministers' wishes. But Commissioners are expected to initiate policy. They must be forever in movement, forever producing new pieces of legislation.

During one of my first Council sessions the Agriculture Commissioner came to my office and begged me to accept the Commission's view on a particular session. I did not think much of the proposals, but they clearly meant a lot to the Commissioner: he had tears in his eyes. He took my attitude as a personal affront.

There continue to be those — in very diminished numbers — who argue that there should be no such thing as a national interest within the EEC. Somehow or other everything should be decided for the benefit of the Community as a whole. In some this is idealism; in others, particularly those farming interests who decided that the EEC could give them things that no British Government would concede, it was cynical self-interest. Whatever it is, it has no real contact with reality.

The reality is that the EEC is, and always will be, an organisation of nations bent upon obtaining the best economic results that they can wring out of the system. The EEC is about money and little else. It is about who contributes it and who receives it, and since nearly three-quarters of the EEC Budget is money devoted to agriculture, and since Britain is a substantial net importer of food, it is Britain who is the prisoner of a system that benefits the other members but not her.

There are those who say we should be enthusiastic members of the EEC because it allows us to work with and support our fellow socialists. When I first went as President of the Agricultural Council to the European Assembly to report on the new farm prices for that year, I quickly learned that the most enthusiastic supporters of the CAP were the Socialist and Communist Parties of France and Italy. Historical differences in Britain — the brutal agricultural revolution of the eighteenth and nineteenth centuries, the cheap-food policies that existed from the 1840s to the 1970s — have meant that there is no common ground with the Labour Party on agriculture. Nor should the Labour Party feel embarrassed about that: the British method of supporting agriculture, which protected farmers at home while allowing imports from abroad, did much to foster agriculture in other parts of the world.

The CAP, with its quotas and taxes, does the opposite. It ensures that affluent European farmers are heavily subsidised, for example, to grow beet sugar at the expense of Third World cane sugar growers who have no alternative crops.

Yet, for all these problems, Britain, of all the EEC nations, is the one that is least prepared to meet the challenge of the EEC straitjacket. The British Parliament has no means of dealing with the sheer volume of EEC legislation that since 1973 has literally become British law. Other nations go to Council meetings not only with expert civil servants, but with expert lawyers as well. A short acquaintance with the rules and procedures of the EEC forces one to the conclusion that a detailed knowledge of Napoleonic law, which is common among all the Continental member states, is needed, with experienced lawyers to deal with the legalistic questions of substance and procedure that arise every minute of the day in Brussels. The United Kingdom has adapted itself about as rapidly as a dinosaur learning to be a mammal.

Edward Heath, for all his blinkered idealism, did at least understand that decisions made in Brussels would have a radical effect upon the structure of British life. Lord Denning, who began to address these problems at least ten years before British entry, said that the EEC was like a tide in the estuary of English law: 'it flows in and affects every single aspect of the rivers of our constitution.'

When Edward Heath signed the Treaty of Accession he set up a Cabinet Committee to deal with EEC matters. Quite rightly, he chaired it himself. When Harold Wilson returned as Prime Minister he delegated the task to the Foreign Secretary. It was an enormous blunder. For all Harold Wilson's qualities as Prime Minister (and his even greater ones as a Party leader) he never understood the forces he was dealing with in the EEC. When leadership on EEC matters went to the Foreign Secretary it went to the Ministry whose sole aim is to appease foreign states — whose motto is, 'If at first you can't concede; try, try, try again.'

This is not to criticise the then Foreign Secretary, Jim

Callaghan: his instincts would certainly have been to stand up for British interests. But he was inevitably overwhelmed by his officials. His successor, Tony Crosland, might have had the will to assert himself, but by then he was ill and losing interest. When Crosland died, he was succeeded by David Owen, one of the most inept Foreign Secretaries that Britain has ever known.

He did everything his officials wished, and will go down in history as the architect of the Hague Agreement, whereby Britain signed away any vestige of defence that remained against the Common Fisheries Policy. By the time the Foreign Office had handed negotiations back to the Ministry of Agriculture, Fisheries and Food, the room for manoeuvre had been greatly diminished.

In my three years as Agriculture Minister I found myself fighting not only the other member states, but the Foreign Office in both London and Brussels. I recall the lady employed in our permanent delegation in Brussels who said she was ashamed of being British, and regarded herself as European. This attitude existed outside the Foreign Office, too. There was one official who believed that the principle of 'rallying to the majority' was more important than the national interest. He spent much of his time warning the other countries of our plans. British members of the Commission regarded it as their duty to support the Commission against Britain, when every other national in the Commission was busy supporting his own nation and giving information to its representatives.

Even when responsibility for the EEC Cabinet Committee left Number Ten for the Foreign Office, the Committee was still serviced by the Cabinet Office. This over-riding, arrogant, and not very experienced body in turn became an instrument of appeasement.

The change in the chairmanship to the Foreign Secretary was frankly a disaster. Foreign Office policy is to agree with any demand made upon it by another Community government. The standard of discussion and expertise was also abysmally low. Too many departments were represented by junior Ministers who had little knowledge of or interest in the subjects they were supposed to be discussing. Senior Ministers, bored by the subjects, preferred not to attend.

The junior Ministers could be relied upon always to support the Foreign Secretary regardless of any arguments put forward. In my time the polarisation between anti-Market and pro-

Market Ministers was very strong, and the anti-Market Ministers lacked subtlety. Outright opposition was never going to succeed against the Foreign Office and the compliant junior Ministers.

I often tried to rescue a sensible policy by offering a compromise, which, while having an element of concession within it, was still robust enough to preserve British interests. I was sometimes lucky enough to take advantage of the Foreign Secretary's total lack of knowledge of the subject. I have no doubt that things are much the same within the Conservative Cabinet Committee.

A lesser but more fortunate influence was that of the Treasury. The Treasury's general philosophy is that anything that costs the Treasury money is suspect. Of all the main Departments of State, it was always the most sceptical of British entry, and shades of this could be seen in its attitude to the problems that arose. When the Foreign Office and the Governor of the Bank of England insisted that we should join the European Monetary System, it was the Treasury who joined with me in opposing this unholy alliance.

Through all this I was fortunate enough to enjoy the support of a Prime Minister, Jim Callaghan, who disapproved of much of what I was doing but nevertheless allowed me to continue. Once, when I had decided it was right to boycott a meeting of Ministers in Berlin, Callaghan came under intense pressure from Chancellor Schmidt. He had great respect for Helmut Schmidt, who wanted him to put pressure on me. Jim Callaghan asked me only one question: did I believe I was doing the right thing? When I said 'yes' he accepted it, and backed me all the way. I was fortunate also in having as my Parliamentary Secretary Gavin Strang, who gave me the benefits of his knowledge and loyal support.

All political parties in Britain keep promising to reform the CAP. It is not a claim I would make myself: the plain fact is that the CAP is incapable of reform, and will not be abolished because it is so much part of the life of the other members of the CAP. In Brussels I was regarded as a disturbing influence, but I neither believed nor said that I could radically change anything. I was only able to make some adjustments at the margins. Preserving the Milk Marketing Boards, doorstep milk deliveries, and the labelling on British ice cream merely saved a small proportion of what would never have been threatened had we not joined the Common Market.

The 'moderate' argument has always been that the EEC can be changed from within. I remember an occasion back in 1967, when the EEC was being discussed in the Parliamentary Labour Party. The EEC might be bad, a Labour MP said, but we could improve it once we joined. An old trade union member, Ernie Fernyhough, took the argument to its logical conclusion. 'We all disapprove of the Tory Party,' he said. 'By the same argument we should join it and change it from within.'

I am not opposed to the EEC. Like the Conservative Party it has a right to exist, and some may find it a congenial home. My opposition is to British membership. The French and the Germans — as Churchill perceptively said in 1946 — need it. It is the core of post-war stability in Western Europe and, because that was the aim from the Common Market's inception, its treaties and institutions are designed to meet the needs of these two countries. That is how it should be.

For the smaller countries of Western Europe, the Common Market offers advantages. It puts their relationship with the big two within a framework of law and peaceful dialogue, which is a distinct improvement over what went on before 1939. With the exception of Denmark, a late entry into the EEC with strong Scandinavian links and maritime traditions (and close trading links with the UK), the smaller countries are staunch supporters of the EEC.

Among the original member states of the EEC there is as much impatience with Britain as we show with them. This is inevitable, and is a problem that must be confronted. One solution is the so-called two-tier Community, with France and Germany and the rest of the core nations of the EEC pressing ahead with integration while Britain and the others settle for a lesser degree of integration. This eminently sensible suggestion causes great alarm in the Foreign Office, where it is interpreted as Britain being 'left behind'.

The reality is that Europe operates as it is on a multiplicity of tiers. The divide between East and West is the most obvious. Within Western Europe there are those nations who adhere to the Treaty of Rome and those who do not. It cannot be argued rationally that Switzerland, Austria, and Sweden are any less 'European' than the EEC nations, or feel themselves left behind. Their common neutrality may be a factor in their decision to stay outside the EEC, but it is not a decisive one, since neutral Ireland, with its farm-based economy, has found the EEC and its CAP a congenial home. Conversely, Norway, a NATO member, has chosen to stay outside. The EEC is such a hybrid organisation that it even contains territory, French-owned, in the Caribbean and the Pacific. Algeria was originally an EEC territory, and Greenland came in with Denmark before going out of its own choosing in 1984.

Even Denmark's position is not immutable. The Danish Minister always has to have his Parliament's consent before he makes a decision, and must often reserve his position for that reason. Danish doubts about the EEC run very deep: when the 1983 General Election was imminent I was sounded out by representatives of the Danish Government, who informed me that if Britain left the EEC Denmark would do the same.

If the EEC is to survive in any effective form, it will have to show in future more flexibility, not less. The degree of integration imposed on Britain at present is already intolerable. Our industry, our regions, our agriculture, our fisheries — all need much more room to manoeuvre.

In an EEC built around France and West Germany, it is hard to see that this flexibility can ever come without harming or even destroying the institutions that benefit them. To ask that of them is unrealistic — and also stupid, since the Franco-German alliance is essential to the stability of Europe.

It is not for us to disrupt that stability. As Churchill said almost sixty years ago, Britain has its own dream and its own task. That dream and task, dictated by geography and culture, existed before the comparatively brief flowering of the British Empire and continues to exist after it. The time has come for action.

Chapter Fourteen

————— ooＯoo —————

Taming the Elephants

To President Nyerere of Tanzania the Cold War antics of the superpowers — the USA and the USSR — were reminiscent of fighting elephants in his native Africa. 'When elephants fight one another,' he used to say, 'they damage not only each other but all the villages for miles around. No village, however humble and uninvolved, can escape'.

In a nuclear war between the USA and the USSR there would be no neutrals: no part of the earth would be able to escape its effects. 'What would be left of Europe and the USSR after an all-out nuclear attack would not be worth fighting for,' Lord Zuckerman wrote in *Nuclear Illusion and Reality*. 'Nor would there be any justification for the price that the USA would have to pay for coming to Europe's aid.'

Zuckerman was writing about the northern hemisphere at a time when some people believed that there could be safety elsewhere in the world. Frightened Americans thought that they could escape if they were to emigrate to New Zealand. Australians viewed the prospect of nuclear war with a kind of detached pity, believing that they and the peoples of South-East Asia would survive. In the last few years this assessment has changed.

The controversy over radioactive contamination from British

nuclear tests at Maralinga in the Fifties has made Australians realise that they, too, are trapped by the nuclear age. The expansion of the Soviet Navy has also made the world appear smaller. 'Although there continue to be powerful constraints against a global nuclear war,' *Australian Outlook* wrote in December 1983, 'the increased tension and arms race between the US and the USSR suggest that some precautionary planning is required in Australia.'

For New Zealand, precautionary planning has meant a vigorously-pursued non-nuclear defence policy, with no nuclear weapons on her soil or in her territorial waters.

And today the theory of the nuclear winter — most prominently articulated in the West by Professor Carl Sagan, but backed by Soviet scientists as well — and growing evidence of the biological effects of nuclear radiation on both human beings and food supplies have brought new fears. In recent years we have seen the climatic effect of a single volcanic eruption: a nuclear war could have the same effect, but many times worse, bringing cold, misery, and death. The Chernobyl nuclear disaster showed how widely and rapidly nuclear pollution can spread.

That is why the meetings between the President of the USA and the General Secretary of the Soviet Communist Party assume such importance to people all over the world. There have been many such meetings, including meetings between Khrushchev and Eisenhower, Khrushchev and Kennedy, and Brezhnev and Carter. The meetings between President Reagan and Mr Gorbachev are, therefore, part of a pattern. The very fact that they meet, whether or not they reach agreement, is sufficient to make the world feel that a great cloud has been lifted. Of all terrors, the world fears most the collision of the two super-powers.

The great dilemma of our age is that the world also has reason to fear the collusion of the superpowers. At a meeting of Commonwealth Heads of Government a few years ago President Nyerere produced his parable of the elephants; another leader, Lee Kuan Yew of Singapore, promptly retorted, 'Yes, but it's even worse if the elephants make love.'

It is frightening to think of the superpowers agreeing between themselves in a new Yalta to divide up the planet, like two feudal barons settling a territorial dispute without any regard for the wishes of the mere peasants who work their land. We are close to that situation already — a situation predicted by Alexander Herzen and other political philosophers a century and more ago, when he foresaw that the twentieth-century world would belong to the Americans and the Russians.

Prophets like Herzen would not be at all surprised to learn that the Russians were still keeping out of South America (President Monroe declared it an American sphere of influence in 1814), or that the Americans, for all their protests, would never dream of intervening in Afghanistan, which is part of the Russian sphere of influence, then as now.

In 1986 the USA, believing that it had evidence that Libya had promoted a particular act of violence against US citizens, bombed that country, after courteously warning the Russians and ensuring that a Russian ship in Benghazi harbour kept its lights burning so that it would not be hit by mistake. Later evidence suggested that it was Syria that had promoted the violence, yet Syria was not bombed. Syria, of course, is part of the Russian sphere of influence; Libya is not, and paid the price for its aggressive independence.

Libya under Colonel Gaddafi is, in a way, a country out of its time. In the Thirties, with the rising threat of Nazi Germany, there was a vocal movement to found a new international order based on the swift dissolution of national identities. There were calls for a nation of all the democracies, for an Anglo-Saxon nation embracing the English-speaking world, for a United Europe. Behind all these schemes was the single idea — much too simple — that one could abolish tyranny and aggression by absorbing the troublesome nation state into a law-abiding union. With no roles for Hitlers and Gaddafis, it was reasoned, international lawlessness would disappear.

But today the most enthusiastic proponents of suppressing national sovereignty are not political idealists but the super-powers themselves, and the price the world pays for this goes beyond the dropping of bombs on Libya.

Nor will matters be improved if instead of two elephants fighting or making love we have three — for there is a third gathering its strength. Within the next twenty years China will be a superpower.

For a brief period of history the European powers and Japan saw China as a place to be plundered and exploited. The Americans had designs on it as well, and among the victims of

McCarthyite witch-hunts were those US State Department officials who were accused of 'losing' China to Communism. Behind this hysteria was an old fear, once expressed by Napoleon: 'Let China sleep for when she wakes the rest of the world will tremble.'

Under orthodox communism China barely began to stir; under more liberal economic policies, intended to end China's isolation from the world economy, the wakening will be swift. It will not make the world a safer place, as three superpowers vie for advantage.

The emergence of China is one of the major reasons why the time is now ripe to rethink the whole question of defence and the world order. The orthodox view of the world that has prevailed for the last forty years — Euro-centric, based on nuclear weapons and East-West confrontation or accommodation — is becoming increasingly threadbare.

For decades it has only been a small minority of people who challenged this orthodoxy — who called for nuclear disarmament and a strengthened United Nations, who pleaded for the Third World to have an adequate share of the world's resources, who doubted if nuclear power was as safe and as necessary as it once appeared to be, who realised that the earth's natural resources were finite and must be conserved.

It is not surprising that these warnings were unwelcome. From the Forties to the Seventies the post-war industrialised world enjoyed an unprecedented period of peace and prosperity. To the developed world, the prospects of another European war receded. The problems of the Third World seemed a long way off. Nuclear power was new and exciting; so too was the apparently never-ending expansion of industry and improvement in the standard of living.

Young people today do not have the same certainty and feeling of security. All over the world they are developing their own attitudes and responses that are light years away from those of their elders. They are aware of the world as a habitat that we must all share. Modern communications — mechanical and electronic — have shrunk the world immeasurably. My father travelled on the last horse-drawn bus in London and lived to see man walking on the moon; even if young people today have not travelled, they have seen the world on television.

It was television, as much as anything, that ended the Vietnam war: it took its horrors into every American living

195

room and mobilised opposition to it. More recently, through television, the world learned of the contemporary horrors of African famine, and then united in a people's response to the problem. In the mid-Eighties, televised rock concerts (Band Aid) and sports events (Sports Aid), which were viewed all over the world, raised tens of millions of pounds.

Before television, the disaster at the Soviet nuclear power station at Chernobyl would have been a distant rumour. World-wide knowledge of it and its effects, more than any other factor, highlighted the need for international co-operation in nuclear power as well as nuclear weapons.

Those who bequeathed us the post-war world should not, however, be judged too harshly. They were, on the whole, determined that the scourge of war should never again affect this planet. Fifty million people had died in the six previous years, and many millions more in Manchuria and China before that.

There was an awareness of the horrifying potential of nuclear weapons — Bertrand Russell even came up with the extra-ordinary proposal that the Western Allies should go to war against the Soviet Union if the Soviets did not agree to international control over all nuclear weapons.

The setting up of the United Nations was intended to free the world from the fear of war. From my office in Dean's Yard in Westminster I can see the plaque on Church House commemorating the establishment of the UN: it is often forgotten that the UN was founded in London. Those who founded it recognised that the pre-war League of Nations had failed to preserve peace because, at the crucial time, it had lacked the membership of both the USA and the USSR. The architects of the UN were determined that this must not happen again. The two powers that had met on the Elbe in 1945 must become and remain active members.

For this a price had to be paid: they were granted a veto over Security Council decisions that they felt might damage their national interests. The other victorious powers, Britain, France, and China, were also given the veto. The two European powers, having suffered twice in thirty years in the European cauldron, would no doubt have been loyal UN members without the veto, but their presence in the élite group did at least give the Security Council some geographical balance.

If, as I have always believed, there is an essential need for the United Nations, the veto was a price worth paying at the time, and is as unavoidable today as it was then. A basis of membership that gives a newly-independent country with a population of a few thousand the same voting rights in the General Assembly as a nation of millions is not tenable when decisions are being made in moments of world crisis, and the interests of the superpowers are at stake. The UN, in other words, can do nothing else but reflect the concentration of power that exists in the world, and channel that power into an arena of peaceful communications, not armed conflict. A UN that attempted to ignore this reality would soon cease to exist.

The permanent presence of Britain and France on the Security Council is, however, an anachronism. To achieve a better balance there should instead be a Commonwealth presence and a Western European presence. Through the auspices of the Commonwealth Secretariat in London and the Council of Europe in Strasbourg, a procedure could be established for nominating a country to represent them on the Security Council for a set term. The countries of Africa and Asia and Central and South America could establish similar procedures, and also have a seat on the Security Council.

This fundamental reform would give the Security Council a federal character. Representing not just their own national interests, but with widened responsibilities, Council members would be challenged to be more responsible.

The Commonwealth seat on the Security Council would introduce a particularly valuable devolving of power from Whitehall to all the nations of the multi-racial, multi-continent Commonwealth. It would strengthen the Commonwealth. The links of history, language, and law would allow this initiative to be smoothly administered. The Central and South American seat would be more contentious, breaking as it would the US pretension that it speaks for all the Americas. The Hispanic bloc in the UN General Assembly is a significant one, and should be given the responsibility of a Security Council seat.

One of the original aims of the United Nations was the establishment of a permanent UN peace-keeping force. It was intended that the Chiefs of Staffs of the member states of the Security Council would form the Military Staff Committee, which would advise the Security Council on the military requirements needed to preserve peace. The Committee's first task was to set up that permanent UN force. These efforts collapsed in April 1947, deadlocked on sixteen points, including total disagreement between all five nations as to the size of the proposed force.

A cynic might say that this did not really matter. No permanent force could have coped with the Korean War three years later, in which half a million soldiers were engaged and perhaps four million soldiers and civilians lost their lives. Yet it is possible that the Korean War could have been prevented had the UN, committed to reuniting the two parts of Korea under democratic government, possessed enough troops in place to monitor all military developments and deter the surprise attack from the North that precipitated the war.

In the event the Soviet boycott of the Security Council allowed the UN to assemble a huge army under US command, which was eventually to re-establish the status quo of a divided Korea.

More lessons were learned after the Suez crisis of 1956. Two Security Council members, Britain and France, had blatantly ignored the UN charter by launching a surprise attack on Egypt. They then used their veto to abort all UN efforts to stop the fighting. Only when their forces became bogged down did they lift the veto.

An ad hoc force was assembled for the role of policing the Suez Canal and the Sinai, through which the Israelis had advanced upon Egypt. Egypt agreed to the UN presence on its territory and could decide which nations could contribute troops (Israel refused to allow any UN troops on its soil). No less than fifteen nations contributed, which led to formidable organisational problems. The troops went in first; logistical support followed: there were shortages of transport and even food. Of the fifteen nations only three, Canada, India and Pakistan, were even capable of providing the level of logistical and technical support needed.

But ten years of peace in the Middle East were to follow. Egypt was no longer able, as she had done before 1956, to mount commando raids into Israel. Then, in 1967, Egypt demanded a UN withdrawal and the Six Day War followed. Much abuse was heaped on the peace-keeping force for its 'failure' to keep the peace. Yet the real failure lay with the statesmen who had not used the ten years of relative calm to promote a lasting settlement to the Middle East conflict.

It was an obvious lesson that should not have had to be

learned the hard way: a UN force cannot in itself create lasting peace. It can do no more than save lives and property and provide a breathing space.

After Korea, the largest peace-keeping operation ever mounted by the UN was in the Congo. Tiny Belgium, so innocuous and put-upon through two European wars, was one of the most brutal and cynical of colonialists. When independence came to the Congo — now Zaire — in 1960 she was totally unprepared: administrators and professional people of all disciplines were lacking — the Belgians assumed they would just go on running the country. It was a tragic miscalculation.

Soldiers of the *Force Publique*, the combined army and police force, mutinied against their Belgian officers. Widespread disorder broke out, and some Belgian civilians were killed. The Belgian response was to fly troops into the two military bases they still maintained in the Congo. The rich Katanga province, led by Moise Tshombe, decided to secede on the stated grounds that the disorder was the fault of Patrice Lumumba's 'communist' central government. He asked for Belgian assistance.

To Lumumba — and to the outside world — it was clear that the Belgians were intent on recolonialising Katanga in the interests of the Western companies that mined the province's mineral wealth. An organised 'Katanga lobby' began to make its voice heard in Western capitals — particularly London and Washington. Its aim was to stop any UN intervention.

Lumumba approached the UN on July 11, requesting both military and technical assistance to save the Congo from chaos. On July 13 the Security Council granted it. Forty-eight hours later the first contingent of Tunisian and Ghanaian troops arrived. By the end of July there were 11,000 UN troops from eight countries in place. By the time of the UN withdrawal four years later, over 93,000 men from thirty-five countries had seen service in the Congo.

The UN task force in the Congo was conceived from the start as a combined military, political, and economic operation. The military presence would provide the basic stability; UN political and technical staff would then work for political conciliation, restore public service, and promote economic revival. Nothing else could possibly save the Congo.

Politically, the country had all the elements of a Shakespearean tragedy. Lumumba, having called in the UN, soon accused it of conniving with his enemies, requested Soviet help, and was deposed. His faction set up a breakaway government in Stanleyville. The young Army Chief of Staff, Colonel Joseph Mobutu, became the most powerful man in the Congo, himself at odds with the UN over its efforts to protect Lumumba. In an extreme gesture of conciliation towards Katanga, Mobutu handed Lumumba over to his old enemy Tshombe for certain execution. Tshombe, however, had no interest in conciliation except as a way of gaining temporary advantage. The UN Secretary-General, Dag Hammarskjöld, died in an air crash while flying to see Tshombe.

For the first time since Korea, UN troops used military force in their efforts to end the Katanga secession. The international criticism this drew was compounded when the operation failed. More violence was precipitated when Western mercenary officers in the pay of Katanga ordered their men to attack UN forces. In December 1962, two and a half years after the first UN intervention, UN troops captured the Katangan capital, Elisabethville, and the secession was at an end.

No UN operation has been more criticised. The conflict was too prolonged, too factious, too bloody, for there to be any other reaction. The superpowers backed the operation at the beginning, but, with no swift solution, soon viewed the Congo with an eye to their own advantage. The Eastern bloc accused the UN of being anti-communist through its failure to preserve the Lumumba government. The USSR boycotted the UN and demanded changes in the way it operated.

There were enormous political and logistical difficulties in mounting the Congo operation. Without US aircraft and ships it would never have got off the ground, but the major powers did not, for political reasons, provide any personnel on the ground. More than 80 per cent of UN troops in the Congo were from nineteen countries in Africa and Asia; there were formidable problems of coordination and supply. Dietary differences were a huge problem in themselves. Canada, India and Pakistan could provide central logistical support of the highest professional standard, but further down the line there were persistent difficulties.

That phrase also describes the history of the Congo/Zaire, both before and after the UN withdrawal. Under President Mobutu's ruthless regime a degree of stability has been achieved, but poverty and regional rivalries still persist. There have been at least two military uprisings in Zaire since Mobutu came to supreme power. Education and public services are still woefully inadequate. In the UK *Pharmaceutical Journal* in 1986 a sad letter appeared from a student of pharmacy in Zaire: in his college, he wrote, the latest pharmaceutical publications dated from 1968, and there was no money to subscribe to new ones — could anyone help?

The help that the UN gave to Zaire was limited, but it did one thing of immeasurable value: it stopped the superpowers from becoming directly involved. Once the UN force was in place, the UN courageously resisted all pressures — from the Katanga lobby in the West, from the pro-Lumumba Soviet Union — to deviate from the task that the Security Council had given it. When the Soviet Union tried to supply Lumumba through a particular airport, the UN closed it down, and international pressure made the Russians desist. Zaire, despite three secessionist movements and political and economic chaos, was rescued from all-out civil war and from becoming a mere pawn in the Cold War.

The tragedy of Zaire is a relic of nineteenth-century European colonialism; that of Cyprus stems from the colonialism of the Ottoman Empire, which bequeathed the island a substantial Turkish minority living alongside the Greek majority, which has populated the island since 1,400 BC. Britain ruled the island from 1887 until independence was granted in 1960 under the Zurich-London Agreements, signed by Cyprus, Greece, Turkey, and the United Kingdom.

During the decade leading up to independence, a Greek Cypriot guerrilla organisation, EOKA, had fought the British in the name of independence and union with Greece. For EOKA supporters, independence as a member of the Commonwealth, with important British military bases on the island, was only the beginning: union with Greece was the goal.

So, for the Turks, independence brought the fear of future rule from Athens. Neither side could agree on the post-independence administration of the island: the Greeks, with most of the votes, were happy with straightforward elections of municipal councils; the Turks wanted to be able to run their own communities, even collect their own taxes. Both camps were secretly arming, and in December 1962 serious fighting broke out in the capital, Nicosia.

The British were reluctantly forced into peace-keeping: they had a lot to lose and nothing to gain by undertaking their old colonial role. They proposed a NATO force to maintain order. The Cypriot President, Archbishop Makarios, rejected the idea, and insisted upon a UN force.

This force came into being with the distinct advantage of inheriting an existing infrastructure from the British, who stayed on to provide logistical support, including food prepared to the individual tastes of the seven-nation UN contingent. The UN soldiers were supported by a military economics branch, there to tackle the economic problems caused by the effective partition of Cyprus, and by a multinational police force.

Thus began years of the thankless task of keeping the Greek and Turkish factions of Cyprus apart. Much of the work was boring, days, weeks, and even months in observation posts between the lines, coping — with scarcely a shot being fired — with situations that could develop into bloodshed. Numerous lives were certainly saved, but, as in the Middle East, the underlying problem was never solved. Greece and Turkey, then as now, could not agree on the future of Cyprus, and among Cypriots themselves the racial and religious divide overwhelmed any desire for genuine independence. Finally, in 1974, the EOKA faction staged a coup against President Makarios, who fled into exile. The Turks invaded and occupied Northern Cyprus, thus cementing partition, although the old, unified Cyprus is still recognised by the United Nations.

In Lebanon in the Seventies and Eighties, UN forces have had little chance of imposing any sort of peace. While Israel and Syria remain effectively at war, the tribes of Lebanon will be exploited by both sides. Direct US intervention in 1982-83 only made matters worse, and emphasised the lack of trust that the superpowers had in the UN peace-keeping efforts.

Looking to the future, what are the factors that would make the UN more effective in peace-keeping? The role of the Secretary-General is crucial. Unfortunately the last and perhaps only Secretary-General who was capable of using the power invested in that office was Dag Hammerskjöld. He proved himself, intellectually and morally, an effective Secretary-General, and in doing so incurred the wrath of the USA and the USSR, who both saw his power and his determination as limiting their own.

Hammerskjöld's determination over the Congo crisis led the

Soviet Union to boycott the UN, and caused Khrushchev to insist that the single Secretary-General should be replaced by a troika of Secretary-Generals, one from the West, one from the Eastern bloc, and the third from the non-aligned world — a proposal that was rejected by both the West and the non-aligned world. President Kennedy and Prime Minister Nehru both spoke out against it.

After the death of Hammerskjöld in September 1961, the Soviet Union pressed for a four-man team to run the UN, drawn from East, West, Africa, and Asia, with the African and Asian delegates — for that is what they would have been — from non-aligned countries.

In the event U Thant from Burma was chosen to succeed Hammerskjöld, and the wrangle centred on who would appoint his advisers, and from which countries they would be drawn. In theory the new Secretary-General finally reasserted the independence of his post, but his authority had been undermined. The last time a UN Secretary-General hit the headlines was in December 1962, when U Thant authorised military action against Moise Tshombe's Katangan forces, but he did this with the official backing of both the US and Soviet Union. The attacks on Thant came from Katanga, not from governments.

All UN Secretary-Generals have been men of great ability, charm, and tact, but the resolution and spirit that characterised Hammerskjöld is now a disqualification to anyone who aspires to the office. Yet there is a desperate need for a Secretary-General with the courage to make decisions and implement them, regardless of what may be felt by member states, however powerful.

Such a Secretary-General would have to work within the limitations of the UN as it is now constituted. He could never go so far as to alienate members of the Security Council. He would have to temper his forcefulness with extreme diplomacy.

Furthermore, he would need to have at his command a permanent UN military force and a UN-controlled satellite surveillance network to match that of the two superpowers. No Secretary-General has ever been so equipped, but without these two essentials he would be unable to strengthen the UN sufficiently to overcome the vested interests of the superpowers.

The key to military victories throughout history has always been knowledge of the enemy's plans and intentions — what is broadly described as 'intelligence'. Today, the key form of intelligence is that gathered by satellite surveillance. Only two nations, the USA and the USSR, can currently afford it.

The superpowers would argue that these systems are entirely for their own protection, but in reality they create a monopoly of a tradeable commodity of great international importance. The superpowers can give information from satellite intelligence to their client states — or withhold it if displeased. In the Falklands War the US supplied Britain with such intelligence, and the USSR, seeing a rift in the Western bloc, supplied it to Argentina.

France is the one major power to support the concept of a UN satellite network. France's close relationship with some of its former African colonies gives force to its views. Chad, for example, is suffering incursions from Libya. Military movements in the Sahara are easily detected by satellite. The last thing France wants is to be dependent upon the USA for such information. Israel, with its remarkable resilience and adaptability, has become a world leader in miniature remote-controlled aircraft equipped with television cameras, but these clever devices are a tactical, not a strategic, military tool.

Certainly the superpowers should be in possession of satellite intelligence. The more they know about one another's movements, the less likelihood there is of a collision between them. But the same holds true for the world as a whole. Every country, for its own security, should have such intelligence available, without pre-conditions or strings attached. A UN satellite intelligence service sharing its information with every country in the world would be in a strong position to deter surprise military aggression.

The major obstacle to a UN satellite surveillance system, apart from the superpowers' opposition, is the sheer cost. But this is bound to drop. The cost of launchers will fall as more countries compete for commercial contracts. In the last five years satellite communication ground stations have spread across the world, and these could form the basis of an intelligence-gathering network. The UN, unlike the superpowers, will not need a vast centralised intelligence bureaucracy to analyse and collate information — nor to keep it secret.

But, even with forewarning of military build-ups and aggressive intentions, conflicts can still start. The UN also needs a permanent peace-keeping force capable of being deployed with great speed, and free from the command of national armies.

A UN force is not like a national army — the UN is not a nation. It requires a military force designed to prevent victory, not to achieve it. National institutions — departments of health, education, agriculture, and the rest — are separate from a national army, which is there to protect them. The institutions of the UN — UNESCO, WHO, the UN Commissioner for Refugees, UNICEF — have a back-up function to the UN's military peace-keeping role. They all function to help create the stability from which political peace can emerge.

Peace-keeping demands a very special type of soldier. Experience in Cyprus showed that professional soldiers often have more trouble in adjusting than volunteer reservists. The professional is trained to kill; the weekend soldier spends most of his time in a normal working environment. Reservists from the Scandinavian countries, especially trained in peace-keeping at home, played a major role in Cyprus.

A permanent UN force will need soldiers who are trained to kill: occasions will arise when an extreme evil must be overcome by force, or made aware that force will quickly follow if the evil is not stopped. The necessity is for an airborne force, capable of getting swiftly to any point on the globe. Unlike past UN forces, this force must not be dependent upon individual countries for transport.

The force would need permanent bases. Some of these could be on territory where ownership is at present disputed, such as Gibraltar and the Falkland Islands. It would operate in the air, at sea, and on land, but the first two would be primarily for transport. Peace-keeping is a matter of confronting people and reasoning with them, not dropping bombs or shells on them from a distance. But it would include a military strike force, in order, at the last resort, to meet aggression with aggression.

Chapter Fifteen

—————————— ∘∘◯∘∘ ——————————

Defending Britain

In 1982 I proposed that a delegation of Parliamentarians from all five inhabited continents should visit Moscow and Washington in rapid succession. The objectives of this Five Continents Initiative were to call for the setting up of a permanent UN peace-keeping force, and for the revival of the McCloy-Zorin proposals of twenty years before — proposals whose terms the two superpowers came close to agreeing — that they should possess arms for internal security purposes only.

The failure of the McCloy-Zorin proposals in 1961 exemplifies a sad truth in the relations between the USA and the USSR. From time to time one or other of the superpowers has been willing to make large concessions in the hope of creating a stable peace with the other. From time to time the leaders of the two nations have seen very clearly not only the frightening possibilities of nuclear war, but also the harsh economic price that is paid in sustaining the Cold War.

But since 1945 these two allied victors of the Second World War have generally been unwilling to make large-scale concessions at the same time. These moments do occur, but they occur very rarely. One such moment came in 1961, when President Kennedy and Mr Khrushchev were in power: John McCloy was Kennedy's disarmament adviser, and Valerian

Zorin was the USSR's UN representative. These two men drafted the principles that bear their names.

The two governments agreed to negotiate to 'ensure that disarmament is general and complete and war is no longer an instrument for settling international problems'. The principles further proposed that 'states will have at their disposals only such . . . armaments, forces, facilities and establishments as are agreed to be necessary to maintain internal order'.

When this was accepted by both national leaders, the United Nations General Assembly gave it an enthusiastic welcome. A draft treaty was drawn up between the two superpowers, embodying the McCloy-Zorin principles. Tragically, the subsequent freeze in East-West relations prevented the treaty from being ratified. The world moved on instead to an even more dangerous phase in its history, with the existence of armed conflict in every inhabited continent.

One day — and for the sake of this planet that day must come before the end of the century — the McCloy-Zorin principles must be revived, ratified, and put into effect. While we wait wars continue, with the superpowers vying for advantage, often backing first one side and then the other. So capricious is the behaviour of the superpowers that, until the United Nations is able and willing to take over responsibility for enforcing peace in the world's trouble spots, each nation will have to continue to look to its own defences.

Very soon after the collapse of the draft treaty negotiations, most politicians had begun to forget not only how near the McCloy-Zorin principles had once come to being implemented; they had even forgotten the names of the participants.

In our attempt to revive these proposals in 1982 the Russians welcomed us; the Americans were grudging. In Moscow I had hoped that we would see President Brezhnev, but he was terminally ill, and his many years in power were followed by the short reigns of Yuri Andropov and Konstantin Chernenko. Instead of seeing Brezhnev we met Valentin Vasilii Kuznetsov of the Supreme Soviet, President Brezhnev's Deputy. Kuznetsov had, in 1961, been the Deputy Foreign Secretary in charge of disarmament negotiations with the USA. He gave us some cause for hope over the issue of nuclear testing for, although the USSR still publicly rejected the idea of on-the-ground verification of nuclear tests, in private Kuznetsov was quite forthcoming. On the other hand he told us that he regarded the

McCloy-Zorin proposals as dead.

The proposals might be dead as far as the leaders of the superpowers were concerned, I told the Vice-President, but such a renewed initiative would certainly be welcomed by the rest of the world. President Echeverria of Mexico rightly made the point that the vast sums spent by the superpowers on arms were at the expense of the Third World and the Latin America he loved so much. Mr N. K. P. Salve, Deputy Leader of the Upper House of the Indian Parliament, added his voice on behalf of the Indian sub-continent.

What gave added symbolism to this meeting was that it took place in May 1982, at the moment when British forces were engaged in active warfare with Argentina to recapture the Falkland Islands. My colleagues and I differed somewhat on the rights and wrongs of this conflict, but it did not preclude rational discussion. My two colleagues could not dispute the fact that the United Kingdom had acted entirely in accordance with the United Nations Charter. We agreed that the Anglo-Argentine conflict, like so many others in recent years, could so easily have been prevented by a United Nations strong enough to impose its will.

On the day I left Moscow I was informed by the British Embassy that HMS *Sheffield* had been sunk — the first British warship to be destroyed in the Falklands War. On the long flight to Washington I reflected that, until the world had a viable peace-keeping force, Britain still needed the means to wage war to defend her people. She needed, particularly, a maritime force. British troops were now engaged in battle 8,000 miles from home in a conflict considered by most Britons as importantly affecting their own country.

It was a forceful reminder that British defence priorities, as developed by a generation of politicians and military experts, were not necessarily in tune with those of the British people. Since 1945 British defence planning has been increasingly directed towards a land war in Central Europe, with the Soviet Union as the only possible enemy.

When the bulk of the British Empire was granted political independence and when later Britain withdrew her forces from East of Suez, the British capability to mount world-wide military operations — even in defence of dependencies we were legally obliged to defend — was diminished. Both the Royal Navy and the Merchant Navy began to be run down.

Astonishingly, this run-down continued after the Falklands War. The Conservative Government has learned nothing. Apparently it does not regard the possession of a merchant navy as important. In the first House of Commons defence debate after the end of the conflict, the Defence Secretary, John Nott, praised all who had taken part in the maritime task force to re-capture the Falklands, spoke of the many lessons that could be learned from it — and then got down to his real brief: to reaffirm Britain's European commitment, which was to be maintained at the expense of maritime capabilities.

Mr Nott quoted a line from the 1981 Defence White Paper: 'The Central Region is the Alliance's heartland in Europe: the forward defence of the Federal Republic is the forward defence of Britain itself.'

'The forward defence of the Federal Republic' is a military proposition that many senior military strategists, including many in NATO itself, believe is outdated — if it ever had any validity. The Second World War long ago showed us how mobile war can be. The forward defence concept smacks of a siege or fortress mentality, which all military history shows to be the most ineffective form of defence open to any power. Even the castles of the pre-gunpowder age were primarily a means of attack, not defence. They were bases from which horsemen controlled the surrounding land, and extended that control by raids against nearby enemy territory.

The fallacy of the fortress mentality ought to be particularly apparent to a generation still close to the Second World War, which witnessed the utter failure of both France's Maginot Line and Germany's West Wall against invading forces.

What created the forward-defence mentality within NATO was not military necessity but political caprice. When it was decided by the Allies that the West Germans should play their part in the defence of their own country, memories of previous German militarism were still fresh. It was considered vital that Allied troops, particularly British troops, should be placed on West Germany's borders to discourage the Germans from ever again being tempted to use these borders to launch aggression against their neighbours. The Germans, for their part, having so recently lost a war, needed political encouragement to rearm. Objections were countered with the promise that British blood would in future be shed in the defence of Germany.

These may have been important political considerations at

209

the time, but they do not now make for a rational British defence policy — a policy designed to defend the state and its dependencies from any potential aggressor. Nor does the reliance upon nuclear weapons of mass destruction add anything to Britain's defence capability — indeed, it detracts from it.

The only circumstances in which a British Prime Minister could even consider the use of nuclear weapons would be if the Soviet Union threatened a nuclear attack upon Britain alone — and only then when the United States had agreed that Britain should be allowed to retaliate. Not only are British-owned nuclear weapons totally dependent upon the United States for manufacture, service, maintenance, and modernisation — it would take at least two years for Britain even to develop its own maintenance facilities — but the power of the United States to destroy Britain economically is also as formidable as ever.

In 1956, when Britain and France occupied the Suez Canal zone, the Soviet Union threatened nuclear war against Britain. The British Government's first impulse was to threaten nuclear retaliation. President Eisenhower stopped all such ideas. He refused to give Britain permission to use nuclear weapons and threatened her with economic warfare if she did not come to heel.

The importance of that precedent is that it occurred in the days when Britain had both her own nuclear weapons and her own means of delivering them. British nuclear weaponry was at that time entirely home-grown, yet still America could give the orders. Today, Britain cannot envisage the remote possibility of using her nuclear weapons without American consent. Had it been otherwise the Falklands War would have been over in twelve hours by the simple threat of using nuclear weapons.

The credibility of the 'independent nuclear deterrent' was removed when the British signed away their nuclear independence by buying American missiles and American aircraft to deliver nuclear weapons.

Unlike Britain, the French have built their own submarine- and land-launched missiles and supersonic bombers, all three of which are in service today. It is something of which the French are immensely proud, and which unites all the main political parties of France.

210

The French, however, also face the problem that Britain faced in 1956: they, too, could not use the *force de frappe* against the wishes of the United States because they could be economically ruined by US hostility. The fact that the *force de frappe* is intended to safeguard France against any threat from Germany rather than from the Soviet Union only makes their difficulties more acute.

What is clear from NATO exercises is that what is envisaged by the strategists sooner or later is a nuclear war; but equally the nuclear weapons used would be American, not French or British. French and British nuclear weapons are regarded as being tiny irrelevances in a major conflict.

It is against this background that Britain's defence policy needs to be framed — a rational defence policy capable of responding to real not imaginary national needs. A policy based on the realities of geography and history.

Britain is an island. Access to Britain, whether for friendly or unfriendly purposes, must therefore be by sea or by air. Such access is vital for the survival of the nation, since we are dependent on imported food and raw materials. Britain, in other words, is an island geographically but not economically. It follows that the basis of any rational defence policy for Britain must have two priorities: the capacity to repel intruders by sea or air, and to maintain access to our islands by the same routes.

These priorities can only be met by maritime defence: the possession of a navy, a merchant navy, and an airforce. Large Continental armies do not keep our supply routes open, nor do nuclear weapons. The lessons of history sometimes change; the dominance of geography does not. What is consistent throughout the ages is the part that geography plays in shaping the defence policy of every country.

Czarist Russia and its successor state, the Soviet Union, alike took as their first line of defence the possession of territories along the borders of European Russia. There, invading armies could be halted before they were able to sweep across the Russian plains. Satellite states, the influence of climate (what Nicholas I called 'Generals January and February'), the pursuit of a warm-water port, the safeguarding of the back door from the Indian sub-continent — these are as important to Soviet military strategists as they were before the revolution to the Czar's General Staff.

The United States, similarly, has not changed its views on defence of its homeland. As when President Monroe was still alive, it sees the whole of the Americas as its border. When the Swiss Commander-in-Chief met his General Staff in 1940 to consider how best to defend their country in the light of German victories in France, it was on the exact spot where William Tell and his countrymen had met to found and defend the Swiss Confederation in 1291.

Britain's geography dictates her defence policy as it has dictated her history. In the present century this has too often been forgotten. When Louis Blériot flew across the Channel in 1909, the *Daily Mail* came out with the headline: 'Britain is no longer an island.' In the Thirties Stanley Baldwin said, 'The bomber will always get through,' and 'Britain's frontier is on the Rhine' — and was proved wrong on both counts. In neither World War did an invading army set foot in Britain. Technology has not changed the rationale of defence in the twentieth century any more than it did in any other century.

Nor does the loss of Empire make the slightest difference. The real threat to Britain in time of war has always been to the homeland, not to the colonies. The homeland is fortunate in being protected by a wall of water. Britain never could win a European war alone, but she has always acted as a beacon of light until an occupied Continent had been liberated.

The Merchant Navy has for centuries been the lifeblood of Britain's defence. This was true in the days of Drake and Nelson, when merchant seamen manned their ships; it was true in the two World Wars. When I was a young officer in the Pacific during the Second World War it was the fleet train of merchant ships that kept us supplied during that war, eight thousand miles away from our base in Sydney. During the Falklands War, when I expressed my anxiety to the Defence Secretary, John Nott, about the state of the fleet train, his reply was depressing. 'What is the fleet train?' he asked.

Britain has another traditional role. She no longer has the most powerful fleet in the world. Her navy has shrunk to the fourth in size, and she is now in danger, through the extravagant Trident programme, of losing even that position among the fleets of the world; but her navy is efficient and is capable in time of war of being expanded to a size where she can send her fleet to every corner of the ocean. She still provides the surest safeguard to the eastern seaboard of the United States, as she has done for two centuries.

Today, with the development of the Soviet Northern Fleet, it would be logical for this role to be stronger than ever, yet the Royal Navy is instead being reduced to little more than an anti-submarine force in the North Sea. If we cannot control the North Sea, then we cannot control the North Atlantic, which means that our island is itself without a defence.

The Thatcher Government, with its belief that industry must look after itself, even if the end result is the total destruction of British manufacture, deliberately allowed the shipbuilding industry to be run down. Not only were ships laid up and left to rust, but the men who manned them were also laid up and left to rust.

In 1979 the Merchant Navy had 1,200 ships; by 1986 the number had shrunk to 550 ships. The always anodyne 'Statement on the Defence Estimates' for 1986 was moved to state that the 'scale of the recent decline has caused some concern' and that the 'serious shortage' of trawlers suitable for conversion into minesweepers was being studied. The need for ships to carry cargo is, of course, as great as ever, so foreign carriers must be used. A once-profitable British industry has been replaced by a balance of payments deficit of around £1.5 billion a year.

The decline in manpower is equally appalling. In 1979 there were 31,439 officers, 28,942 ratings, and 6,318 cadets registered. In 1986 there were 13,371 officers, 17,680 ratings, and 1,016 cadets. On current trends what is left of the Merchant Navy will, in five years' time, be serving under foreign flags.

Britain continues to have a defence role around the world, most notably in Hong Kong (until 1997), the Falkland Islands, Cyprus, Brunei, and Belize. The British base in Cyprus is a key facility for United Nations peace-keeping and observer operations in Lebanon, Sinai, and Cyprus itself. Brunei and Belize are now independent, but have requested a British military presence to guard their sovereignty. British forces in Belize have been able to play a valuable role in disaster relief in Mexico and Colombia.

The British military presence in the Falklands is fairly criticised as being an expensive way of defending a small territory with an even smaller population. The truth is that the huge post-war expense is as unnecessary as the war itself. The Tory Government's insistence on withdrawing the solitary survey ship *Endurance* from the South Atlantic as a cost-saving measure, coupled with the passage through Parliament of a Bill to deprive the Falkland Islanders of British nationality, was read as a clear signal by the fascist junta in Buenos Aires that Britain would not oppose an Argentine invasion. Before the war took place I had pointed out that the decision to withdraw HMS *Endurance* would be seen by the Argentines as a green light to go ahead. The same view was taken by Jim Callaghan and Keith Speed, a former Conservative Navy Minister. A ship on patrol, like a policeman on the beat, is a restraining influence out of all proportion to its size. Its withdrawal was bound to be interpreted as a sign of weakness. When during the extraordinary session of the House on Saturday 3 April 1982 I wound up the Debate it was in the knowledge that the Tory Prime Minister and the Defence Secretary had, in neglecting a cornerstone of British defence policy, made a war inevitable.

Britain is in a strong position to help small countries that are under military threat. Such countries do not want superpower involvement, for the superpowers are expansionist in outlook and wish to exercise total control over the countries they claim to help. The United Nations, still lacking the permanent peace-keeping force that its Charter demands, cannot yet help.

Britain, with the imperial phase of her history behind her, with the goodwill created by the Commonwealth, with continuing access to world-wide bases, can and should offer help where needed. This help, a useful adjunct to the UN, is also of immense importance to the defence of Britain itself. In any wars of the future, as in wars of the past, Britain's only hope of survival would be in playing it long; in lasting out until defensive alliances become effective and our enemies begin to tire.

It is from that perspective, one in tune with geography and history, that the defence of Britain should be organised.

Epilogue

ooOoo

John Silkin died suddenly on 26 April, just before the 1987 General Election. He had no confidence in the Labour Party's ability to win that election; he believed that the Party's failure to do the groundwork in the years beforehand would cost it its victory. His abiding fear was that, if the Labour Party did not start to do the groundwork after losing, it would be out of office for a good twenty years.

John saw the Labour Party in government as a way of changing society: of giving everybody in Britain economic freedom and self-respect. Unlike many professional politicians, he cared more about that than his own political career. In the last ten years of his life he campaigned for Labour Party reforms, knowing his actions would make him dangerous enemies and damage his political future. He decisively blocked Tony Benn's bid for the Deputy Leadership in 1981, he challenged the hard Left over *Tribune*, he refused to bow to hard Left pressure in his own Constituency Party. He did not quarrel with the broad thrust of Labour's policies, but with the obsessively self-destructive way in which some Labour activists sought to implement them.

The Party, which started as the party of organised labour, has in recent years become the party of disorganised labour. If Labour is again to become a party of government it must start by getting its organisation in order. If the organisation is in order, its membership will be more representative, its policies

215

more relevant, and its image more attractive.

An essential step towards Labour's recovery is a system of one member/one vote in the selection of candidates. Without a central, computerised list of members this is not practical; it will just lead to argument and court cases. Without this reform the Party is likely to be doomed to permanent opposition, for many of the candidates selected will be out of touch with the electorate.

Neglect of Parliament and of the need to be an effective opposition as a prelude to government has been a predominant feature of the Party since the introduction of mandatory reselection and the electoral college. Introduction of one member/one vote and proper membership records would enable MPs to give the time they should to their Parliamentary responsibilities instead of being diverted to pandering to the various interest groups. Those interest groups, rather than the Party itself, have been allowed to dominate Party publications such as *Labour Weekly* and *New Socialist*. If those publications return to their prime task of giving information about what Labour is achieving in Parliament, the ordinary Party member will be better able to persuade his fellow voters of the wisdom of electing more Labour MPs.

But who is the ordinary Party member? At the moment it is too easy to get into the Party. All you have to do is fill in a form, then your name and address is read out at a ward meeting and a later GC meeting. In most cases nobody has the faintest idea who the names going forward are. This means all sorts of people can join the Party for all sorts of reasons.

John Silkin wanted the Labour Party to introduce a system of candidate membership, during the two years of which new members would not be permitted to vote on selection of candidates for election and Party office, or on policies. All but the most determined infiltrators would thus be deterred from joining; and Parties would be able to identify the few people who join determined to destroy rather than promote democratic socialism.

Changes should also be made to the procedures of the electoral college. The present procedures are tailor-made for someone who is good at manipulating pressure groups rather than someone with the ability to give an effective lead to the whole Party in Parliament and in the country. Clear rules on expenses, canvassing and meetings also need to be adopted before there is another contest.

It is no good decrying the waste of time and effort spent on peripheral groups if the Party is itself divided into factions. Party conference overwhelmingly voted against black sections, which are racist and divisive. Yet the NEC has not had the courage to close down those unconstitutional black sections that have sprung up. This lack of guts has lowered the status of the NEC and of the Party's regional officers in those Constituency Parties, particularly in London, that do have black sections. It has also alienated voters of all colours.

Women's sections should go too. The majority of Labour's women members do not join women's sections. The Party has not attracted women's votes as much as it should partly because many of the most vociferous women activists have a very strange idea of what women's issues really are. Sadly there are men in office in the Party who, while knowing that these women are out of touch, defer to them because they have a power base in the women's conference and as delegates to the national conference.

During the 1987 Election Campaign the Party's divisions were forgotten or obscured. The moment it was over they came back. It is all very well to stop insulting each other on television for the duration of an election campaign; but that moratorium will have minimal effect if, in the four years before, the voters are treated to a regular diet of the 'comrades' knocking hell out of each other.

The Party also needs to use the next few years to get its regional organisation right. That means devolving staff and responsibility to the regions. The stranglehold of the National Union of Labour Organisers, the tiny union that represents Labour Party agents, on regional appointments must be broken. The staff of regional offices must consist of more than experts in election law and Party constitution; among them must be people who can put Labour's case on local issues to the regional media — newspapers, television and radio. Mrs Thatcher's declared aim of taking seats from Labour in the northern inner cities at the next election makes this particularly important.

Together with the strengthening of the regional staff should come a streamlining of head office, including a reduction in the number of researchers. There are too many head office researchers with too little to do. Keen to contribute, they become instrumental in setting up committees, producing policy discussion documents and other writings on a vast scale. Much of this provides material for opponents in other political parties, or for those within the Labour Party who want to undermine the Parliamentary leadership by setting up an alternative power base, or ends up in wastepaper baskets. The last reform of Labour's research and policy-making structure made next to no difference. Labour's researchers are still wasting and duplicating resources and devastating vast tracts of Canadian forest.

One of the great problems at the next election will be Labour's lack of experience in central government — which is very different from local government. There has been a tendency for some Party members to sneer at the achievements of past Labour Governments and to belittle the value of the experience of those who served in them.

The fitness of Labour for government needs to be stressed throughout the years leading up to the election and not just in the campaign itself. Moreover the message must be got across not only on television but, as far as the Tory press will allow it, in the newspapers. That means making a distinction between the ownership of newspapers and individual journalists.

Labour must listen to people, not lecture them. It must guide, not dictate. At least in the 1987 Election middle-class policy-formers stopped telling the working class how wrong it was for them to want to own their own homes. There are other policy areas where similar radical thought is desirable.

Labour must also stop fawning on opinion polls and opinion pollsters. Far too much of the Party's resources and energy is spent on private polls and their analysis, when a good read of the published polls plus innate common sense, bolstered by chats in the local shops and pub, would be infinitely more useful.

If this book helps the Labour Party to power in 1991 or 1992 by eliminating some of the follies of the past ten years, John Silkin would have thought his purpose in writing it had been achieved.

Ann Carlton

Ann Carlton worked with John Silkin when she was Local Government Officer of the Labour Party (1967-74) and as a special adviser (1974-87).

Index

———————— oo◯oo ————————

Index

Index

Index

Index

Morris, Charles, 48
Morris, William, 3
Mortimer, Jim, 18, 53
Motorcycle industry, 100
Mullin, Chris, 54, 148-149
Murdoch, Rupert, 139
Muslim League, 165
Mussolini, Benito, 24, 159, 172

Napoleon, 195
National agency service, see Labour
 Party
National Government, 1931-35, 85,
 87
National Front, 29
National Health Service, xii, 136-137
National Plan, 11-12, 86, 87
National Union of Agricultural and
 Allied Workers, 54
National Union of Journalists,
 140-141
National Union of Labour
 Organisers, 7, 64-65, 217
National Union of Mineworkers, 20,
 96-97, 98, 140, 148
National Union of Public Employees,
 48, 54
National Union of Seamen, 54
NATO, 174, 191, 209, 211
Naumann, Friedrich, 171-172
NEDO, 145
Neighbourhood councils, 118
Netherlands, 183
New Building sub-Committee, 70
New Socialist, 147, 216
New Statesman, 31, 147-148
New technology, 94, 100
New towns, 127, 132-134
New Zealand, 112, 163, 192-193
News Chronicle, 159
News International, 139
News of the World, 139
Newspapers, 6, 139-142, 151-156,
 217, 218
Nicaragua, 162
Nigeria, 167
North Sea oil, 91-92
Norway, 104, 191
Norwich, 3
Nott, John, 209, 212
Nuclear energy, 161, 195, 196
'Nuclear winter', 193
Nyerere, Julius, 192, 193

Obote, Milton, 167
One member/one vote, see Labour
 Party, reselection of MPs
Open University, 138
Opinion polling, 6-8, 12-13, 218
Orme, Stan, 45, 46, 48
Orwell, George, 31, 150, 163
Owen, David, 37, 38, 144

Pacifism, 160
Packer, Richard, 182
Pakistan, 166, 198
Palestine, 166
Pankhurst, Emmeline, xii
Parliament, see House of Commons,
 House of Lords
Parliamentary Labour Party, 30, 34,
 38, 41, 42, 43, 48, 57-62, 69-74,
 76-80, 179, 217, 218
Pendry, Tom, 48
Pension funds, 101
Pitt, Terry, 16
Poland, 88
Poplar, 121-122
Porsche, 94
Postal services, 96
Powell, Enoch, xv
Prescott, John, 56
Price, Christopher, 55
Prices and Incomes Policy, 87-90
Private Notice Questions, 152
Proportional Representation, 68
Proudhon, Pierre-Joseph, 117

Race, Reg, 44, 55
Radio, 13-14, 154, 217
Radice, Giles, 50
Rank and File Mobilising Commit-
 tee, 34, 43, 80
Reader's Digest, 174
Reagan, Ronald, 193
Redcliffe-Maud Report, 124-126
Reform Acts, passing of, 4, 13
Regional government, 126-128
Revolutionary Socialist League, see
 Militant
Rhondda Valley, 3
Richardson, Jo, 55
Roberts, Allan, 55
Roberts, Ernie, 55
Roberts, Gwilym, 55
Robinson, Kenneth, 164-165
Rodgers, William, 38

Index

Index